Whitney,

REVIVAL ON KING STREET

Always follow your Passion!

Suzie

Revival
ON KING STREET

Book 1 of the Lowcountry Liaisons Series

Suzie Webster

Palmetto Publishing Group
Charleston, SC

Revival on King Street
Copyright © 2018 by Suzie Webster
All rights reserved

First Edition

Printed in the United States

ISBN-13: 978-1-64111-247-5
ISBN-10: 1-64111-247-6

For my husband Drew who has weathered my whimsy and adventurous spirit with patience, love and endless support. My dreams are his dreams and I know I am one of the lucky ones to have found my true other half. Together we are Two Fish.

Also, to the three most important ladies in my life; Ryleigh Katie and Reese. You inspire me to write strong and beautiful women. Women like the ones you are growing to be. You continue to inspire me with your humor and grace, kindness and love. I am one lucky "cool" Mom.

Lastly, thank you to my Mom, Bonnie. You never fail to believe that whatever I do will be amazing. I appreciate your never-ending confidence in me and the heartfelt love you have always shown me.

The characters in this book are fiction, but I cannot deny being inspired by the beautiful people of Charleston, South Carolina. I moved here in 2006 and I have never felt more at home in any other town. The people of the south are like nowhere else in America and I feel lucky to have landed here. I am a gypsy and I love to travel the world, but the Lowcountry will forever be my home.

CONTENTS

Chapter 1: Charlie 1

Chapter 2: Charlie 8

Chapter 3: Charlie 19

Chapter 4: Charlie 34

Chapter 5: Luke 47

Chapter 6: Charlie 58

Chapter 7: Luke 71

Chapter 8: Charlie 82

Chapter 9: Luke 90

Chapter 10: Charlie 99

Chapter 11: Luke 111

Chapter 12: Charlie 118

Chapter 13: Luke 127

Chapter 14: Charlie 138

Chapter 15: Luke 148

Chapter 16: Charlie 164

Chapter 17: Luke 175

Chapter 18: Charlie 185

Chapter 19: Luke 202

Chapter 20: Charlie 213

Chapter 21: Luke 226

Chapter 22: Charlie 242

Chapter 23: Joe 256

Chapter 24: Luke 263

Epilogue 273

CHARLIE FINLEY had an idyllic life. At 23 years old, she was married to her childhood sweetheart, was a successful real estate agent and lived in the beautiful city of Charleston, South Carolina. Some days she wondered if she should pinch herself because it was such a dream. But sometimes when things seem too good to be true, they often are, and Charlie's perfect life came crashing down around her when she walked in on her husband, Joe, on top of his secretary in their bed. Two years later, single and a successful interior designer, Charlie was celebrating the high-profile remodel of her parent's Bed and Breakfast, Southern Lady Inn, with her two best friends, Everleigh and Chase. The unveiling of the newly refurbished inn was the talk of Charleston high society and all of the movers and shakers were at the party toasting Charlie's success. Charlie felt like everything was finally clicking for her again, she even had the inside track on a brand-new condominium conversion in the heart of downtown that would take her business, Whimsical Designs to a whole new level. As she slid into one of her parent's guest rooms to catch her breath and take a break from all the well-meaning guests, she never expected the heart racing encounter that would change everything.

LUKE COLEMAN didn't care about being Charleston's most eligible bachelor. His heart and soul belonged to the business he had built with his best friend Ethan and more importantly, to the apartment community they had just acquired in the hottest part of downtown. He had big plans for his little piece of historic Charleston and no one was going to get in the way of his success. Luke loved women and he especially loved to walk away after an evening of mutually satisfying consensual fun. Nearly every mother in Charleston society had tried to throw their beautiful single daughters his way and he had no interest. So when he wandered into one of the guestrooms at the Southern Lady Inn relaunch party, he never expected to have his world rocked by just one kiss. The last thing he was looking for was a complicated relationship, but that was before he laid his eyes on one fiery redhead. Suddenly, both his brand-new project and the heart he worked so hard to protect were at the mercy of Charlotte Finley.

Chapter 1

CHARLIE

*And one day she discovered that she was fierce, and strong,
and full of fire, and that not even she could hold herself back
because her passion burned brighter than her fears.*
—Mark Anthony

Music blared from Everleigh's bedroom, distracting me as I
rifled through my closet looking for something to wear to my
parents' grand reopening party tonight. "Good lord," I muttered under my breath. "I might as well join her, so I can enjoy
the tunes too." I grabbed a couple outfit possibilities and made
my way to the other side of the house to Everleigh's room.

My best friend was completely unaware of my arrival as
she danced around the room in fuzzy shorts, tank top, and slip-
pers. I cleared my throat loudly, and when that didn't work, I
grabbed Everleigh by her arms and started to swoop around
the room with her. Everleigh giggled as we both shimmied

across the cluttered room acting like a couple of fools. "E, I really appreciate how much you need music to inspire your every activity, but it's so loud, I can't even focus on picking out the perfect outfit." I laughed.

Everleigh smiled sheepishly. "I am so sorry, I just can't get enough of this new Kayce Musgraves song, and I need all the help I can get trying to figure out what to wear to this high society event."

I laughed again (my laugh was trademark loud and a bit like a cackle). "Chill out, sugar pop, it's just a small little celebration at my parents' place, no big deal."

"Ha, no big deal is the understatement of the decade, Charlotte Finley. Not only is this the debut of the new and improved Southern Lady Inn, it is also the official coming out of Whimsical Designs." Everleigh did a little bounce and clapped her hands. "I can't wait to see the finished product, and even though I wanted to strangle you for not letting me visit to see the progress, I am actually pretty stoked to see what your creative genius has cooked up."

I playfully punched her and laughed self-consciously. "Hopefully the remodel will live up to your overinflated expectations. I think 'creative genius' is a bit much, Ever."

"Well, the way your mom was gushing at lunch, it seems you may have really outdone yourself this time. And judging by the elite guest list, you're likely to find yourself off-the-charts busy here soon."

I got quiet for a second, wondering if I should mention to Everleigh that Ethan Grant would be at the grand reopening. I'd spent the last six months working with Coleman

Grant Homes & Remodeling on the massive undertaking of renovating my parents' historic Charleston bed and breakfast. Widely considered one of the best in the country, with accolades and awards to prove it, my parents' decision to close for four months to fully remodel and redecorate was not an easy one. In my opinion, the smartest move they made was hiring Ethan Grant to handle the construction side of the project, and he proved his worth right away by recommending architect Sebastian Waters. Needless to say, my fledgling interior design business did not have nearly the resume to take on a high-profile project like Southern Lady, but my parents had complete faith in me, and after yesterday's final walk-through, I felt fairly confident that the outcome lived up to their expectations.

Working with Ethan and Sebastian had been a pleasure, and we made a great team. But while my dear friend knew my parents had hired Coleman Grant and could certainly deduce that I was working with Ethan, she had deliberately not asked about him, and I wasn't about to bring him up. Because although Everleigh had not said very much about her very brief affair with the handsome contractor, I have little doubt that he was a big factor in her decision to quit real estate and start her own baking business.

Everleigh had decided after college to get her real estate license and had taken a job with Coleman Grant Homes. I had had some success in real estate, having worked for a large firm for several years after high school, and Everleigh thought she would enjoy following in my footsteps. I tried to convince her to come on board with my company, but she thought that the more boutique Coleman Grant would be a better fit for her. That was three years ago, and while Everleigh had some success and seemed to enjoy working for both Luke Coleman and Ethan Grant, after a year, she suddenly decided to change course, resigned from the company, and left the real estate business altogether.

I couldn't help but feel guilty about not questioning Everleigh more about her reasons for leaving. Maybe if I had pushed her a little harder, she would have opened up to me. Unfortunately, I was distracted by a meltdown in my own personal life. A seemingly normal afternoon ended up becoming the end to what I had thought was my perfect marriage, and I was struggling to face my own reality. So, I took it at face value that my friend wanted to pursue her passion for baking, and I encouraged her to spread her wings. It was hard to miss the sadness behind her eyes, and I knew at the time that there had been something going on between Everleigh and Ethan, but I never pressed her and focused instead on my own problems.

The downhill spiral of my life began one beautiful April afternoon when I spontaneously decided to go home for my lunch break. Never did I imagine an innocent turkey sandwich could turn into divorce after I walked in on my husband, Joe, mid-stroke on top of his secretary in our bedroom. Like a fool, I stood there watching as his ass bobbed up and down in our bed; it was almost as if I were frozen in place. Eventually, I shook myself out of my trance, stepping inside the room and slamming the door behind me. I didn't think I had ever seen Joe move faster, and his secretary, Michelle, couldn't meet my eyes as she grabbed her clothes and ran out of the room. I could hear her pulling on her clothes as she ran down the stairs, but

I was literally unable to move or even react. The most difficult thing two years later was the awful visual that still lingered in my head. It no longer made me angry that Joe hardly seemed to feel bad that he had ripped our marriage apart so grotesquely, but I was sure I would always feel hurt and betrayed. In the end, after two years of perspective, I couldn't help but feel grateful for how things had turned out.

After my divorce, I moved into one of my parents' investment condominiums, and through a fortuitous break, I was asked by a real estate friend if I could decorate a model home for her company. The friend had been to my house with Joe and was really taken with my decorating style. She was in a bind, and they needed to hire someone quickly to get the home ready for the grand opening of a new home community. A little overwhelmed with my first foray into decorating, I still managed to jump in with two feet. My side project not only wowed my friend but also the owners of the home building company. It wasn't long before that one project expanded to two more and two more after that. I started to get so busy that I reached out to my best guy friend from high school, Chase, to see if he was interested in helping me part time. My real estate clients were getting pushed to the back burner too, and I made the decision to hand them off to other capable agents to focus solely on decorating. Within six months of joining me, Chase quit his job in hotel management (he hated it anyway), and together we formed Whimsical Designs.

During my transition to Whimsical Designs, Everleigh had started baking. Her side hustle was turning into something bigger, and after leaving Coleman Grant, she too began a new venture, opening a bakery and coffee shop on Sullivan's Island. In addition, after college, her grandmother had passed away and left her a small cottage near the beach, also on Sullivan's Island. At the time, she had been renting an apartment downtown and was working for Coleman Grant. She decided to make the beach house a vacation rental for the time being because she liked the pace better downtown and wanted to be close to the office. After leaving her real estate job to try her hand at baking full time, she knew she needed a larger kitchen. She took out a small loan against the Sullivan's house and renovated the kitchen to give her the space and commercial appliances she needed. Everleigh knew I was itching to get away from downtown Charleston and all my memories with Joe, so she invited me to move in with her and be roomies. It had been two years, and we'd had so much fun supporting each other's growing businesses and just hanging out on Everleigh's rustic deck and drinking margaritas while enjoying the view of the intercoastal waterway. Reconnecting with my best friend was the greatest thing to come out of my messy divorce, and I surrounded myself with that thought whenever I started to feel bitter or sad.

I shook off my trip into the past, remembering that Everleigh had still not asked me about Ethan being at the party. She seemed carefree, and while it had been two years, I was pretty sure she had gone out of her way not to see Ethan since she left Coleman Grant Homes. I worked closely with Ethan for six months and mentioned Everleigh a few times to him in passing. I noticed that he seemed to perk up a little when I brought up her name, and he even casually asked a few questions to try and get more details about Everleigh's current situation. He tried hard to make it seem like polite interest, but I felt a weight behind his questions, and he listened intently to every detail I shared. We were comfortable working together, but I just didn't feel close enough to him to pry about their history, and it felt a little disloyal to Ever for me to do that. Frankly, I was surprised he had not been into Everleigh's bakery. Because although Ethan lived downtown and the bakery was on Sullivan's Island, I knew that Coleman Grant had several jobs on the island, and it seemed rather deliberate that Ethan would avoid the only coffee shop/bakery in the tiny beach town. Call me Sherlock Holmes, but this added up to a whole lot of avoidance between two former good friends.

As I watched Everleigh carelessly tossing clothes from her closet to her bed, I sighed inwardly and decided to keep Ethan's presence at the Southern Lady Inn grand reopening party to myself. I couldn't help but wonder if there might be some fireworks at the inn tonight. Little did I know that the sparks wouldn't be coming from Ethan and Everleigh.

Chapter 2

CHARLIE

*If I had my way, if I was lucky enough, if I could be on the brink
my entire life—that great sense of expectation and excitement
without the disappointment—that would be the perfect state.*
—Cate Blanchett

After trying on several outfits a piece, we were finally on our
way downtown. Everleigh, as usual, did not stray far from her
uniform of an A-line short skirt and conservative blouse, but I
managed to convince her to wear my turquoise cowboy boots
to "give her outfit a little more personality."

"Charlie, I never know if it is a blessing or a curse that we
wear the same size shoes."

I couldn't help but laugh at her grumbling. "Ever, you
needed those boots; otherwise you would have completely
faded into the background, and tonight is not the night for
that."

"If I am hanging around with you, that is unlikely to happen." Everleigh smirked, looking at my sparkly ensemble.

I gave an exaggerated toss of my hair and smiled at her mischievously. "Well, you certainly never know who might show up to this thing, and as two single girls ready to mingle, we need to look the part."

Everleigh smacked her palm to her forehead as she drove over the bridge, too distracted to admire the beautiful marsh views. "It isn't like we have much free time to consider romance, Charlie."

"Who said anything about romance, E? It's been far too long since either of us have had even a sexy diversion," I responded, my many bracelets jangling as I waved my hands for emphasis.

Everleigh snorted loudly. "I think you get all the sexy you need from your oversized pink vibrating companion, and truly, I'm not judging. Who really needs the complication of anything more?"

I nodded, feeling my mood get more reflective. "You may be right. After all, even after two years, I am so skittish at the thought of putting myself out there that way again." Everleigh reached over and patted my leg as I continued, "I thought Joe was the love of my life; I never even considered he didn't feel the same way. Finding out he had been fucking his secretary for six months really sent me into a tailspin. I hardly expected him to be such a cliché, and the fact that he married Michelle last year doesn't make me feel any better. How could I have been such a fool, E?" I shook my head, forcing out a smile. "But let's not think about that; both of us are in a great place professionally, and we're only twenty-seven years old. We're great catches, and there are dozens of eligible hot guys in town that we haven't even met yet. There's nothing wrong with giving the pink beast a break and having a little fun with the real thing, don't ya think?"

Now it was Everleigh's turn to laugh as she shook her head. "I don't know if that's me, Charlie. I dipped my toe in that pond one time, and it didn't turn out so well. But I am here to support you, if you find a hot stud for yourself. More importantly, I cannot wait to see the metamorphosis of one of the oldest and most revered homes in Charleston. I know you made your parents proud, and I am looking forward to basking in the glow of your success."

And Ethan Grant's success, I thought to myself. It was clever architect Sebastian Waters who put my parents' visions on paper, but it was Ethan and me who brought them to life. I knew how challenging it would be to renovate an historic home, especially one as old and high profile as Southern Lady Inn. I watched mostly from the sidelines as Sebastian and especially Ethan went before the architectural review board numerous times to gain approval for even the smallest changes. When the board wouldn't allow the old wood windows to be replaced, Ethan spent days trying to come up with ways to redo the windows and make them more efficient. Finding materials for the exterior that didn't take away from the historic preservation but were aesthetically pleasing was not an easy task. So often, I would come up with design ideas, and it was Ethan who would spend hours researching to make sure the architectural review board would accept the changes. I had really grown to respect and admire Ethan over the six months we spent working together, and it didn't hurt that he was easy on the eyes. It was really no surprise that Ever fell for him with his rugged good looks and easy-going manner. I just hoped it wouldn't be awkward when Everleigh and Ethan saw each other tonight.

As Everleigh (no surprise) turned up the volume on the radio and sang along, relatively on-key, my thoughts turned to the night ahead. As much as I tried to make a big deal about us being on the prowl for hot single guys, my mind was laser-focused on the magnitude of tonight's event. Everleigh was right that my parents were over the moon about the outcome of my designs and how beautifully it had all turned out, but I knew that Charleston was a small Southern town. All the movers and shakers would be at the grand reopening tonight, and the future of my company rested on their opinion of what I'd done to one of the city's most beloved homes. Their approval could take my small two-person interior design firm to the next level, and the idea of that was both exciting and terrifying.

My mind drifted again, thinking about my parent's decision during my senior year of high school to pursue their dream of owning a bed and breakfast. I had changed schools more times than I could count during my childhood. Dad was an admiral in the Navy, and we were constantly moving to new cities and had even spent time overseas in Japan. Being an only child, I'd always been very independent, and my parents never really treated me like a little kid, so I was comfortable around adults even at a young age. But I wasn't going to lie and say that constantly changing schools and having to make new friends didn't wear on me. So, I was thrilled when the summer before

I started high school we moved to Charleston and my dad announced that this would be our last move. Dad had always loved being on the water, and so the Navy was the perfect fit for him. He also loved to travel and wanted to see the world. I never resented that part of our life; I still got the itch to travel several times a year. However, I was excited at the prospect of putting down roots and making some lifelong friends. When I was in the tenth grade, my father decided to retire from the Navy, and to my surprise, he and my mom announced not long after that they were buying a bed and breakfast.

I guess it shouldn't have been so much of a shock. My mother had always been the rock of our family. Organized to extremes, she made moving seem like a breeze. Military life was full of parties and social events, always welcoming new families and often saying goodbye. Mom became an expert hostess, and our house was frequently the center of all social activity. It wasn't a stretch to see Mom and Dad as the host and hostess of a bed and breakfast. My father loved to putter, always fixing things and working in the garden during his free time, and as the go-to bartender for their many parties and a charismatic leader, he was the perfect host to travelers looking to visit historic Charleston, South Carolina.

When my grandparents passed away years before, they left behind a farm in the Midwest, and my parents quickly sold it and invested the money. This along with their savings allowed them to purchase the beautiful house on the desirable Queen Street in the heart of downtown Charleston. It was not origi-nally a bed and breakfast, but it was set up perfectly, a detached guest house had plenty of room for my parents plus there was a spacious rear yard between the main house and the guest house. The main house had six good-sized bedrooms, each with its own en-suite bath. Mom and Dad invested in some updates to the common areas, creating a welcoming entry/check-in space and enlarging and updating the kitchen. They also removed an interior wall between the dining room and a sitting room to create a larger dining space to accommodate several round tables. In addition to renowned breakfast spreads, Southern Lady Inn was also famous for its high tea on the weekends and happy hour seven nights a week.

The inn opened about nine months after I graduated, and in the beginning, my parents did everything. I moved in with Joe to an apartment downtown and took classes at the local community college while I helped my parents get the inn ready to open. Even then, I was most interested in the decorating. I loved choosing themes for each room, helping to create the perfect individual oasis for visiting guests. I was also pretty good at social media and had a little skill in graphic arts, so I helped my parents build their website and set up Facebook and Instagram pages. I was even a sounding board for them as they decided where to spend their advertising dollars. They didn't really need to worry about the advertising though, because Charleston's tourism was booming, and with its quaint charm, central location, and delicious food, Southern Lady Inn took off from opening day.

Although my parents felt guilty for distracting me from going away to college, I knew that the inn was the perfect excuse not to leave my boyfriend since the tenth grade, Joe Patterson. I met Joe when I tried out and got a small role in the school play. Joe worked on the tech crew, handling the lights. Really, it was an underwhelming experience, except for the fact that at the end of it, I got the boy. Literally, at the post-show cast party, I found myself in a corner with Joe watching the upperclassmen celebrate. When he put his arm across my shoulders and bent down for a soft kiss, I was gone. It's funny because while I noticed him during our many rehearsals, we hadn't really talked until the night of the party. But for some reason, once we started talking, neither of us wanted to stop. We spent hours that first night sharing silly stories and just getting to know each other. Surprisingly, up until we crossed paths during the school play, I had not had any classes with Joe. He was an honor student, and his interests strayed more toward math and science, while I was much more into literature, the school newspaper, and art. When his guidance counselor suggested he should diversify his extra-curriculars, Joe decided to get involved with the tech club, which led him to the school play and me, his future wife.

Despite barely knowing each other before, after the cast party, you couldn't pry us away from each other. I smiled wryly at the memory. *Just look at us now*, I thought. It was amazing how well he fit in with my friends, but we were such a diverse group, and I shouldn't have been surprised. Plus, Joe was funny and clever, handsome in a subtle way, tall and lean with a quick smile and engaging dimples. All the girls loved him because he was easy to be around and was as comfortable with girls as he was with the guys. His quick wit was legendary, and he was even close to my and Everleigh's best friend, Chase, the quarterback of the football team. He charmed everyone, especially my parents. I quickly realized that Joe's home life was very different from my own. His father always seemed to be angry and it was clear that Joe preferred to spend as much time as possible at our house and away from his own. As their only child, my parents were obviously very protective of me, but Joe was laid-back and genuine and seemed to be completely enamored with me back then. By graduation, Don and Judy were treating him like the son they had never had and he equally loved their attention.

As high school wound down for us, Joe decided to study environmental management at the College of Charleston. He had always had an interest in social and environmental issues, and with his love of science and our proximity to the ocean, it made sense for him to stay in town. This made me very happy because it meant there was no fear of a four-year separation during college. Joe was my first, and after two years together, I had no interest in playing the field, and he seemed to feel the same way. I've always considered myself a one-man kind of girl, and I never really cared to date around. While I helped my parents get the Southern Lady Inn off the ground, Joe immersed himself in college. Life became a comfortable routine, and I felt like everything was perfect. My two best friends, Chase and Everleigh, went away to college, and I missed them, but the inn and Joe kept me busy. Eventually, the inn really didn't need me. It was open and thriving; my parents had things under control and had even hired a chef to handle the breakfast, high tea, and happy hour food. I started to feel restless and decided that real estate might be a good option for me. I loved interacting with people, and I thought my personality was suited for sales. So, I got my license, joined the premier real estate company in Charleston, and set out to build my career.

I never doubted that Joe and I would get married after college, but I never expected him to be so anxious. Red flag? It was Christmas during Joe's sophomore year at CofC. My parents hosted a beautiful holiday party, and I was shocked when Joe stepped forward to make a toast. The tears in Mom's eyes and Dad's intense focus should have clued me in that something was up, but you could have knocked me over with a feather. I mean, we were barely twenty at that point. It was romantic and sweet, and all the people I loved were there. Joe got down on one knee, emotional and serious, telling me all that I meant to him. When he dropped to his knee, I thought my heart would leap out of my chest. Never for a second did I question that we should be together. Joe and Charlie forever, right?

Joe and I had our dream wedding at the inn. My parents pulled out all the stops, Joe's family had always had their issues, but they loved me and seemed happy to see Joe settle down with a well-established Charleston family. Joe had one more year of college, and with an internship at an established environmental nonprofit, he was likely to have a good job after graduation. I was having some success in real estate, so money was not a problem. My parents gave us a generous wedding gift (and a thank you for not having to pay for college), which helped us get started. We used their generous gift to buy a cool townhouse in an emerging area of downtown. I was living my bliss and could not have been happier at the age of twenty-two.

"What are you thinking about over there, sweetness?" Everleigh had turned down the music and was regarding me with concern."

"It's all good, Ever, I was just thinking about my parents and how they started the inn. I am just so happy about their success. I love that they followed their dreams and really made it work; they are truly an inspiration."

Everleigh smiled fondly; she was nearly as close to my parents as I was. "I know, Charlie, and I am sure they love that you were such a big part of this new evolution. What a wonderful gift for your family."

I smiled at her, thinking about Everleigh's traditional suburban family. Her parents were both teachers in the Charleston suburb of Mount Pleasant, and we only ended up at the same high school because we all went to a local private school. Even our best friend, Chase, who lived next door to Everleigh, went to our school. I guess his parents felt that if two public school teachers were sending their daughter to private school, maybe they should do the same. Everleigh's parents were sweet but very conservative; they were quite in awe of my parents, who they considered major risk takers, but they applauded their success. I knew they had gotten an invite to the grand reopening, and Everleigh told me that they were giddy to be included in such a fancy event.

My heart started to pound as we crossed the Ravenel Bridge into downtown Charleston. I had crossed this bridge thousands of times, and it never failed to take my breath away as I gazed out over the water across the marsh grasses to the lights from the city. It was early March, and with the party starting at 7:00 p.m., it was already getting dark.

Everleigh reached over and squeezed my hand. "This is going to be an epic night for you, Charles. I am so happy to be a part of it."

I started to feel giddy as we got closer. For the first time since my divorce from Joe, I felt optimistic. My life spread out in front of me, and everything seemed to be perfect. Little did I know that this was only the beginning.

Chapter 3

CHARLIE

Fashion is the armor to survive the reality of everyday life.
—Bill Cunningham

Since childhood, I have always used my clothing as both an inspiration and a shield. Some days, I would wake up and my mood would dictate what I would wear. Did I need to be fierce today? Black leather leggings and an off-the-shoulder sweater with cowboy boots would do the trick. Did I want to look sweet and vulnerable to get some attention from Joe during our early days? A J.Crew button-up, knee-length pencil skirt, and sparkly Keds with a statement necklace usually got his attention. I'd never met a sequin I didn't love, but even in high school, I knew that moderation was key. If my eyeshadow was bold, then my lips were neutral. If I had bracelets jangling halfway up my arm, then I wore modest gold stud earrings. I loved to shine, but I knew enough to dial it back just so. Clothing was how I put myself in the right frame of mind for what I wanted to accomplish. I used it to activate whatever superpower I needed for the day. I never shared this with anyone, but I think my close friends knew that clothing was my shield, and while they sometimes laughed at my more questionable choices, they never made me feel foolish or insecure. They championed my love of dressing up and seemed to enjoy the little surprise in seeing what I would come up with for the bigger events in our young lives.

Chase, especially, was my fashion muse, and while many were shocked when during our sophomore year in high school he came out as gay, I wasn't really all that surprised. He confided in me and Everleigh before rocking our classmates by bringing a boy as his date to our homecoming dance. I think many of our fellow students and teachers were surprised because in school, Chase was Mr. Popularity, the captain and quarterback of the football team, very athletic and sort of macho. While Ever and I considered Chase our third musketeer, he had a wide circle of guy friends and spent a lot of time hanging out with them after football practice, etc. I'm not sure exactly where Chase met his homecoming date, and I don't think he ever saw him again after the dance, but I know it was just easier to share his secret in that very public way. He never shied away from conflict, and I knew he didn't want to have to hide who he was.

I would love to say nothing changed for Chase after everyone knew, but as is often the case in small towns, there were some cruel and ignorant kids (and adults). He rarely let it get him down, and while he shared some of his sadness and frustration with me and Ever, he continued to be the same awesome and studly Chase Billings.

Like me, Chase had an undeniable creative streak. I expected that he would pursue something in the arts in college, but I think he just wanted to make his parents happy. His sexuality was not an easy thing for them to deal with, and I always got the impression that the opinions of others carried a lot of weight with Chase's dad. His father had been in hotel management most of his career, and it seemed an easy choice for Chase to follow in his footsteps. He studied hospitality and hotel and restaurant management at the University of South Carolina and after graduation, his dad got him a job in sales and marketing at a prominent hotel in the city.

I knew Chase was good at his job, but whenever we hung out after work, he seemed restless and not very happy. One thing I did know was that he loved the access his job gave him to meeting potential lovers. Yep, Chase was definitely the slut of our trio. It was rare that he didn't have a hot guy waiting for him somewhere in town. Everleigh and I would just shake our heads in amazement over his success rate.

A couple months after I had completed my second big decorating job, the three of us were out at our favorite downtown spot, 492.

"Chase, how is it in this conservative Southern town, you always manage to find the hottest guys ready to jump in bed with you?" Everleigh asked, as the waitress set our drinks in front of us out on the patio. "Charlie and I can't even get the barista at Starbucks to look at us twice. What the hell?! Tell us all your secrets."

Chase just laughed. "It helps when you aren't looking for strings, plus there are so many hotties traveling through town and staying at the hotel. Discretion is key, and I am always quite careful when the situation calls for it. Maybe you bitches need to broaden your horizons, go to more parties and events. Your entire social life consists of each other and your hot gay bff, which doesn't help your odds."

"It is slim pickings out there, I agree, but I am glad someone is getting satisfied. Although, sometimes I think you sell yourself short Chase, you're a great catch and you deserve to be with someone who appreciates all of your fine qualities." I said.

"I appreciate the sentiment, my sweet little romantic, but I am quite happy playing it fast and loose for the time being. Perhaps you girls should stop looking for Prince Charming and lower your standards a little. There are of plenty of hot straight guys; you just aren't letting your guard down. Especially you, Charlie—not every relationship will end up like you and Joe. Just give someone else a chance," Chase responded.

I knew he was right, but tonight I didn't want to talk about my asshole ex-husband. Our divorce was imminent, and the pain of his infidelity was still too fresh. I was here to celebrate my blossoming new business, and I had exciting news to share. So, I smoothly changed the subject, grabbed my glass, and lifted it toward my friends. "I have some news, and I wanted you both to be the first to know." Chase and Ever grabbed their glasses, ready to toast my news, and they looked at me expectantly. "As you know, I just finished my second big project, and my clients have several more homes for me to decorate this year. I was also approached by another custom homebuilder who wants to work with me on some upcoming model homes. I had to decide whether this decorating gig is just a hobby or I want it to be my career. And honestly, guys, I really get so much more satisfaction decorating versus selling real estate. So . . . this week, I handed off my clients to some of the agents in our office, and I have decided to focus on decorating full time."

Everleigh's drink was spilling out of her glass as she bounced in her seat during my announcement. Chase's smile was genuine, and he raised his glass and toasted my choice. "I always thought you were missing something when you went into real estate, but of course you crushed it for so long, it didn't feel right to say anything. I'm glad you've found something that makes your eyes sparkle again, Charlie."

"Well, I can only think of one other thing that would make me happier." I smiled. "If you would consider helping me part time? I have too much to handle alone, Chase, and I have always trusted your sense of style and creativity more than anyone. I am not busy enough to replace your income at the hotel, but maybe with the two of us working, we can eventually get there."

Chase was shocked, and I could see his mind working. He was well liked at the hotel, the hours were flexible, and since so much of his income was commission-based, they practically let him write his own schedule.

"Right now, I just need help with installs and maybe some of the design work, but we can do that around your schedule at the hotel. I just want you, Chase. I know we would be an amazing team!" I leaned forward in my chair, grabbing his muscular forearm enthusiastically. He smiled wide at me, and as usual, I was bowled over by how handsome he was.

"How could I say no, Charlie? I can't think of anything more fun."

Everleigh giggled happily as we all clinked our glasses. "Look at us," she said. "For the first time, it feels like we are all doing what we are meant to do. This is the best night!"

It was a great night for us, and it only got better. Six months after that evening, Chase left the hotel and we became partners in Whimsical Designs. Now here we were meeting at my parents' amazing inn to hopefully celebrate our greatest success to date. I knew Chase had likely gotten to the inn hours ago, needing to be certain that everything went off without a hitch. Even though we had spent all day yesterday adding finishing touches and making sure the inn was perfect, Chase had a hard time not overthinking the placement of every throw pillow and candle.

As Everleigh pulled into the private parking lot behind the inn, my heart started racing. "This seems so big, Ever. I pray this night goes well. My parents had every design firm in the southeast begging for this job. I hope we did it justice."

Everleigh punched my arm. "Please, girl, there is no duo as fierce as you and Chase. Plus, you have your heart in this job, and that is what made you the best choice to do it right. Now let's get in there so I can finally get the reveal I have been waiting for."

Just as we stepped out of the car, Chase sauntered out the back door. It was six thirty, so the first guests had still not arrived, and I was excited to give Ever the tour without the intrusion of outsiders. Chase grabbed me and lifted me against his strong torso. I could tell that he was anxious but in great spirits. "I really think we did it, Charlie. Our vision is even better than I anticipated, and even the caterers were gushing about how amazing everything looks," he said, beaming at me.

"Well, come on." Everleigh grabbed both of our arms. "Show me!"

I nearly fell, my heel catching on the driveway. The concrete was swirled with colorful beach glass and seashells, making small cracks and pits that caught my spiked black patent leather heel.

Chase laughed and scooped me around the waist. "Taking the fashion risks as always, Charlie. Maybe I should carry you so you don't break your neck in those four-inch heels. I mean, Christ, you are almost as tall as me and I'm six foot two!" He smiled at me, and it was true—we were almost eye to eye.

"You know I need my heels so I can boost my confidence. Being tall makes me feel powerful!" I pumped my fist for emphasis.

"Well, you should be mighty confident," Everleigh said, looking up at me. "Us little people are definitely intimidated."

"I offered you my sparkly Jimmy Choos, Ever, but you picked the cowboy boots, so you might as well enjoy the view down there and stop complaining." I laughed as we walked up to the front porch.

My breath caught in my throat; the stately elegance of Southern Lady Inn never failed to move me. It was one of Charleston's oldest homes, and my parents had done everything to bring it back to its original glory. The wraparound porch gleamed, and the wide planks were perfectly weathered but felt strong and solid beneath my feet. The light blue beaded ceiling soared twelve feet over our heads, making the enormous walnut door look even more grand. I smiled happily at my two best friends as we stepped into the spacious yet cozy entry.

Everleigh gasped, her hands covering her mouth as she surveyed the new and improved foyer. It had always bothered me that when you walked into the inn, the first thing you saw was the staircase. While it was a sweeping and glamorous staircase, it was stairs nonetheless. Through some clever maneuvering from Sebastian and Ethan, we managed to curve the stairs off to the side, opening the entry and allowing for a sweet little sitting area and handsome registration desk in the expanded entrance. I had found a clever little umbrella stand/coat rack at one of my favorite antique stores which stood in one corner, and a miniature potted palm completed the look in the other corner. It all felt very Southern and Charleston without being an over-the-top cliché. A gorgeous green, blue, and gold pineapple needlepoint rug graced the entry and was the perfect finishing touch. Chase and I both had a fondness for blue, and after we discovered the splendid rug, we used the colors as inspiration for all the common areas of the inn. The golds and tans mixed with the greens and blues gave the entire home a subtle beachy air and lightened the heavy antique wood doors and paneling throughout.

As Everleigh exclaimed over the new pieces, the elegant curved stairway, and the seagrass wallpaper, I led the way into the great room, just behind the entry. I almost wanted to save this room for last because it just might be the space I was most proud of. The room was very large, a perfect space for entertaining, with cozy pockets for groups to gather and sitting areas around the two fireplaces flanking either side of the room, just right for afternoon tea or evening cocktails. Originally, the walls had been covered in dark wood paneling stretching all the way to the twelve-foot-high ceilings. Rather than tear down the beautiful wood, Chase and I had decided to paint the paneling white, making the whole room feel larger and brighter. The two fireplaces were updated with recycled glass surrounds, glittering with beautiful blue and green sea glass and shells, a polished version of the updated driveway. The original heart pine floors had been refinished and shone, looking both new and old at the same time.

I repurposed some gorgeous antique rugs my parents had purchased in their many travels overseas, and the colors meshed perfectly with the velvet and leather sofas scattered purposefully around the room. Overstuffed chairs beckoned with brightly colored ottomans nearby to rest one's tired feet after a long day walking the historic streets of downtown. Antique tables mixed with more modern wrought-iron pieces, and the hand-hewn rustic fireplace mantels tied in with the oversized bookcase designed and built by my favorite local craftsman, Piece of Work. A whimsical card table repurposed from whisky barrels found on one of the old plantations stood in the corner, waiting for an impromptu game of chess or cards (also courtesy of Piece of Work). Each of the sitting areas had a scattering of colorful lamps, and scented candles were lit throughout the space, wafting the smell of cedar and the sea throughout the room. Two enormous ceiling fans circulated air throughout the room, and their adjustable lights brought a soft light down from above.

Everleigh pointed to the fans. "I don't think I have ever seen fans quite that large. Wherever did you find them?"

I patted Chase proudly. "This guy is relentless in his research, and he can find a needle in a haystack. It was amazing he found something that worked in scale but didn't detract from the historic vibe of the house."

"Truly, they are amazing, Chase, what a find!" Everleigh gasped in delight.

Chase just laughed modestly. "The whole project has been a dream. I am not going to say it was always easy or smooth, but it sure was a blast. Seeing everything come together has to be one of the more satisfying things in my twenty-seven years so far."

Everleigh sat in one of the dark-teal leather wing chairs near the card table. "Everything is so welcoming, you guys. Comfortable and yet still elegant. It feels lived in, but I know so much of it is new. The colors make it feel fresh, and I love the fabrics and those beautiful fireplaces! It's hard to believe it's the same space."

I started toward a tall arched opening. "Come and see the kitchen and dining space. The guests will be here soon, so you may have to tour the guest rooms on your own, Ever." We walked into the dining space, which was bustling with caterers, who were also starting to filter into the great room. My parents had enlarged the dining room years ago, when they had first bought the inn, so Chase and I didn't feel it needed much updating. The wood paneling only extended four feet from the floor, so we left it the deep mahogany color. We painted the walls above a beautiful, light blue-green to lighten the space from its original dark red, and I had my craftsman build a new large dining table from reclaimed heart pine barnwood. It was the centerpiece of the room and was surrounded by smaller round tables. The room could accommodate thirty people seated, and it would be nice to have the one larger table for family gatherings so we could all sit together. With six guest rooms, sleeping a total of sixteen, the dining room was plenty for all the guests during breakfast. However, with the addition of a chef a few years ago, the inn also took outside reservations for brunch on the weekends and occasional special dinners.

We walked through the dining room, and I pushed open the swinging doors into the kitchen. The kitchen remained the same since my parents had updated it twice, once when they purchased the inn and again for the new chef. But I knew Everleigh would want to check on the desserts she had sent over earlier in the day. The large kitchen bustled with activity as I walked over to kiss the leather cheek of our resident chef, Frederico.

"Ahhh, how is my sweet Charlotta?" He smiled at me fondly, grabbing my hands. "I am so proud of how you have brought this place to new life," he exclaimed. "And you," he reached out and grabbed Chase by the arm, "such a talented duo I have never seen!"

Everleigh laughed, butting in, "But what about me, Freddie? Have you tasted my new raspberry almond cake with Italian buttercream icing? I wanted to come up with something special for the big night."

"Oh, my little plum, of course I tasted, first thing. It is sublime, like everything else your talented little hands whip up." He blew a kiss with his fingers for emphasis. "I am so pleased to have you as my little dessert goddess because this is one chef who does not like to bake!"

Everleigh giggled again. "I am always happy to be your dessert goddess, Frederico. Do you think I made enough desserts for the party?"

The chef waved over to the table laden with cakes and pies and cookies. "My dear, I think you made enough to feed all of Charleston, certainly South of Broad."

I noticed Chase looking at his watch. "Well, Frederico, we will leave you to it. I want to find Mom and Dad before the hordes descend." I grabbed Everleigh away from her scrutiny of the dessert buffet, and we swept to the back of the house.

On the other side of the dining room and just behind the great room was a light and airy sunroom. It had originally been a screen porch, and with my parents' blessing and our architect's creative genius, we had raised the ceiling to mirror the twelve-foot height of the great room and extended the room's depth by another four feet. The porch flanked the rear of the house, and an ancient wisteria vine ran along a trellis the entire width of porch. We hired Charleston's premier landscaping company to carefully relocate the vine/tree, allowing us to enlarge the room.

Ethan recommended the incredible Austin McDonnell, who ran his family's pool and landscaping business. Since we had to move the vine and remove much of the rear landscaping, we hired McDonnell Landscaping to design a new plan for the rear yard. It included a stunning waterfall and koi pond that blended perfectly among the soaring oak trees surrounding the inn. Natural rock and ground cover made the water feature look like it had always been a part of the landscape. Cattails and numerous water plants and lilies spread out around and in the pond, and beautiful koi weaved in and among the greenery. It really was a breathtaking change that took the backyard to another level.

The sunroom was all white, with beadboard on the walls and whitewashed wide plank wood floors. It felt completely different from the rest of the house, yet somehow it worked perfectly. A relaxing and happy space with brightly colored cushions on the love seats and rocking chairs scattered about. One end of the sunroom had a huge buffet that was currently set up as a bar but on most days would hold refreshments like lemonade, Everleigh's famous chocolate cookies, and afternoon coffee and tea. The other end of the sunroom hung a bed swing that I'd had custom made to tuck in perfectly. Made of whitewashed wood to match the floors and piled with pillows atop a bed-sized cushion, it just beckoned guests to take an afternoon nap in the sun streaming from the floor-to-ceiling windows.

Of course, it was evening, and the sun had gone down, but the landscape lights twinkled in the backyard and spotlights shone on the koi pond, highlighting the Japanese maple draped over the top of the waterfall. Chase and Everleigh each rested a hand on my shoulders as I watched my parents walk over from the cottage in the back. I was surprised they weren't already at the house, but I couldn't blame them for enjoying their last few minutes alone. I knew their evening would be filled with excited friends and well-to-do Charlestonians extending their congratulations and angling for reservations in the already-packed summer calendar.

I smiled to myself as I watched them walk over holding hands, like they so often did. I knew I was fortunate to have such loving, wonderful parents. They weren't always perfect, and my dad had a way of looking at me with a raised eyebrow and pursed lips that would make someone who didn't know him better quake in their boots. He was, after all, the admiral and had commanded the respect of many men for decades in the Navy. But when it came to his precious Charlie, his heart was soft, and he was putty in my hands.

As they came from the stone patio into the sunroom, there were only smiles for me and my friends. My Dad reached out with two hands to Chase, shaking his hand with one and patting his shoulder enthusiastically with the other.

"Hello, Admiral. Nice evening for a party, wouldn't you say?" Chase smiled as he responded to my dad's enthusiastic greeting.

"How many years have I told you to call me Don, Chase? After all, you've spent almost as much time in my house as Charlie and Everleigh here. You're practically a son to us. After what you and Charlie did for Judy and me, fixing up our inn, I don't think I could love either of you more." His green eyes twinkled as he looked around, shaking his head. "We just couldn't be happier with how it all turned out, and I know Charlotte couldn't have done it without you."

I nodded as my dad spoke. "No doubt about it. You guys were some tough customers, I'll tell you that."

Mom laughed and smacked me playfully. "I think we pretty much let you two have free reign, and it was clearly a good decision. I can't wait for everyone to see the finished product. In fact, I think our first guests should be arriving in minutes, so we better get in there." She turned to my dad. "Honey, I'll check on Frederico if you could just walk through and make sure all the rooms are well lit and open."

My dad smiled fondly down at my mom as he gave her a slight nod and headed toward the front of the house. He looked back at me. "I think Charlie and Chase should go to the foyer and start welcoming our guests. After all, this is really their big night." I could hear him whistling some old Navy song as he headed up the stairs, and Chase, Everleigh, and I headed toward the front door just as the bell chimed, announcing the first guests.

Chapter 4

CHARLIE

The moment eternal—just that and no more—When
ecstasy's utmost we clutch at the core while cheeks
burn, arms open, eyes shut, and lips meet!
—Robert Browning

My friends and I greeted the first flood of arriving partygoers, but eventually we went our separate ways. Chase and I spent much of the evening acting as tour guides, and I saw Everleigh wander into the kitchen, her comfort place. As I watched her retreat, I felt a firm hand on my shoulder. I turned around to see two ruggedly handsome men smiling at me.

"Ethan Grant and Austin McDonnell, aren't you two a sight for sore eyes. And you both clean up so well." I gave them a deliberate once over as they laughed at my flirtatious words. Even though I was joking around, I nearly had to do a double take. It was hard to miss the fact that these were two very good-looking men. I was used to seeing Ethan in jeans and a button up, often a little beat up from spending the day on the jobsite and tonight he was wearing a suit and wearing it amazingly well. Austin, who spent his days outdoors was the bigger surprise. He was also wearing a suit, his large body filling it out so well, my mouth nearly watered at the sight. It was hard not to ogle his clean-shaven face sporting a rare smile. I felt a little like I was looking into the sun, a very dark and manly sun.

"I'm glad you two were able to make it out. You certainly deserve to revel in all the accolades. Everyone is marveling over how seamlessly you relocated the staircase and what a tremendous improvement it is when you walk in the front door, Ethan. Our guests can't stop talking about the craftmanship and care you put into your work. I think I've handed out a dozen of your cards. I hope you are ready for the onslaught of new business. Both of you." I smiled as they high-fived one another before turning back to me.

Ethan's voice was deep and warm, and as he spoke, his eyes traveled around the great room. "Thank you for all the credit. I had a feeling things would turn out well, but the finishing touches really brought it all together. Most of the credit goes to you and Chase, it was your vision. Oh, and by the way, you are also looking beautiful on your big night." He winked at me and it was impossible not to feel a few butterflies from his attention. I gave myself an internal shake, nope, no way, not going there, too much baggage with Everleigh. Even though they were no longer an item, Ethan Grant was off limits. Austin on the other hand... I turned my attention to Ethan's companion.

Austin was examining me with his usual serious expression, but I saw him smirk a bit as he noticed me clearly checking him out. I guess I needed to work a little harder on being subtle, but it was difficult not to admire his square jaw that always seemed to have just the right amount of stubble and those chocolate brown eyes that drooped just a bit in the corners, making any girl want to fix the sadness that was behind those intense eyes. I cleared my throat and smiled at him to let him know that I realized I was caught in the act. Why not? The job was over, and I had been the one lecturing Everleigh on the way over about putting ourselves out there. Nothing wrong with flirting with a handsome, single, ex-special forces soldier. It was important to keep my options open and I was very open to the appealing Austin McDonnell.

"Austin, the courtyard has been the hit of the night. The koi pond and waterfall are just breathtaking, truly the perfect finishing touch. I know my parents are excited for the parties they will have back there." I gave him another smile, hoping to coax one back from him. I really wanted to see him smile again. I was rewarded with a dimple in his left check, totally unexpected. His smile was warm and practically made my toes curl.

"Just doing my job," he said modestly. "It was a fun project. I'm kind of sad it's over." He shrugged. "But I guess it's on to the next one. They can't all be a dream job, sometimes it's just mowin' a lawn or trimming some hedges." He chuckled, as he looked at Ethan. "It sounds like Ethan has a fun proposition in the works. Hopefully he and Luke will let me play in their sandbox."

I turned back to Ethan raising an eyebrow. "Ooh, I'm intrigued. What's in the works for Coleman Grant after this?" I asked.

His smile widened. "Well, since you asked, we just acquired an old apartment complex in an amazing location here downtown. Luke had an inside track, and we managed to snap it up before it even went on the market. We're planning on converting it to upscale condos, complete with security in the lobby and a rooftop deck."

"Wow, that sounds amazing. What an exciting project." My mind whirled with the numerous design opportunities. "How many units?"

"We just started working on the plans with Sebastian, and we may want to combine some of the units on the upper levels to make penthouses, but it looks to be around eighty or so," he answered as he combed his fingers through his hair thoughtfully. "As a matter of fact, I invited Luke here tonight so he could see the amazing work you and Chase do. We will need an interior designer to work with us on the project, and I would love it if you would put in a bid. It's hard to believe that you and Luke have never managed to meet. I thought he would be here by now, maybe I missed him and he's out back?" He looked at Austin. "We should probably try to find him, he's always getting cornered by someone's wealthy mother trying to do a little match making for her single daughter. He's likely to need rescuing."

I hardly heard what Ethan said after the part about needing an interior designer for their new project. My pulse jumped with excitement. An eighty-unit upscale condo reno was bigger than anything Chase and I had taken on so far. An opportunity like this could carry our company for eighteen months or more. "I don't know what to say, Ethan, this is an incredible opp—"

Before I could finish my sentence, I noticed a change in Ethan's expression. His eyes softened, but his face tensed up and he seemed immediately on edge. I looked over my shoulder to follow where his attention had drifted and saw Everleigh coming out of the dining room headed toward us. I doubted that she could see Ethan since I was blocking her view, and it was likely she only saw Austin and was coming over for an introduction. I knew it wouldn't be long before she realized who else I was talking to and I was a little curious to see her reaction.

I put my hand on Ethan's arm, preventing him from leaving, as I turned to greet my friend. Her eyes got big, and I could see her hesitate. I smoothly reached out to her. "Ever, come over and congratulate Ethan. He was such an important part of this renovation, and I know you have just been blown away by the changes."

Everleigh smiled, but I noticed it didn't reach her eyes. She looked up at Ethan, crossing her arms awkwardly like she was trying to comfort herself. "Hello, Ethan, congratulations on a job well done. It's no surprise that things turned out so well; you've always been great at everything you do."

Her praise was no doubt sincere, but I felt there was more meaning behind her words, especially when I noticed Ethan wince. Just as I was considering making an escape in order to give Everleigh and Ethan some space, Austin leaned forward reaching a hand towards my friend.

"Hello, I'm Austin McDonnell, I don't think we've ever met."

Everleigh's eyes grew wide as she took in Austin and her small hand was swallowed up by his huge one. "H-h-hello," she stuttered as I elbowed her in the ribs in an attempt to drag her attention from Austin. He was starting to look uncomfortable as she continued to clutch his hand and stare.

I jumped in trying to smooth over the awkwardness. "Austin owns the landscaping company that designed and built the gardens out back."

Everleigh's eyes kept darting nervously to Ethan, even as she seemed to gather her composure. "Wow, I was just talking with some friend's about how amazing everything looks back there. You've created quite the oasis. It's hard to believe we are in the middle of the city." She smiled enthusiastically and Austin visibly relaxed.

Out of the corner of my eye, I noticed Ethan studying Everleigh intently while she was distracted by Austin. I decided it was time for me and Austin to make our escape and give the other two a chance to catch up and maybe smooth things over. Clearly Austin had the same idea and spoke up before I had the chance.

"Hey Eth, I'm gonna go see if I can find Luke. I'll catch up with you in a bit." He flashed a dimple at Everleigh. "By the way, I heard you were responsible for the desserts. Your chocolate chip cookies are the best I've ever tasted."

She smiled flirtatiously. "Maybe you should come by my bakery on Sullivan's and try out some of my other desserts, there's plenty more to choose from."

He laughed, a disarming sound that changed his whole demeanor. "I just might do that, Everleigh." He gave Ethan a nod as he walked away.

Everleigh turned to me clearly prepared to make her escape, but I smiled and put my arm around her keeping her in place. "I need to go check on the music; it seems to have stopped. Why don't you catch up with Ethan and I'll see you in a bit." She gave me a dirty look as I patted her arm reassuringly, but she nodded and turned back to her former boss as I left the room. I felt a little guilty for abandoning her, but damn it, Everleigh needed to put her past with Ethan behind her and move on. There was no better way to do that than to clear the air. I just hoped nothing would get broken in the process.

It took me a good ten minutes to get to my mom's iPhone so I could figure out why the music had stopped playing, this was due to the numerous well-intentioned party guests wanting to congratulate me and talk about the remodel. After rebooting Spotify, I decided to sneak up the back stairs. I was hoping to grab a few minutes to catch my breath, and since the party had been in full swing for a good bit, I figured it would be much quieter upstairs. Perhaps I could even sneak into one of the guest rooms to grab a few solitary minutes. I slid over to one of the side bars and grabbed a glass of champagne (my first one) and piled some fruit and chocolate from the chocolate fountain onto a plate. I made my way to the second floor and slid into the third guest room, partly because it was farther from the stairs, but also because it was my favorite of all the rooms.

The walls were a soft cream, with oversized white trim along the ceiling and bright white wainscoting offering an elegant contrast to the walls. A gorgeous chandelier with sprays of crystal cherry blossoms hung over the antique walnut four-poster frame. The bed was layered with goose down and piled high with pillows in various patterns of soft red and gold. An elegant red throw weaved with gold thread lay across the foot of the bed, and diaphanous cream-colored fabric draped along the top frame of the bed, creating an utterly romantic visage.

Angled in one corner of the room was a deep scarlet chaise lounge in plush velvet, also piled with cozy goose down pillows. It was an inviting space that included antique pieces with simple clean lines, my favorite being a dressing table and mirror; plus there was a chest of drawers made of a rare and gorgeous tiger maple.

The room opened to a spacious bath with a claw-foot tub in one corner and a modern shower with multiple showerheads and steam features in the other. Dual porcelain vessel sinks flanked a long antique chest that continued the feel of old world elegance and luxury. The cream marble floors were inlaid with a black fleur-de-lis design, which, combined with the gold and cream wallpaper, really took your breath away.

I spent a long time searching for the perfect paintings to fill the space, veering toward romantic landscapes and beautiful couples walking through cities that sparkled in the night sky. I loved to support our local artists and was pleased with some of my finds in Charleston's galleries. It truly was our most romantic room, and I knew my parents planned to use it for couples visiting to celebrate their birthdays, anniversaries, and wedding nights.

I stepped inside, and not seeing anyone, I quickly shut and locked the door behind me. It was only then that I noticed a man standing across the room, leaning against the chest of drawers. He was standing so still I had missed him in my initial perusal. I was caught off guard and attempted to stutter out some sort of greeting as I looked him over. I felt even more awkward as

I stared a bit too long at his handsome face. My eyes traveled down, taking in his broad shoulders; obviously fit torso that tapered down to a trim waist; and wide, muscular legs straining against his perfectly fitted dress pants. *Wow, he is tall,* I thought as my eyes traveled back up to his face. As I got there, I realized his full mouth had twisted into a bit of a smirk and his bright blue eyes regarded me sharply, but with a twinkle.

"I am so sorry," I said breathlessly. "I thought there was no one in here. I was just trying to get away from the crowd for a couple minutes." I stood there, awkwardly holding my plate of fruit and my champagne, and he quickly crossed the room, taking my plate and setting it on the dresser.

"I guess we both had the same idea," he said. "These types of things are not really my cup of tea, but unfortunately, it seems like I end up at a lot of them. I was just thinking I should head back down when you stumbled in and saved me from more senseless small talk with the Charleston elite."

"They aren't all bad," I responded a bit defensively.

"I can see that now," he said, his mouth lifting in a small smile. "Clearly I have not met the most interesting and beautiful party guests tonight."

Now it was his turn to check me out, and I felt my cheeks getting warm at his very frank assessment. His eyebrows raised as he looked me over from the tip of my head to my patent leather heels. I decided now was a good time to take an unladylike swig of my champagne. I needed something to cool me off and slow down my rapidly beating heart. What the hell was wrong with me? I was feeling like a nervous schoolgirl locked in a closet with the captain of the football team—geez.

He walked toward me as I finished my gulp of champagne and reached up to brush aside some of my hair, which had swept into my face in my frantic effort to take a drink. "I don't think I have ever seen such a beautiful shade of red hair." He said it so softly that I believed he was, in fact, talking to himself.

"Excuse me?" I said nervously, smoothing an invisible wrinkle in my leather pencil skirt.

He chuckled deeply, and his warm voice flowed over me, surrounding me like a blanket. "I am sorry, I didn't mean to say that out loud, but I was just admiring your hair. It's such a beautiful color. I mean, if I'm being honest, it wasn't the only thing I was admiring, but fortunately I didn't express those thoughts out loud."

I felt my face getting hot again, and maybe it was the champagne, but suddenly I was angry at his impertinence. After all, I was just trying to get a few minutes alone, and this obviously very confident—no, scratch that—egotistical man was intruding on my space and making me feel off balance. I needed to pull it together and get a handle on this situation. "Now, listen, Mr. Whoever You Are . . . " He started to speak, and I held up my hand. "I'm sure you're used to having women fall all over you, what with your chiseled chin with its little dimple and your blue eyes and strong biceps, but I am not one of those women." He was really smiling now and looking a little dangerous as I continued. "I came in here to enjoy a little champagne and strawberries in solitude, and the last thing I need is your unwelcome flirtation."

I found myself backed up against the bed as he stepped closer, and my heart started to beat faster again as I smelled his musky aftershave. Wait—was that grapefruit mixed with cedar-wood? I shook my head, trying to get control over myself, as he ran a finger down my arm and grasped my fingers.

"I see there's a spitfire in there to match all of that red hair. It is quite interesting how green your eyes get when you're all worked up." He dropped my hand and walked over to the dresser to grab my plate. Why did my hand suddenly feel cold once he let it go? What the hell was happening to me? I watched him as he picked up one of the biggest strawberries on the plate and brought it to his lips to take a bite. My body was starting to betray me, as I felt my nipples get hard and moisture surge between my legs. This was ridiculous; I didn't even know this guy!

As I was trying to form a coherent thought, he was back in front of me, holding out another strawberry. "I think you had the right idea, these really are delicious; you should try one. There is nothing better than a local South Carolina strawberry in March."

I looked up at him (yes, he was that tall), not really comprehending what he was saying. I mean, his lips were wet from the berry, and I couldn't seem to drag my eyes away. I realized that he was putting the strawberry to my lips, and like a crazy person, I bit down on it, my lips caressing his fingers.

I could see him suck in his breath, and I felt some satisfaction knowing I had shaken him too. He dropped the stem onto the plate and leaned back toward me like he was going to kiss me. *Is he going to kiss me? Do I want him to kiss me?* His piercing blue eyes were inches from mine, and I could see the question there. *What am I doing?* I felt myself leaning in, and then it was happening.

He took my proximity to mean approval and he gently laid the plate behind me on the bed and circled one hand around my waist. His other hand was behind my neck, and his firm full lips came down on mine gently at first. He was tentative, slowly testing out the situation, probably thinking I might push him away, (like a rational person). But not me, I couldn't seem to stop myself from responding. I wanted to blame it on my lengthy dry spell, but I had never felt a kiss so completely; it rolled over me like a wave and traveled down to my toes. Instead of doing the sane thing and pulling away, I leaned in seeking more of his firm lips. I felt a rumble in his chest as he deepened the kiss, his eagerness matching my own. Going completely off the rails, I decided to venture out with the tip of my tongue. That seemed to set him off, and he dragged his mouth over mine and down to that most wonderful spot below my ear. He was tasting me like I was the strawberry, and suddenly I was on fire.

I could feel his hands roaming down my waist and curving around my ass as he tried to pull me closer. I felt his erection pressed against me, and even in my haze, I was intimidated by the size. My own hand had traveled up around his neck, and I ran it through His soft dark blond hair. My other hand still held my champagne, forgotten in this crazy frenzy. I brought my hand down to his chest . . . boy, was he built. His muscles flexed beneath his shirt as his hands ran up and down my spine. His lips were back on mine, my head was tilted as we nearly devoured each other's mouths. I heard soft sounds echoing in the room and realized it was me responding to his kisses.

I started to feel out of control, wanting to take it further, when I heard noises coming from the hallway. Clearly, he heard the voices too because his hands dropped, and he groaned as he pulled his lips away from mine. "Shit, that was unexpected," he said as he ran his hands through his hair.

"You can say that again. Definitely a first for me and not what I had planned when I came in here," I responded, taking another swig of my champagne, thankful that I hadn't dropped it on the floor.

I quickly reached over and unlocked the door. I certainly didn't want anyone to suspect what we had been doing. I brushed my hands down the front of my clothes and smoothed my hair, praying that I looked presentable. My lips felt swollen and really quite wonderful, still aching from where his lips had been. I wasn't sure whether to feel embarrassed or angry, so I settled for sarcasm. "I suppose you kiss every new girl you meet that way?" I said, cocking an eyebrow at him.

"Not a chance—just the sassy, beautiful ones." His eyes glinted as he smiled mischievously.

He reached for the door as the voices got closer. "I certainly hope we can do that again some time; this is the most enjoyable encounter I have ever had at one of these dreadful parties." Opening the door, he practically hit Ethan and Chase, chattering as they walked down the hall. As he winked at me, I realized I didn't even know Casanova's name. Just as the words came to my lips to ask, Ethan came in the room and saw me.

"Oh, Charlie, this is great, I see you and Luke have finally met," he said happily.

Chapter 5

LUKE

The sound of a kiss is not so loud as that of a
cannon, but its echo lasts a great deal longer.
—Oliver Wendall Holmes

"So, you never told me your thoughts on the Southern Lady Inn remodel last night." Ethan wiped the sweat from his neck as he walked toward me. We had just finished up a punishing CrossFit workout, but as usual, Ethan seemed barely winded. I, on the other hand, was bent over, still trying to catch my breath after our last set of clean and jerks. I held up one hand as I grabbed my water with the other, then took a long swig.

"I was too busy trying to recover from my encounter with that feisty interior designer," I said, still trying to calm my heart rate.

Ethan scratched his head. "Yeah, you never did tell me how you ended up in that guest room with her. What's the story?"

I felt my pulse start to speed up again. Now was not a good time to reflect on one of the hottest kisses I could recall having . . . maybe ever. I certainly couldn't ever remember getting a hard-on from a simple kiss; that was new. "It was just a strange coincidence. I had wandered in there to get a breather from all the glad-handing, and I guess she had the same idea. Although I'm sure with it being her parent's inn and her project, she was fending off a lot more people than I was," I answered vaguely.

"I think you were running from Martha Winston, who seemed to be desperate for you to meet her very single, youngest daughter. I managed to avoid her when she tried to grab my attention. Sorry I didn't warn you, buddy." Ethan laughed a little too gleefully as I tiredly rubbed my hands over my face.

"It does seem like there is a never-ending stream of Charleston moms with single daughters they're trying to unload. For fuck's sake, this isn't the seventeenth century. Can't they just let their daughters find their own husbands?"

"Speaking of single daughters, you did seem to be hitting it off with the very sexy Charlotte Finley. I sensed some sparks between you two. Am I wrong?"

Clearly, I had not dissuaded his interrogation. "Hitting it off might be a bit of a stretch. I think I pissed her off more than anything. I recall her calling me egotistical." *I also seem to remember liking it*, I thought. "Of course, that was also before she realized who I was, and I may have been flirting with her just a little. So it was probably deserved."

"Leave it to you to hit on the girl, the first time you meet her. Geez, you're such a player." Ethan laughed. "It seems to me, if you got her riled up, then she probably thinks you're hot, either that or more likely, she's not into players. I hope you didn't offend the woman I am interested in hiring for our King Street job." He said, shaking his head.

I'm not so sure offended is the right word, I thought, recalling her eager hands running through my hair and across my chest. Her tongue sneaking in between my lips nearly caused me to take her right there on that very convenient bed. Wouldn't that have been a fun one to explain to our friends? I seriously must have been possessed last night. I looked over at Ethan as we re-racked our weights. "Listen, Eth I agree, that it's always best to have a hands off policy regarding anyone we work with. Now that I know who she is, I have no plans to do anymore flirting." *Or anything else for that matter.* I thought.

"Since we are supposed to be discussing her work, now that you've seen the before and after of Southern Lady, what are your thoughts?" Ethan responded attempting to get us both back on track.

I reflected on my self-guided tour of the inn during the party last night. That was not my first visit, as Ethan knew; I had stayed there pre-renovation. About a year ago, I had met a very sexy flight attendant on one of my business trips and asked her to look me up the next time she was coming into Charleston. She called me about a month later, and, hoping to seal the deal, I booked her a room at the Southern Lady Inn. I had a rule about women sleeping over at my place. It no longer happened. After a couple encounters that got sticky when I wanted them to leave, I vowed to never put myself in that position again. So, I rarely invited women over, preferring to go to their place or book a hotel room, allowing myself the luxury to leave at any time. I did manage to get lucky at the inn with my very willing flight attendant, and while the details of the accommodations were fuzzy, I do remember thinking it was cozy and welcoming.

My reintroduction to the inn was a much more memorable experience; aside from my encounter with the redheaded Charlie, I was pretty blown away when I walked in. I knew before Ethan dragged me there that he was interested in hiring the decorators, so I walked through the space with a critical eye, and it was hard to find a flaw or misstep. I understood from both Sebastian and Ethan that Whimsical Designs had a large hand in the changes to the structure, and obviously, the finishes were all them. It was clear that Chase and Charlie had an impeccable eye. Everything flowed beautifully and felt like it had been there forever without feeling old or worn. I had been touring the guest rooms when I ran into Charlie, and I had just returned to the red bedroom after visiting them all. Each room felt like opening a new and different present with little surprises and treats in each one. But I had gone back to the red room because I had really loved it and wanted to see it again. I was surveying the space, trying to determine just what made it feel so special, when Charlie rushed in, shutting and locking the door. Not what I was expecting at all.

Just as my mind was once again headed back to last night's kiss, Austin made his way over to us from the locker rooms and distracted me from my reminiscing.

"Nice work today guys. You both headed to the office?" He asked giving us both the pre-requisite fist bump for good measure.

I tried not to roll my eyes. Like Ethan, Austin barely broke a sweat in our workouts, his military training made him a beast, especially when it came to endurance. He nearly always wiped the floor with me and while Ethan could throw around more weight, Austin was one fast dude.

Ethan tilted his head in my direction. "Luke and I were just talking about the party last night and the remodel of the Inn. He was about to give me his thoughts on the outcome." He said.

"I have to admit, I really loved it." I responded, as both men looked at me expectantly. "I thought the changes were smart and added to the space. The decor was near perfect and felt cohesive, yet visiting each room felt like a fun adventure. It was everything I would want if I were staying in an historic house in Charleston. And by the way McDonnell, I never told you last night, but great work on the yard. That waterfall was killer."

"Thanks man," he said. "It was one of my favorite jobs to date."

I turned back to Ethan. "Did they seem interested in bidding on our project?" I asked.

"I think they would be foolish not to. Their firm is fairly new and still small, but I think we can capitalize on their talent and get a better price than some of the interior designers with more overhead. I also have to tell you, I really enjoyed working with both Charlie and Chase. Their ideas are great, and they are both down to earth and fun. It was one of my favorite remodeling projects. I also think they made us look good on this one. I've already had people who were at last night's grand reopening reaching out about remodels they want us to look at," Ethan responded.

I grabbed my gym bag and headed for the door, Ethan and Austin followed closely behind. "Give Charlie a call and set up a time for us all to meet. I'd like to give them some more details and hear their ideas firsthand. Then we can decide if we want to put it out to bid or just let them run with it." I couldn't help but wonder what getting Charlie involved with this project might mean. I couldn't ever recall having been more anxious to see a woman again, especially after such a brief meeting. But I was curious to see how it felt being in the same room with her a second time. I wondered if it had just been the romantic room and Charlie's sexy red hair, combined with that leather skirt and heels. I thought about the little sounds she'd made while I was kissing her and the feel of her firm round ass when I pulled her closer. Yep, I was definitely anxious to look into those green eyes again, and the sooner the better, because our one encounter was already way too distracting. "Oh, and by the way Austin, we would also love for you to bid on the landscaping and the pool. The rooftop recreation area is going to be epic and I also want to incorporate some greenspace up there."

He responded with one of his rare smiles. "Cool, have Sebastian send over the plans and I'll put together some numbers."

Ethan was able to set up a meeting for the following afternoon with Whimsical Designs, and both of us were already in our conference room when Charlie and Chase showed up.

It had been momentarily awkward when we ran into Ethan and Chase outside the guest room at the inn. Clearly, our telepathic communication had been working, though, and we both played it off as a funny coincidence that we had run into each other—not letting on that until the moment Ethan let the cat out of the bag, neither of us even knew the other's name. So, I was a little curious to see Charlie's demeanor today.

As our bubbly receptionist, Crystal, brought them into the room, I noticed Charlie was focused entirely on Ethan, so naturally, Chase came over to shake my hand in greeting. "Thank you both so much for giving us the opportunity to learn more about your condo project. We cannot wait to hear your plans. It's an amazing location."

"Well, I was mighty impressed at the outcome of your remodel of the Southern Lady Inn. I had gotten updates from Ethan and seen photos along the way, but the finished product was truly special. You both should be very proud, and the town is just buzzing. I saw that a few of the local papers already posted pictures online," I responded.

Ethan was still standing in the corner chatting with Charlie, who was clearly avoiding me. I tried to appear casual as I checked her out. It was rare for any woman to catch my attention so fully, but I couldn't seem to stop looking her over. I was starting to find it quite aggravating; I hoped our first encounter had just been a fluke. Clearly not the case, since I was already starting to imagine myself grabbing her around the waist and pushing her up against the wall and . . .

"So, should we get this thing started?" Ethan interrupted my inappropriate thoughts. "Luke and I have printed out some of Sebastian's initial floor plans and renderings for you to take a look at, plus we have included some ideas for the lobby and common areas of the building." Ethan looked over at me. "Are you okay, Luke? You seem to be a bit distracted."

I grabbed the chair at the head of the table, as far away from Charlie as possible. "Of course, I was just thinking about a phone call I forgot to return. No big deal, I'll take care of it when we're done here." I smiled at the group, trying to appear more relaxed then I felt.

I let Ethan take the lead, explaining to Charlie and Chase our vision for the project. This allowed me to sit back and watch her without appearing too creepy. She was clearly excited to talk about the design possibilities, and I found her ideas and contributions to be clever and insightful. She and Chase both seemed to have a good grasp of our concept and thought it was a good one. Although I knew they were partners, Chase seemed more comfortable letting Charlie run the show, just leaning in to offer suggestions or to agree with her ideas.

I had spent some time yesterday doing research into Whimsical Designs and Charlotte Finley, and I had been impressed with what she had accomplished in a short amount of time. I was surprised that we had never crossed paths, but like me, she seemed more interested in the work and stayed out of much of the Charleston social scene unless absolutely necessary.

As I watched her, bent over the drawings, her long, slender fingers pointing out different areas as they talked, I felt my chest tightening. I had been with many women, some more beautiful than Charlie, but something about her was knocking me off kilter. That long, thick, auburn hair brushed the tabletop, and she kept throwing it impatiently over her shoulder. She was wearing a sleek, form-fitting dress, just low-cut enough to make me wish I was able to see more of her full breasts. Every so often, her tongue would flick out and touch her top lip, especially when she was getting into what she was saying. I remembered what it felt like to have that tongue in my mouth, urgently seeking mine.

Oh, boy. I leaned back in my chair and brushed a hand through my hair, trying to shake off my train of thought. Charlie looked up at that moment and smiled right at me. It was as if she knew what I was thinking. How could she? I pulled out my best cocky Luke Coleman smile and tried to throw her off. "So, Charlie, what are your thoughts about our plans for the rooftop?"

"Well, Mr. Coleman, it's funny you should ask. We were just getting to that." She gave me a little smirk as she said it.

Before she could continue, I said, "Please call me Luke. It'll be much easier if we're all on a first-name basis, don't you think?"

"Of course, Luke." She gave me an even bigger smile and continued, "At this point, there are no other buildings offering a rooftop recreation area, and the footprint is large enough that you can put in not only a pool, but also a running track around the perimeter. At one end, you could include an outdoor kitchen and a large bar area for the residents to use for parties, and over here, there is room for a grilling area for individuals or smaller groups. You can have seating areas and tables with umbrellas away from the pool and surround the pool deck with

lounge chairs and perhaps a screened-in cabana at either end."
She smiled up at me again, and my heart beat a little faster as
I watched her rosy lips curl up. I couldn't help but smile back.

"That all sounds incredible, providing, of course, that the
city will give us a permit allowing us to do all that. I only know
of two other rooftop pools, both in hotels. What do you think,
Ethan? I know you have been doing some research on that
topic." I forced my eyes away from Charlie's mouth and over
to Ethan.

He scratched the stubble that always seemed to be perma-
nently on his chin and looked back down at the plans. "There
is certainly the space for it, and provided we are able to get the
insurance we'll need and proper barriers around the perimeter,
I can't imagine why it would be a problem. But you never know,
the Charleston Architectural Review Board is a fickle bunch."

"Do we have any friends on the board who may be willing
to advise us on the best approach to get a yes?" I asked with a
wink. "So much political bullshit in this town."

Ethan laughed. "Of course we do; I can make some calls
this week."

Chase and Charlie asked a few more questions about the
building's exterior and plans for landscaping as the meeting
started to wind down. Ethan looked pleased, and fearing he
was about to close the deal, I decided to jump in before he
said anything he couldn't take back. I felt very good about
Charlie and Chase's ideas, but I thought we still needed some
time before offering them the job. *Or maybe you just need some
time to decide if you can work with the enticing Charlotte Finley,*
I thought.

"This has been very fruitful, and I have no doubt that Whimsical Designs has a lot to offer our project, but let Ethan and me discuss a few things, and we will be in touch very soon." I extended my hand to Charlie, who hesitated briefly before reaching out and taking it. I saw something flicker in her eyes. Was she nervous? But then she relaxed and smiled up at me.

"Thank you both again for allowing us the opportunity to hear more and share our ideas." She was still holding my hand as she glanced at Ethan. "We look forward to hearing from you." She said as she let go of my hand. *Oh, fuck, why did she have to let go? And why did it bother me when she did?*

Ethan and Chase shook hands and said their goodbyes, and Ethan opened the door and escorted them out.

Charlie didn't glance back as she walked away, thank goodness, because it would have been awkward for her to see me so clearly staring at her gently swaying ass. I sighed and rubbed the back of my neck. Thank God it was five o'clock because I really needed a drink. My favorite barstool was calling my name. I went to my office to shut things down, grabbed my coat, and went in search of Ethan. I also needed a drinking buddy.

Chapter 6

CHARLIE

A strong woman is one who feels deeply and loves fiercely. Her tears flow as abundantly as her laughter. A strong woman is both soft and powerful, she is both practical and spiritual. A strong woman in her essence is a gift to the world.
—Native American saying

As I headed back to Sullivan's Island, I wanted to bang my head on the steering wheel. What in God's name had possessed me to kiss a strange man at my parent's party? And just my luck that said man turned out to be Luke frickin' Coleman. How had I not realized who he was? Granted, I had never personally met him or, to my knowledge, even been in the same room with him, but I was sure I had at least seen his picture. After all, his company had been written up several times in the local paper, and I was fairly sure he had received an award for being one of the thirty under thirty to watch a couple of years ago.

I guess I was just so thrown off guard to find him in the guest suite that my mind didn't connect the dots. Besides, we were too busy making out to exchange names.

I wondered if our little encounter would impact Luke's decision to hire Whimsical Designs. Normally, I might have just laughed the whole thing off, but I would kick myself if we missed out on this amazing opportunity due to my impulsive actions. Should I reach out to Luke and make sure he understood that I was a complete professional and didn't normally do that sort of thing? I mean, I NEVER did. Since Joe and I split up, I had only dated a few men. One guy, who shall remain nameless, ghosted me after I slept with him on our fourth date. That was not great for my ego, and I decided to take a break from dating and focus on work.

I couldn't imagine what Luke thought of a woman who practically threw herself at him the first time they met. *Wait a second*, I thought, shaking my head, *he was kissing me too, and I distinctly remember his large hands cupping my ass and an obvious erection pressing against my stomach. Why am I the bad person in this scenario? Ugh, I do need to call him. I cannot let this jeopardize such a great opportunity for me and Chase. This is stupid, there is no reason we shouldn't be able to work together and be professional.* I decided that tomorrow I would call him and straighten this whole thing out. I would not think about how my breath caught in my throat and my heart sped up when he shook my hand. Nor would I remember how incredible he looked in his suit at our meeting today, his blond hair ruffled from running his hand through it. That reminded me of running *my* hand through his hair as he kissed me up against the four-poster bed.

STOP THIS. I needed to not think about him this way. Whew, I could do this. I could do this. Yes, I could.

I had been in the office for three hours the next morning before I finally got up the nerve to call Luke at his office. Part of me hoped he wouldn't answer and I could just leave a message, but deep down, I knew I had to put this behind me. Fortunately (or unfortunately), his receptionist put me through to his office, and my heart skipped a little when I heard his deep voice on the other end of the phone.

"Hello there, Ms. Finley, what a pleasant surprise it is to hear from you."

I knew I was in trouble when the sound of his voice flowed over me like expensive scotch and sent shivers down my spine. Everything I had rehearsed flew out the window and I burst out with a quick, "I think we should meet and talk about what happened at the inn. Or if it's not convenient, we could just talk now on the phone." I heard him chuckle softly, which naturally pissed me off. Why did I let this guy get me so riled up? "And I thought we agreed to use first names," I continued. I could hear him actually laughing now.

"Calm down, little firecracker, I'm happy to meet you. It's close to lunchtime, why don't we grab a bite at Butcher & Bee and clear the air?"

I was caught off guard by his agreeable response. *Better sooner rather than later*, I thought. "Fine, good, that sounds good. Should we make it one o'clock?" I could see him smiling in that cocky way.

"Looking forward to it; see you at one."

I got to the restaurant a few minutes early. I wanted to be seated and get myself together before Luke got there. Clearly, he must have had the same idea because as I walked in, I immediately saw him at a table across the room. I was relieved he hadn't chosen to sit at the bar because I wasn't sure that my nerves could handle being that close to him, and I needed to keep my wits about me. "Think professional, Charlie," I muttered under my breath as I lifted my chin and walked over to the table. His eyes never left me as I walked over and sat down, but I refused to let that shake my resolve. He was just a regular guy, albeit a very appealing one, but I interacted with handsome guys all the time. Hell, Ethan was incredibly hot, and even Sebastian was quite handsome in a kind of nerdy way. Luke was just another hot man that I had no interest in. *Yeah. Right.*

Luke's eyes crinkled in the corners as he smiled at me while I took my seat across from him. "My day has just gotten so much better. And to think, I assumed I would be stuck in my office staring at spreadsheets and working on budgets all afternoon. Thanks for enticing me away from all that." He disarmed me so easily, and I couldn't help but smile back. Maybe this wouldn't be so hard.

"I really just thought that we needed to talk things out." The waiter walked to over to take our drink order before I could say any more. I decided to break my day-drinking rule and ordered a sparkling rose. I needed some liquid courage, after all.

Luke watched him walk away and then turned back to me, lifting one eyebrow and waving his hand, encouraging me to continue.

"I'm not going to lie to you, Luke, landing your King Street project would be a game changer for Whimsical Designs. And right now, for me, nothing is more important than my business. I've spent the last two years with Chase working around the clock trying to create a name for ourselves in Charleston. I would love to see us get to the next level, and I think your job could get us there. I also think we have what it takes to help make your King Street Condos the talk of the town." I took a deep breath as I saw the waiter heading back over with our drinks. After taking our order, he again left, and Luke smiled at me encouragingly, so I continued. "I want you to know that what happened between us at the inn is not a regular occurrence for me. I've never in my life kissed a man I didn't know, and I definitely wouldn't have done so, had I known who you were." I smiled wryly and attempted to soften my words. "Not to say it was an unpleasant experience."

Luke nodded thoughtfully, and he seemed to choose his words carefully, "Look, Charlie, I understand where you're coming from; I mean, I really get it. Ethan and I scrounged and scraped to get Coleman Grant off the ground, and a couple lucky breaks and a lot of long days and nights got us to where we are. I wouldn't want to jeopardize that for anything. I'm not sure what got into me the other night, and while I have some experience with women . . . "

I almost spit out my rose when he wiggled his eyebrows at me. *Wow*, I thought, *he's pretty funny too.*

"I have never done anything like what happened between us. You looked kind of sexy standing over there getting all feisty, and I just gave into an impulse. As enjoyable as it was,

I would like to think we can control ourselves if we decide to work together," he said.

The waiter delivered our food, and we both started eating in silence. I was thinking about what he had said. He seemed very confident that what happened was a one-time thing, and I needed to believe that too. I couldn't imagine the complications of us getting involved during such a big and important project for both of our companies. Not to mention, Chase would kill me. Also, I had discreetly asked around about Luke Coleman, and there was no doubt he was way above my pay grade. He seemed to squire around some of the most beautiful and successful women in Charleston, and I didn't doubt that many of them ended up in his bed.

I finished my bite of food and decided to get right to the point. "So, I guess what I'm asking you, Luke, is if our initial encounter is going to affect your decision to hire Whimsical Designs for this project?" He looked at me steadily, taking another bite of his salad. *How on earth can a guy look so sexy eating salad?* I thought. Shit, there I went again, but damn, he was looking at me so intently and his eyes were just so . . . blue.

"Charlie, I know Ethan wanted to hire you and Chase yesterday. I just thought it would be wise to think on it for a day or two. That's how I roll—I like to think things through—and yes, Ethan says I tend to, in his words, 'mindfuck' everything." He smiled, and I laughed; he really was easy to talk to. "However, in this case, I happen to agree with Ethan and with you. I'm sure Whimsical Designs will do amazing things with our condo community. I'm also confident we can both be professionals and work together without feeling the need to grope each other at every opportunity." He set his fork down and rested his square chin on his hands. "But I sure am disappointed we won't have the chance to do that."

After my lunch with Luke, I decided to skip going back to the office. I knew Everleigh's coffee shop tended to be quiet before the early evening rush of commuters returned to the island. I decided I needed a sounding board, and I knew that while that she might shake her head and laugh at my foolishness, she would never judge me. As I drove home, I used my Bluetooth to call Chase.

"Hello, darlin'." His Southern drawl sounded thicker than usual.

"Hey, babe, I wanted to be the first to share the good news." I smiled into the phone. I hurried on before he had a chance to interject, "We should be getting all the details on the King Street project from Coleman Grant by the end of business tomorrow. They want us to look things over, then schedule a meeting with Luke, Ethan, and Sebastian to go over more details so we can put together a bid. So long as we can agree on the budget, they won't interview any other designers."

"Woohoo!" Chase shouted into the phone. "Things are really looking up for Whimsical Designs, baby doll! We are going to go from the little guy trying to get noticed to the hottest design firm in Charleston overnight." It wasn't hard to imagine him dancing around his office.

"Apparently, they were impressed with our ideas, and I think our boutique size is appealing as well. Hopefully, we can live up to their expectations. Chase, this is by far the biggest thing we've done. We're going to have to put any other jobs on hold for a while."

Chase was quiet for a minute. "I guess I'll put a call in to Tad. He had a project he wanted us to look at after seeing the inn the other night. I know it wasn't nearly the scale of the Coleman Grant job, but I'm sure he won't be happy."

"Why do you say that? I'm sure he can hire one of the many other designers in town," I responded.

"I know you tend to stay out of the local gossip, but it's well known that he and Luke are bitter rivals—mostly on Tad's end, I think—and I'm sure his knickers will be in a twist that his favorite little designer is going to be working for the enemy." He sighed. "Oh, well, Tad is just going to have to get over it. As you said, we aren't the only game in town, and he will just have to try a different tactic to get in your pants."

I bristled. "That's ridiculous, Chase. He and Britt have been an item for years; he's just a flirt."

"Whatever you say, Charlie, but I have a feeling this is going to cause a bit of a stir. But no worries, your boy Chase is always on board for a little Southern drama." He laughed loudly at his own joke.

"Everyone is just going to have to get over themselves, because you and I are going to knock this one out of the park and really set the Lowcountry on its head!" I exclaimed, pumping my hand in the air for good measure, even though the only one who saw it was the elderly man in the Volvo next to me. I gave him a friendly wave.

"I'm heading over to see Everleigh at the bakery. I need a little girl time before things get too crazy," I said, preparing to hang up.

"Girl time without me?" Chase huffed, pretending to be offended.

"Oh, please, Chase, we can all gossip and giggle this weekend. Not everything is meant for your judgmental ears. Hopefully we'll get all the paperwork early tomorrow so we can start working on it. I don't have any appointments until later in the day. The sooner we can get this contract nailed down, the better."

Chase snickered. "I'll pretend to ignore that comment about my judgment because you called and gave me such good news, but don't think you haven't piqued my curiosity. Something is going on with you, girl, and don't think I haven't noticed. I'll see you in the morning. Say hi to my bestie!"

I laughed as he hung up in my ear. I really didn't think there was any reason to get Chase all riled up with stories of Luke; after all, it was essentially going to amount to nothing, right?

I sat at the counter at EverLand Coffee & Sweets while I waited for Everleigh to finish stocking the case. She had two part-time employees working this afternoon, and I managed to convince her to take a walk with me on the beach before she had to come back and close up at 7:00 p.m. I even offered to help her shut down, so she could send her workers home. Fortunately, Ever nearly always wore leggings with some kind of funky top and tennis shoes, so she was all set for a walk on the beach. I looked down at my skirt, blouse, and heels and shrugged. At least I could just carry my shoes, and luckily, my skirt was flowy, so it wouldn't hinder my stride. It was a beautiful, warm, spring day, and I planned to sink my toes into the surf.

As Everleigh untied her signature frilly apron, I pulled a hairband out of my purse and tied my hair off my face in anticipation of the breezier beach air. Ever came from behind the counter and grabbed me by the arm, looping her arm through mine and pulling me close. As an only child, I never got tired of her affectionate hugs and touches. We had been friends for over a decade, and I felt so fortunate that we had always shared all our secrets and heartaches. I corrected my thoughts: *Well, except where Ethan was concerned.*

"So, what's the big news?" Everleigh asked as she led us out the door into the bright sunshine. "You hardly ever ask me to ditch work to hang out, and a walk on the beach seems kind of . . . unexpected." She wriggled her nose at me, trying and failing to look serious.

"Well . . . "I said slowly as we walked briskly toward the beach. "Whimsical Designs got some great news today."

"What, wait . . . let me guess!" she squealed, bouncing as she walked. She still held my arm, so I had no choice but to bounce with her. "You landed the deal for the Coleman Grant condo job!"

I smiled, nodding. "Yep, you guessed it. We sure did, girl-friend. Chase and I are excited, overwhelmed, and terrified already."

"Wow, Charles, this is the greatest news ever!" She was practically shouting now. "You guys are going to be the talk of the town!"

"Yeah, well, according to Chase, not everyone in Charleston is going to be pleased," I added.

"What do you mean?" Everleigh looked puzzled.

"According to Chase, he had set up a meeting with Tad to talk about a project his real estate firm was working on, and he thinks Tad is going to be bent that we're going to be unavailable. He seems to think Tad has a thing for me and he also has a big grudge against Luke Coleman."

Everleigh's eyes grew wide with understanding. "Fuck, that could be awkward, Charlie. I agree with Chase. Tad definitely is hot for you; maybe Britt isn't doing a good enough job in the sack. I always thought she was a cold fish. Chase does keep his ear on all the town gossip, so if he says Tad has a boner for Coleman Grant, it's probs true. But I wouldn't worry about that, girl, just focus on doing a great job for Luke and Ethan, and nothing else will matter. Other companies will be clamoring to hire you, and you'll just have to hire more designers to keep up with demand. You can build an interior design empire." She swept her hand through the air in a grand gesture as we walked along the beach, heading for the water so we could dip our toes.

"There's one other teensy-weensy complication." I looked out at the ocean to avoid looking her in the eye. "Remember how I mentioned meeting Luke at the grand opening of the inn?"

"Yeah, so?" she said, shrugging.

"There was a bit more to it." I blew out a breath before continuing, "He actually kissed me, or . . . I kissed him, or . . . we kissed each other."

"What, wait, I'm confused. I thought you said that was the first time you met him?" Everleigh was probably looking at me now in amazement, so I avoided her eyes.

"It was, it's . . . hard to explain, kind of a 'I guess you had to be there' sort of thing. Also, I should mention, it was a toe-curling, face-exploding kind of kiss—possibly the best of my life." I decided to take a peek at Everleigh's face. Bad idea. Her mouth formed a circle, and her eyes were really wide. Then she squealed a little.

"Are you kidding me!" She laughed. "I can't say I'm surprised. Luke Coleman is the hottest of the hot. I mean, that ass and those big arms, I just can't."

"Well, I did, and I'm afraid I liked it. But it's not going any further. We had lunch yesterday and agreed that we would put aside our weird attraction for the sake of working together on this King Street project. I just can't jeopardize this opportunity, Ever." I sighed again. "But, man, it was a great kiss. I nearly wrapped my legs around him and climbed him like a tree."

Everleigh put her hands on her cheeks and looked at me incredulously. "Charlie, how can you walk away without exploring this? I am so jealous; it sounds amazing. Luke is successful, not to mention so sexy."

I made a face at Everleigh. "Who's to say it would even go anywhere? We both know Luke has a rep for being a player, and that's just not what I need right now. I have finally managed to reassemble my damaged ego post-Joe, and I am not about to set myself up again. Even if the idea of a good solid fuck is appealing . . . "

"Never doubt the healing qualities of a good one-nighter," Everleigh agreed.

"Besides, I'm pretty sure we're on the same page, that this was just an unexpected impulse moment that won't be repeated, so there's that," I responded firmly.

"If you say so, Charlie, but that ass . . . just sayin'." She laughed as I punched her in the arm.

Chapter 7

LUKE

If you take time to realize what your dream is and what you really want in life—no matter what it is, whether it's sports or in other fields—you have to realize that there is always work to do, and you want to be the hardest working person in whatever you do, and you put yourself in a position to be successful. And you have to have a passion about what you do.
—Stephen Curry

As Ethan and I wrapped up our meeting with Sebastian to iron out all the details for King Street, my mind drifted back to yesterday's lunch with Charlie. Compared to our impromptu meeting at the inn, she seemed so uncertain during lunch. I had definitely seen her fiery temper flare a couple of times, but she'd clearly been out of her element. This surprised me because I had been blown away by her self-assuredness at our first meeting, and she'd seemed more subdued and controlled at lunch. It made me curious to peel back the layers. Of course, now that we were planning to hire her company to manage the design aspect of our project, this might prove a bit complicated. This project was my baby, and I was already heavily invested in its success. I planned to be 100 percent involved in all the decisions regarding the remodel and design. This would require me to work very closely with Charlotte Finley.

I rubbed the stubble on my chin and closed my eyes for a minute as I thought about how adorable she looked at lunch. Clearly, she had tried to dial down the sexy, but that was impossible in my opinion. Even in a simple olive-green skirt, off-white blouse with little birds on it, and low pumps, I still imagined bending her over the table, lifting that skirt, and exploring what was underneath.

I was jolted out of my dirty thoughts by Ethan's fingers snapping in front of my face. "Hey, dumbass, where'd ya go? Sebastian has another meeting to get to, and we need to wrap this up so we can send it over to Charlie and Chase."

"He must be daydreaming about one of his hot hookups. Another flight attendant, Luke?" Sebastian smirked.

"Not hardly," I answered drily. "Just drifting off—I didn't get much sleep last night, and no, it had nothing to do with a hookup."

"I think we have enough info to give to Whimsical so they can get us some numbers. Unless you need to add anything, Luke?" Ethan looked at me as he closed his folder and stood.

"Nope, I think we're good to go. Let's get this ball rolling; I'm ready to get moving on this thing," I responded as Sebastian and I both stood and headed for the door.

Sebastian reached over and patted my shoulder. "I expect we'll have preliminary approval from the city in a few days. Once we get the bid back from Whimsical Designs, we can start working on the details to submit to the architectural review board. That's where the fun begins." He laughed without much humor. "Hopefully, I can pull some strings on the board to move things along for you. Try not to piss anyone off in the meantime." He looked pointedly at me. "We need all the help we can get."

After saying goodbye to Sebastian, Ethan and I stopped to talk outside his office.

"Listen, I think we should deliver a copy of the plans and the other documents to Whimsical in person. They should have a full set of plans so they can put together an accurate bid. Aren't you heading out to meet a customer for a walk-through not far from their office?" Ethan asked.

"Yep. How quickly can we pull it all together? I only have about forty-five minutes until my appointment."

"I have most of it assembled; I just need to grab another set of blueprints and print out the nondisclosure agreement and you're good to go." Ethan turned to head into his office. "Just swing by on your way out, and I'll have it all here for you."

"Thanks, buddy," I responded. "I'll be back in a few."

Fifteen minutes later, I was on my way to see Charlie and Chase. I decided to drive so I didn't have to walk and carry a full set of blueprints. I thought I would see about leaving my car at the Whimsical office so I could walk from there to my appointment. The fewer times I had to look for parking downtown, the better. One of the main reasons I enjoyed living in the city was that I could walk most anywhere. Despite the fact that I loved to walk, I owned a small sports car and an SUV. I often left my sports car at the office so I would have it when I needed it, but my house was just a ten-minute walk to my office. I lived on the water in the Wagener Terrace neighborhood of Charleston. It was a more family-friendly part of town, with larger lots and homes with front and backyards, a luxury in the city. A couple years ago, I rescued a pit bull named Sadie, and I wanted to have a yard for her and to be near Hampton Park so I could take her for walks. I found an amazing property right on the water, but the house was rundown, so with Ethan's help, I tore it down to build my dream home.

I always loved homes, and in my younger years, I would tour model homes and open houses, admiring the architecture and the luxury features. I hoped to someday own a home of my own, but I never imagined having such a special place at only thirty-one years old. But Ethan and I had worked hard, and I had made some outstanding investments early in our business that have paid tremendous dividends, allowing me to enjoy some unexpected luxuries. I love mid-century modern design, and with Sebastian's help, my house has beautiful clean lines with dark wood and metal accenting the moss-green cement siding. Despite the modern aesthetic, it still has an historic Charleston feel with multiple porches and large, airy doors and windows. Being on the water, the house is built above a four-car garage, with a staircase in front that widens at the bottom. There is a rarely used circular driveway at the bottom of the steps that wraps around a landscaped garden with a beautiful koi fish fountain I'd found during a trip to Maine. The entry to the garage is along the side of the house, and most of my friends park on the side when they came to visit. I rarely have more than a few friends over for an occasional poker night, so the driveway is a bit more for show.

Inside the house, it's fairly modern, but the decor is warmed up by some mid-century pieces and a few antiques I'd stumbled upon during my travels. The main floor is very open, with the kitchen overlooking the spacious family room and a large, handmade, wood table with iron legs just off the kitchen. I liked to be relaxed, the upholstered furniture is oversized and comfortable. I have two big leather chairs that recline, and I admit to owning an Xbox because I love to play sports-themed video games—sue me. A huge floor-to-ceiling stone fireplace flanks one end of the main living area, and while it rarely gets that cold in Charleston, it is nice to be able to build a fire on the few cold nights in the winter. The kitchen is sleek and high-end, but with a funky, bright-blue apron sink. I'm not much of a cook—it is hard to get excited about cooking for one person—but I have a weird obsession with cookware, and I have a rather large collection of blue Le Creuset. The only cooking I love to do is on my Big Green Egg smoker. Grilling is a great excuse to invite the guys over to watch sports or play Xbox.

There are no formal areas in my house, but the living area is quite large, and I have a separate office space on the main level. It feels very old-school "library" with dark paneling and built-in bookcases made of reclaimed wood that look vintage, even though they were custom-built for the house. Sebastian found the desk at one of Charleston's many antique malls, and it is one of my prized possessions. A dark walnut, it has surprisingly smooth lines with wide, sturdy legs and a slight curve around the edges to soften it up. It has a long drawer in the middle and deep drawers on either side. It is surprisingly functional for an antique and is a great centerpiece in the room. Dark-blue leather chairs flank a small chest of drawers in one corner, and a large display case houses my antique gun collection that I inherited from my father, in the other. It is definitely the coziest room in the house, and I spend a lot of time in there, working or reading.

My favorite room of the house is the master suite. It is also on the main floor, and while the room is by no means grand, it has a sweeping balcony overlooking the pool and the marsh as well as a luxurious bath with all the bells and whistles. My bedroom even has a little nook with an oversize dog bed for my best girl, Sadie.

For those naysayers who thought I couldn't have a committed relationship, well, they clearly haven't met my dog. Several years ago, I went with Ethan to the animal shelter so he could surprise his wife with a kitten on Valentine's Day. He walked out with a fuzzy kitten, and I walked out with a mixed-breed pit bull. She is my favorite companion, and we love walking around Hampton Park together and playing ball in the dog park.

In addition to Sadie's dog bed, I'd also splurged on an adjustable Tempur-Pedic mattress and the most comfortable bedding I could find. Just off the bedroom is a master bath with an amazing steam shower and whirlpool tub. Hey, no shame in a post-gym soak, and that steam shower is the bomb. I spend my days helping other people buy and sell homes, and my love for sticks and bricks has carried over to my own space. Having grown up with very little in the way of luxuries, I feel lucky to be able to enjoy the fruits of my labor.

At times, I am maudlin about the fact that both my parents are dead. I would have loved to have been able to share some of my good fortune with them. They spent their lives working long hours to provide for me and my two brothers, and they were never able to just relax and enjoy their years of hard work. I seldom dwell on the accident that took their lives when I was in my last year of college. My brothers were older and lived in my hometown in Maryland when it happened. I'd been in South Carolina in college, and my oldest brother, Jack, had called me at school. It had been late at night, and I remember being asleep when I'd gotten the call on my cell. I'd been confused as to why Jack was calling me so late. Apparently, my parents had been on the way home from a rare night out when they'd been T-boned by a driver who had run a stop sign. According to the hospital, the impact killed them instantly. The driver was in a big Ford F-250, and my parents' little Honda Civic didn't stand a chance.

My parents' death impacted my last year of college, but Ethan helped pull me through, and I was still able to graduate in May. Both of my brothers came to my graduation, and I know they were proud. I was the first college graduate in our family. But looking out into the crowd and knowing my parents weren't there left a mark. I often thought about how much they would have enjoyed my and Ethan's success—they'd loved him like a son. It killed me knowing they would never be able to enjoy it firsthand. My mom always loved the water, and some nights when I would sit on my deck looking out at the marsh grasses burning copper and gold as the sun set, I would think how much I would love to have her sitting next to me, drinking a glass of pinot and soaking it all in. I am sure my dad would have been puttering in the kitchen—he so rarely sat still—but Mom, she would have really enjoyed that view.

I attribute much of my success to my parents. They had a work ethic I couldn't help but admire and although we didn't have many extras growing up, my brothers and I always felt loved. I never really bemoaned the things I didn't have. My parents never complained about their long hours or made us worry about how much three big growing boys ate every day. There was always food on the table, a slap on the back from my dad, and a gentle hug from my mom to get us through the day. I missed them, but I know they would have wanted me to move on and enjoy my life. I just wish they could have been here to see how far I have come.

I was still a little distracted by my thoughts of the past when I walked into the offices of Whimsical Designs. Charlie and Chase didn't appear to have a receptionist, but they obviously anticipated the need for one eventually because they had a cute little lobby area with a funky desk in the corner. I chuckled to myself, imagining a kooky, middle-aged woman with large, brightly colored accessories and cowboy boots answering the phones. I passed through the lobby to look for Chase or Charlie, and as I turned the corner, I ended up with a handful of sexy curves and a face full of red, silky hair. I couldn't help but breathe in the sweet smell of lavender and eucalyptus as I grabbed her shoulders to keep her from falling.

"Oh, shit. Luke, I am so sorry." She stumbled over her words, clearly surprised to see me.

I smiled down at her, enjoying our unexpected collision. I knew it was probably not a good idea, but it was great having an excuse to touch her, and I could tell by the pulse in her throat that I might be having an effect on her too. I was trying to decide how long I could keep my hands on her without becoming obvious when she gracefully extricated herself from my grasp and sidestepped around me. It was clear she was trying to get control of the situation, where I just preferred to revel a little longer.

I gestured to the satchel that was thrown over my shoulder, blueprints sticking out of the top. "Ethan asked me to drop all of this off for you, so you can get started on putting together your bid. I was just looking for your office."

"Oh, yes, wonderful." Her smile nearly knocked me over. "That's so nice of you to bring it by." She gestured behind me, toward the lobby. "Chase is interviewing potential assistants this week; we figured it was time to bring in some reinforcements. Did you have any items you want to review with me? Chase is out, but I can share any updates with him when he gets back."

I nodded. "Ethan sent over the full set of blueprints. I have a few minutes if you want to quickly go through and see if you have any questions while I'm here." I smiled, trying to put her at ease.

"Sure, that would be very helpful. Let's just go in the conference room," she said as she quickly turned to head back down the hall.

Mmmmhmmm, I thought to myself as I followed behind, admiring the view. This girl really had my attention. I could already see that working with Charlie was going to be a blessing and a curse. Her backside gently swayed, hypnotizing me as we walked. Most of the women I had "dated" tended to be very tall and thin—lots of models and socialites who probably never ate more than a few pieces of lettuce and drank their weight in chardonnay. Charlie was also on the taller side, she had generous curves, and I imagined she could throw down a steak or two. My mouth started to water thinking about taking her out for a nice steak dinner and then heading back to her place for dessert. Geez, I needed to think about something more appropriate. Luckily, we were walking into the conference room, so I could turn my attention to blueprints.

Charlie waved me to one of the chairs, indicating I should sit down, and I did so after pulling the plans out of my bag and rolling them out onto the table. Charlie leaned in front of me to get a better view, and once again I got a whiff of lavender—it must be her soap or shampoo. Whatever it was, I could have sat there and smelled it all day. We spent a few minutes combing through the plans with Charlie asking a few questions and clarifying some of our design ideas. I found that I was really enjoying talking with her; her observations were refreshing, and she was clearly a very intelligent woman. It was nice to be close to her when she was relaxed and enthusiastic about my project.

I hated to leave but realized when looking at my watch that I was going to have to walk fast to make my next meeting on time. I leaned back, preparing to get up, and felt my shoulder brush across her soft breast as I stood up. Charlie jumped like she had gotten an electric shock and quickly moved away.

"I'm sorry, I didn't mean to startle you." I said laying my hand on her shoulder trying to get her to relax. "I just have to head out to a meeting down the street. Do you mind if I leave my car in your lot? It's just a couple of blocks away." Her skin was warm beneath her thin sweater and I resisted the urge to stroke her skin temptingly within reach above her neckline.

She had recovered her composure and gave me a shy smile, as I dropped my hand regretfully. "No, of course, it's fine. We aren't expecting any clients, so there's plenty of space."

"Great, I'll just grab it on my way back. Let me know if you have any additional questions after going through that pile that Ethan and Sebastian sent over. I know it's a lot of information to take in," I said as I headed for the door.

She followed me and held out her hand. "I feel like I keep thanking you, but we are so excited to work on this project, so thank you once more."

Her smile was sincere, and her hand was soft and warm in mine, and I thought, *Right now, I would give you most anything you asked for.* I shook my head slightly and smiled back. "I know we're going to have a blast bringing this vision to life, and I'm looking forward to working with you and Chase. I'm glad that Ethan recommended you." I turned and walked out before I said something foolish because I was feeling sort of warm and fuzzy, a very unnatural feeling for me. It was time to get my head back in the game, and I headed to my next appointment with a determined stride.

Chapter 8

CHARLIE

Between the wish and the thing the world lies waiting.
—*Cormac McCarthy*

My head felt a little light as I watched Luke walk away. I was puzzled by the effect he had on me. I spent years with Joe, and I had always been comfortable with him, I never had this shaky feeling of being just a little off-kilter. I was used to being in control, and aside from my divorce, I worked very hard to keep everything in my life on track. My friends thought of me as a free spirit, but in my own head, I always knew exactly where I was going. Every time I was around Luke, I just felt a little out of control, never sure what he might do and how I would react. Maybe it was because of our first encounter. I'd done something impulsive—out of character—and I had actually enjoyed it, in the moment. It seemed like whenever he came around, it was difficult for me to focus. On the other hand, when we started talking about the King Street condos, I felt my juices start to flow and I was into the work, but the minute we stopped talking business, I felt that weird little sizzle just being near him. When he brushed against me at the conference table, I nearly made a fool of myself with my over-reaction. It was just . . . every time he touched me, I wanted . . . wanted more. Ugh, I needed to get out of my own head. After all, he was like any other smart, successful, good-look-ing (really good-looking) guy. I worked with them every day; why did this one make me feel like I was about to melt into a puddle every time he came close?

I looked at my watch; it was after 4:00 p.m. Clearly, Chase was not coming back to the office after his meeting with Tad. I grimaced, hoping it had not gone too badly. Chase had felt it was best to let him down in person; he'd seemed convinced that Tad was going to be upset that we wouldn't be available to help with their townhome infill project. I wasn't so sure. It seemed like they had numerous other options, and I was sure one of the many other interior design companies would be glad to work with him. After all, his family's real estate holdings were vast, and their company had lots of upcoming opportunities. I, however, was happy to have an excuse not to work with him. Ever since high school, when he tried to kiss me after a football game, I had just never felt comfortable being around him. He was just so sure of himself and when I pushed him away that day under the bleachers he got really angry and acted like I had led him on. Since then, every time I was around him, I got a slimy vibe and he looked at me like he was picturing me naked, ugh. It was the opposite problem to the one I had with Luke, which, while off-putting, was at least sort of fun. With Luke I wanted to run at him not away.

I decided to spend the next hour going through all the paperwork Luke had brought over; that way, I could give Chase a rundown on Monday (or tomorrow, if I could convince him to come in for a bit). It was Friday night, and I knew Everleigh probably wouldn't want to come into town, but maybe I could track down Chase and convince him to meet me for a drink. I could dangle all my new intel as an incentive. With that decided, I put my head down and lost myself in work for a bit.

I'm not sure how long I had been at it, and I found myself getting excited about this project the more I read. I couldn't seem to put it down. I was so engaged in what I was doing that I didn't even notice I was no longer alone in my office. I looked up to find Luke quietly and intently watching me. I admit, I jumped a bit because I wasn't expecting anyone, and I had no idea how long he had been standing in the doorway. One side of his mouth turned up in what was clearly the signature Luke Coleman cocky grin.

"It looks like you're working on something very interesting there. Anyone could have snuck up on you."

"How long have you been standing there?" I stammered in my usual, awkward-around-Luke manner.

"Relax, little firecracker, I just walked in. I was about to announce myself when you looked up. Since I had to swing by and get my car, I figured I would check in and see if you had a chance to look over the stuff I dropped off. I can see you're all over it." I was still letting my head wrap around the nickname he seemed so fond of using for me, when he caught me off guard again. "I was going to head over to 492 and sit on the patio and enjoy some appetizers and maybe a scotch on my Friday evening. Perhaps you'd like to join me?" He quickly added, "We could talk about the project."

I considered his offer. Whimsical-Designs Charlie was dying to talk more about the project, especially with the man who had all the answers. Sex-deprived Charlie, who was absurdly attracted to aforementioned man, was jumping up and down, waving her arms and screaming, "DON'T DO IT!" I wondered if I could convince Chase to join us or if maybe Ethan was a possibility. I needed a buffer.

"Sure, I would love to join you and talk about the project. Maybe I can get Chase to join us," I responded after a minute of internal deliberation.

He shrugged. "Of course—the more, the merrier."

"Okay, I'll text him. Can you give me about five minutes to freshen up?"

He smiled. "I think you are quite refreshing as you are, but I'm happy to wait. I'll just hang in the lobby and check my messages."

I gathered all the papers into a neat pile and headed for the bathroom. "Perfect, I'll be quick . . . and thanks for the compliment." I smiled back at him.

Chase responded to my text to say he was headed out on a hot date with some sexy Latin guy he had been pursuing for a couple of weeks. Since I had failed to fill him in on my Luke drama, I really didn't have any reason to insist that he join us so I didn't have to be alone with Luke I-Could-Bounce-a-Quarter-Off-of-His-Ass Coleman. Not that I had spent too much time looking at his ass, ok maybe a little time. I considered texting Ethan and inviting him, but I felt that might come off as desperate, and the last thing I wanted Luke to suspect was that I was afraid to be alone with him. So much for being able to be professional. After touching up my lip gloss and putting some concealer under my eyes to hide my end-of-week shadows, I headed out.

Luke stood quickly as I turned the corner into the lobby and held out his elbow. "Shall we go?"

I tramped down any misgivings and confidently reached for his bicep. "Lead on, fine sir."

Luke and I had spent the last hour talking intently about his plans for King Street. I was warmed by his enthusiasm and maybe a little bit by the direct way he looked at me while we talked. I had never been with a man who made me feel so alive, so in the moment. I realized I was actually having fun. Luke was amazing to look at, yes, but he was interesting, too. He had already had tremendous success in business, but it was clear that this project meant so much more to him. This was his vision from the start, and if it worked, it would mean some amazing opportunities for Coleman Grant. I began to understand the weight of his trust in me and Chase. This was not just one of many projects for Luke—this was his baby, and we would have a big hand in its success. I felt pressure in my chest at the thought of it.

I must have let some of my feelings show on my face because suddenly Luke reached across the small table to touch my arm. "Charlie, are you okay? You look a little lost."

"No, no, I'm fine. Good, actually." I smiled, hoping to reassure him. "Actually, Luke, I'm having a great time." I loved how his eyes crinkled in the corners as he smiled back at me. I felt my heart beat a little faster as his face lit up. I was afraid I might start melting into a puddle again. His deep voice washed over me as I tried to keep from turning to mush.

"I am quite pleased to hear that. I was starting to feel like you wanted to run in the opposite direction every time you saw me."

His hand was on top of mine, and I was drawn to the visage of his large hand on my smaller one. Slowly, he turned my hand over and ran his fingers along the inside of my wrist. So much for not turning into a puddle. *Should I be saying something?* I thought. I looked away from his fingers and back up to his face. His blue eyes scanned my green ones, missing nothing. I smiled hesitantly; I suddenly felt shy and uncertain. My heart fluttered in my chest as he held my hand and stroked my wrist. I felt the wall I had tried to erect against him crumbling a bit.

He moved his chair closer to mine, invading my space. "Charlie, I know what we said, and I heard you, believe me, but I feel so drawn to you. I know it sounds like a line, but I'm a little out of my element here. I don't usually get involved with people I work with, and I'm not great with commitment, so my taste in women can be rather, ah . . . shallow."

I was trying to focus on what he was saying. It was hard to concentrate since his hand was traveling up my arm now, and he was twirling my hair in his fingers. "What do you want me to say, Luke?" My words sounded hoarse to my ears. I cleared my throat and reached for my drink with my free hand. I took a generous sip. "What is it that you want?" I continued, feeling the alcohol warming my insides. I felt my defenses crumbling.

For the first time in my life, I wanted something so badly even knowing that it could be so problematic. I felt like I was on the precipice of doing something reckless, but as Luke continued to touch me gently, I was finding it hard to care. I held my breath waiting for his answer.

He leaned into me to whisper in my ear, "Charlie, I want you to come home with me. I want to get to know you better. I want to run my hands through your hair, kiss your neck. I want to taste you, Charlie. Please, just come back to my house. We can stop for takeout, whatever you want, let's just see where this goes. I know it's complicated, but the way I feel about you is simple. I want you." I felt myself shiver from his breath on my ear—or maybe it was his words. My insides heated up even as I tried to put the brakes on.

"But what about being professional? What if we crash and burn or one of us gets hurt, Luke? We will have to work together for months; how can we do that?"

"I can't make any long-term promises right now, Charlie. I just know I need you. It's selfish, but I want to touch you. I want to feel you under me. It will happen tonight or soon, but we will be together eventually, you know it and I know it. Who knows? Maybe it will ease some of this tension."

His fingers were stroking my neck now, the sensitive skin under my ear. I literally felt like I might explode; I was burning for him too. Maybe he was right, maybe we could get each other out of our systems, burn off a little of this energy between us. Was I justifying? Where was Everleigh when I needed her? Who was I kidding? She would tell me to go for it, get a piece of that. I turned my head toward him, feeling the heat of his gaze burning me, waiting for my answer.

"Yes, okay," I whispered. I lifted my chin. "But we are definitely stopping to get some food on the way."

He threw back his head and laughed.

"What's so funny?"

"Not a thing, baby," he answered, still grinning. "How about if I call ahead to Halls Chophouse and get us some steaks. We can pick it up on the way to my car."

I relaxed a little. "Sounds perfect, I love steak."

He laughed again and signaled for the waiter to bring out the bill.

Chapter 9

LUKE

A gentleman holds my hand.
A man pulls my hair.
A soul mate will do both.
—Alessandra Torre

The drive to my house was quiet. I hoped that Charlie wasn't having second thoughts. A small part of me worried about the outcome of this evening, but the more persistent part was semi-hard with excitement at getting a go at the sexy lady beside me. Deep down, I knew Charlie was different from the other women I had dallied with. She didn't seem like the type to have a one-night stand, plus the fact that we would be working closely together in the coming months certainly made things a little stickier. I reached over to lay a reassuring hand on her knee. She wore jeans tonight. It was nice to see her in more casual attire, and the jeans did wonders for her assets. She smiled over at me, and I detected some heat in her eyes. Maybe I wasn't the only one following my baser instincts.

We pulled into my driveway, and Charlie gasped. "Oh! Your house, it is so . . . elegant. Not at all what I was expecting."

For some reason, her reaction made me happy, and I realized this was the first time I had invited a woman to my home. I decided not to dwell on that and instead pulled into the garage, got out, and circled around to open her car door. Her eyes were large as she looked around. "Even your garage is beautiful."

"Why, thank you," I said. "Sebastian helped me design the house, and being on the water required a raised elevation, so I decided to use the space to store my toys." Charlie glanced over at my boat, a Yamaha AR210, bright blue. I had not yet dropped it in the water, even though the weather had started to consistently warm up. Finalizing the deal for King Street had not left much time for recreation. "Yes, I do enjoy the occasional cruise or fishing with my buddies, and it's nice being able to take off behind the house at high tide," I acknowledged.

"Sounds fun," Charlie agreed, taking one more glance at the boat before following me up the stairs and into the house.

"I need to prepare you before we go inside," I said, turning to Charlie on the landing outside the mudroom.

"You have five kids and a secret wife?" she said, laughing.

I made a face at her. "Hardly, but I do have a forty-five-pound pit bull named Sadie, and she gets a little enthusiastic when I have houseguests." I wasn't sure how Sadie would react to sharing my attention with another female, but I decided not to mention that. I opened the door to the mudroom, bracing myself for Sadie's usual enthusiastic greeting. I heard

Charlie giggling behind me as a gray blur launched itself at me with abandon. I grabbed her wriggling body and gently but firmly put her on the floor. "Settle down, girl, we have a guest."

Charlie came from behind me, unafraid, and reached out a hand. "Hello, pretty lady," she said softly. "I'm Charlie, what's your name?"

I chuckled as Sadie wagged her tail and started licking Charlie's hand. "Her name is Sadie, and she is the other woman in my life."

Charlie raised an eyebrow at me, still petting Sadie. "It seems like you have rather good taste in female companions. I approve."

I laughed out loud, placing my hand on the small of her back to lead her into the kitchen. "It's quite obvious that she approves of you, too, firecracker."

As I led Charlie inside, with Sadie close at her heels, her attention was immediately drawn to the floor-to-ceiling windows. The kitchen, family room, and master bedroom all faced the water, and during the day, the views were breathtaking. It was dark now, but the lights from the city twinkled and the view of the Ravenel suspension bridge was still amazing. I silently thanked my house for doing a great job setting the mood for me. I had not been prepared for visitors, but the backdrop still wowed Charlie.

"What a gorgeous setting, Luke!" she exclaimed. "I would never leave this view."

I raised an eyebrow at her. "There's a similar view from the bedroom."

I was relieved when she laughed. "Maybe we should have a little food first. We don't want that award-winning steak to get cold," she responded as she lightly patted my cheek.

Oh boy, am I in trouble, I thought.

I walked over to a cabinet to pull out some plates and utensils as Charlie slid into a barstool on my expansive island. The countertop was a hearty weathered butcher block that Ethan had salvaged for me; it was a nice contrast to the gray quartz in the rest of the kitchen.

"I like the blue accents; clearly you have a favorite color," she observed as I put a loaded plate in front of her and reached into the wine fridge for a bottle of red wine.

"Are you a fan of red?" I asked. "I have a wonderful bottle of Purple Angel from Chile; it's my favorite."

"I love red wine, but I have never tried Purple Angel. I would love to try some."

I could see she was waiting for me. "Please eat," I said. "I don't want your food to get cold."

She smiled and took a generous bite of food. I couldn't help but smile; it was so nice to see a girl enjoy a healthy plate of food.

We were both ravenous since we had never gotten those appetizers at 492, and it wasn't long before we had finished eating. I managed to save a few scraps for Sadie, who was behaving wonderfully and deserved a reward. I cleared our plates and rinsed them off to put them in the dishwasher. It felt strange to have a woman in my house, and I was surprised to realize I was enjoying it.

"Why don't you grab your glass and I'll show you the view from the deck," I said, coming around the bar to take her hand.

She was quiet but seemed relaxed, so I took that as a good sign as I led her out for a closer look at my view. She just shook her head as she looked out to the water.

"I love our view from the cottage on Sullivan's, but this is really another level. I think I would just sleep out here if I could."

"This portion is screened in; I just need to get one of those hanging beds like your parents have at the inn, and that could be arranged. Maybe you can help me find one of those?" I asked.

She turned to me, and I felt my heart jump in my throat as her emerald eyes looked seriously into mine. I could almost see them growing darker as she studied my face. "Well, perhaps—"

I never let her finish because I just couldn't hold back and I leaned down to catch those perfect lips in mine. It had only been about a week since I'd last kissed her at the inn, but I was as excited as a schoolboy about to have his first kiss as I slid my lips over hers. Her lips were soft and gentle at first, but she quickly responded as I deepened the kiss looking for more, needing more. She answered me with fevered kisses of her own; her small tongue slid between my lips, and I groaned. I couldn't help myself—this woman took me completely by surprise. I hardly noticed the warm spring breeze circling us as her hands crept up my chest and around my neck, her fingers tugging my hair. I wanted to touch her everywhere. I was anxious and even a little frantic as she pressed against my rapidly expanding erection. The sweet noises she made in the back of her throat as I ran my lips down her neck and to the soft skin beside her ear were making me crazy. Lavender and spices assaulted my nostrils, and I drank her in. I had been dying to do this for days, and it was even better than I imagined.

I pulled away gently, looking down into her large eyes, which were swimming with arousal, mirroring my own. "Would you like a tour of the master bedroom?" I asked, smiling. "Otherwise, I am liable to just lay you down right here on the deck."

She ran her hand down my chest, causing my cock to lengthen even more, pressing uncomfortably against my zipper. "Yes, Luke, I would be delighted to see your bedroom." She gave me a seductive smile, different from the other women I had been with because I didn't think she was trying to be sexy—she just was. I had an urge to swing her into my arms and carry her to the bed. I definitely needed to review that later, but instead, I grabbed her hand again and led her out onto the terrace and into the bedroom from the balcony. Her head turned once more to the view, and I saw her smile as she followed me.

I waited for awkwardness to overtake us, but it never did, because she came quickly over to me and reached out for the buttons on my shirt. I chuckled as she eagerly fumbled with my shirt, trying to get it off.

"We are certainly an anxious little firecracker, aren't we?" I said. I grabbed her fingers, placing them against my lips and sucking the tips into my mouth. I heard her gasp, her mouth making a small "O." I dove in for another kiss, and this time, it was more like thunder as we explored and plundered, nipping and sucking each other's lips. I grabbed her shirt at the waist, sliding it up over her head, eager to get my hands and mouth on what was underneath. I walked us over to the bed as I undressed her. Then I pushed her gently back as I ran my hands down her torso to the button on her jeans. She was looking up at me, eyes wide and eager.

"Is this okay?" I asked, praying she would say yes.

"Please," she said, her voice raspy, "don't stop, Luke. Please, don't stop."

That was all the invitation I needed. I stripped her of her jeans, and she removed her bra as I quickly divested myself of all but my boxer briefs.

Charlie's hands reached eagerly for me, running up my chest, circling my nipples, sliding down to the top of my briefs. I looked down at her full breasts and dark rosy nipples, so full and ready for my tongue. I rolled the peaks between my thumb and forefinger, and she moaned below me. I felt like a teenager ready to explode, it was so unnerving. At thirty-one, I felt as if I might blow my load just looking at her soft skin and beautiful curves. I leaned down to suck on her slender neck, enjoying her quiet sounds of encouragement. I made my way down, covering her with kisses, and circled my eager tongue around her hard nipple. Her back arched up toward me as she put her hands on the back of my head. God, she was so willing. My hands were everywhere as I slid my tongue back and forth between her full breasts. She gasped as I slid my hand down into her panties. I didn't get far before I felt how slick she was. I groaned.

"Oh, Charlie, you are so ready for me. Tell me what you want, baby."

Her cheeks were flushed; I wasn't sure if she was embarrassed or aroused, but I didn't care. My fingers reached inside, pushing into her tight channel. She moaned even louder, "Please, Luke, I just need to . . . I just need."

I pulled off her underwear and spread her legs, sliding down in between. I placed my tongue on her swollen nub. She nearly levitated off the bed, one hand grabbing my shoulder, while the other fisted in my hair. I pushed my fingers in and out, hard, and used my tongue to tease her clit. She was moaning and tossing her head; I could tell she was close, and I wanted so badly to feel her come on my tongue. She let out a shout throwing her head back into the pillow as I sucked her into my mouth while curling my finger inside, stroking her in the spot I knew would send her over the edge. I felt her shudder as she moaned softly once more, and slowly I released her. I looked up at her. Her skin was flushed, and she panted gently, her eyes closed. I loved how relaxed she was in that moment. My body throbbed, reminding me that it had needs to be fulfilled. I crawled up the bed and lay next to her, kissing her softly, letting her taste her juices on my lips. She didn't seem to mind, and she kissed me hard, reaching her hand between us to stroke my pulsing cock through my briefs.

"Please, Luke, I want you inside me. I want you to take me . . . and don't be gentle."

Without hesitation, I reached into my nightstand to grab a condom with one hand as I pulled off my underwear with the other. Charlie watched me with hungry eyes as I rolled the condom on.

"I'm not sure how long I'll last." I smiled ruefully. "Maybe I can last longer the next time." I gave her a wink as I slid into her in one stroke. She gasped and dug her nails into my shoulders. God, she was so tight. I took a deep breath, trying not to move as her hips arched against mine.

"Do it," she begged breathlessly.

I started slow, but her frantic wiggling caused me to lose control and I pounded into her, burying my face in her neck. I could hear her moans, and her breathing sped up, so I could tell she was getting close. I gritted my teeth, trying to hold back for just a little longer as she ground against me. I captured her lips, my tongue diving in her mouth as she arched against me furiously, moaning louder now. I felt her tighten against my cock, and that was all I needed; I lost myself. I pounded into her harder as I felt the tingling in my spine, and I couldn't control the roar that tore from me as I released into her. We were both breathing hard as I collapsed gently on top of her. I rolled off slowly, my arm falling against my forehead. We looked at each other and laughed.

"I guess we both needed that." I chuckled, reaching for her hand.

"I don't know about you, but it's been a while for me," she said.

I smiled at her, enjoying the flush on her cheeks and her sparkly eyes. "I hope it was as good as you remember."

"I would say, it's better than I remember, Mr. Coleman. You are quite impressive, in more ways than one." She responded as she pretended to ogle my still semi-hard cock. Suddenly, she was laughing at something over my shoulder, and I looked over to see Sadie's head on the foot of the bed; she looked at us both with interest.

I lay back into the pillow, laughing with her. "Geez, Sadie, a little privacy?" I said to my dog.

Chapter 10

CHARLIE

"Push me up against the wall and do dirty things to me."
Anonymous

I lay in Luke's bed, his naked body next to mine. We were both still coming down off the high from our love making. *Is that actually what you call this?* It was definitely the hottest sexual experience I had ever had, but maybe love making was a premature definition. I really hadn't expected to be here, in his home, his bed, with his dog staring at us, no less. I covered my eyes with my hands—boy, my resolve didn't last long in the face of one Luke Coleman.

"Hey, don't do that. There are no regrets in this scenario," Luke said as he pulled my hands from my eyes. He leaned over me and dropped his lips gently on mine. Seeking . . . distracting, harder now. I felt my blood start to heat up again as his kisses grew more persistent, and I couldn't help but respond.

This man, his lips, his hands running up my body, squeezing my breasts—I couldn't help myself. My mind wanted to slow things down, but my body was already in fifth gear, revving into overdrive. I was instantly wet again, yearning to feel him against me.

He pulled back, smiling, that cocky grin taking over his face slowly. "This time, we're going to go slow. I want to taste every part of you. I want you on your hands and knees. I want you on top of me. I want to make you come again and again." I could feel my nipples getting hard; it was impossible to hide my reaction to his words. His hand reached between my legs, and he was greeted by my juices flowing freely down my thighs. He groaned. God, I loved the sound of his excitement. I had never had a man who was so free with his desires. He was un-ashamed about his need to tell me what he wanted and what he wanted to do to me. It was really freeing. I rolled onto my side, my movements knocking away his probing fingers. I wanted to see him and run my hands along the hard planes of his body, to feel his muscles clenching. I wanted to be in control and see him weak with need. Getting married at such a young age, my sexual experience was limited to mainly one person. Our sex had always been good, or so I had thought. Now I wondered how any man was ever going to live up to Luke.

I thought this as I sat up and ran my hands up his chest. My hair fell forward and followed the path of my hands as Luke moaned, his hands in my hair and on my shoulders, encour-aging me. I dropped my lips to his perfect nipple, and it be-came rock hard under my tongue. I put my teeth on it, and his hips arched off the bed. His erection had returned and pressed against my hip as I explored the crevices along his chest and stomach. I didn't think I'd ever seen a man more beautiful—just the right amount of golden chest hair and the line of darker hair leading from his belly down to his now-hard cock. His head rolled back into the pillow as I circled my fist around it, rubbing my thumb along the tip.

"Charlie . . . oh God, you're killing me." He moaned, and I felt powerful. I bent down and touched the tip with my tongue, swirling around the head. His hands ran up my back to my head.

I pulled my head back. "No, no, no touching," I said, pushing his hands down on the bed.

He growled at me but cooperated, clutching the sheets as I bent back down to take him deep in my throat. I marveled at his size; I could only go down a little more than halfway, but I used the wetness from my mouth to pump his base with my hand. I could tell he was struggling to keep it together, but his hips were pumping almost involuntarily into my mouth. It was such a rush, and I couldn't remember ever being so turned on while giving a blowjob. Maybe it was because he always seemed so in control that I loved making him lose it a little. He tossed his head, moaning, his hands clutching the sheets.

"Please, Charlie, I need to be inside you," he begged.

I lifted my head, and he let out a great puff of air as I released his cock from my mouth with a pop. I peppered it with kisses and slid my tongue from base to tip as he grew more agitated.

"What's the matter Luke? You don't like my tongue on you?" I stroked him slowly with my hand, the saliva from my tongue making it slide slowly up and down.

He moaned again, and his voice was hoarse when he spoke. "No, I love it, but I love the feeling of being inside you more, and I'm gonna lose it if you keep that up."

Deciding to show a little mercy, I reached over to the nightstand to find another condom in the drawer. I ripped it open and smoothed it slowly down his length, my eyes locked onto his.

"Yes," he groaned softly as I rose up to position myself over top of him. My body was clenched in anticipation, and I don't think I have ever been more wet. I smacked his hand away as he tried to help, and I could feel him shift in agitation. I wrapped my fingers around him and rubbed his head against my wet opening. I could feel him shiver, and he groaned with a mixture of pleasure and frustration. I slid down slowly; he was so large, and I reveled in the feeling of him filling me up slowly. As much as I enjoyed torturing Luke, my body, too, was begging for release, and I wasn't sure how much longer I could wait. I rose back up and slid down just an inch or two, and then, with a sigh, I slid all the way down in one smooth motion. The feeling of relief was palpable, and I leaned forward to slide my tongue in his open mouth. He was beside himself as I bounced up and down and rubbed my clit against him.

I leaned into his ear. "Fuck me hard," I whispered urgently.

His hands shot up off the bed, clutching my hips as he frantically drove up into me. It was all I needed; I felt the telltale clenching of my abdomen and nearly saw stars as my orgasm gripped me. I clung to Luke as he pounded into me, seeking his own release. Our lips were seared together, tongues tangling furiously as we both moaned endlessly. I gripped his broad shoulders as I felt him tighten, and as he exploded into me, I prayed the condom would hold against the fury of his orgasm.

As I felt him relax, I collapsed on top of his muscular body. I wasn't a small girl, but I felt somewhat fragile as his big arms circled around me and he kissed my forehead and my cheek. He reached up and smoothed my now-tangled hair away from my face and gave a small sigh as he kissed me gently on the lips.

"Holy hell, that was amazing, Charlie. I'm not sure I'll ever recover." He sighed again, so deep in his chest I could feel it expand underneath me. I found myself feeling a little self-conscious; I mean, I barely knew this man. I attempted to roll off of him, but his strong biceps were like iron as he tightened them to prevent my retreat.

I buried my face in his neck, and he rubbed the back of my head. "Charlie why are you hiding? That was incredible, and I know you enjoyed it too. If you were faking it, I think there's an Academy Award in your future."

I lifted my head to look in his eyes. "I'm just not sure where this is supposed to go from here. I've never been in this position before. My experience is limited to one marriage and a couple of bad dates. I know who you are, Luke, and I know not to expect anything from you." I gave him a lopsided smile and shrugged, trying to lessen the judgment in my words.

He cocked an eyebrow at me. "I didn't think you were the kind of girl to listen to gossip, Charlie. But I'm not going to lie to you: You are the first woman to visit my home and lie naked in my bed. Not to say that there haven't been women, it's just we've enjoyed our, ahem, activities elsewhere." He looked a little sheepish. "That's not to say I have any regrets about bringing you here. This has been a very satisfying evening, and I would do it all again." He nuzzled my neck, nipping at my shoulder. "I may just need a sandwich first."

I couldn't help but laugh. Some of what he said made me feel uncomfortable and raised the invisible red flag I was already holding behind my back, but at least he was being honest. "So, would you like for me to go?" I asked "I probably should go anyway. Everleigh is my roommate, and she doesn't actually know where I am, so she'll probably be worried."

"Then I guess you better call her because you aren't going anywhere," he growled as he flipped me over onto my back. "I am not nearly done with you. There is so much more ground to cover before you escape my bed, darlin'." He was rubbing his hands all over me as he said this, and I shivered—maybe from the cold, but mostly from the anticipation.

I went into the bathroom to call Everleigh, and the conversation was brief—partly because I didn't want to go into too much detail, but mainly because I was anxious to get back to Luke. I felt like a magnetic field was drawing me to him whether I liked it or not. I reassured Everleigh that we would catch up after she came home from the bakery tomorrow afternoon and I would fill her in on all the details. I grimaced to myself, realizing I was going to have to get Chase up to speed too. It looked like a happy hour for three was in order for tomorrow night.

I peeked out the bathroom door to see if Luke was still in the bedroom. He looked very comfortable (and mouthwatering), lying on the bed scrolling through his phone. One arm was behind his head, an optimum position for maximum muscle definition, and the sheets were casually thrown over his waist, but the rest of him was on glorious display. Sadie had retired to her bed in the corner, apparently over the intrusion of a strange woman in Luke's bed. I was able to enjoy the view for a minute or two before he noticed me in the doorway.

"Hi." I said, feeling a little unsure of myself; this was a first for me. "Ummm, I was thinking I might take a shower and clean up. Is that okay?"

My stomach dropped as he stretched his arms over head, flashing tight muscles everywhere. My mouth suddenly got very dry as he got out of bed, dropping the sheet. I was amazed to see he was already semi-hard . . . what the hell?

"Let me give you a hand; the shower is a little complicated with all the knobs and sprayers. In fact, perhaps I could join you and wash your back?" He posed it as a question, but he was already stepping in the shower, fiddling with the knobs. As I admired his very fine muscular backside, I quickly followed him in.

"What happened to needing a sandwich?" I asked, laughing.

"Aren't you a very naughty girl? And here I thought we were just going to wash up." His eyes were wide, trying hard to look innocent, but I didn't miss the glint in his eye, and his cock was hard and heavy against his thigh.

"Ha," I said, "sounds good to me."

As the water poured out of multiple showerheads, Luke pulled me up against the hard body I had been admiring earlier, running his hands slowly down my backside. "Not so fast, little firecracker. Teasing will only get you in trouble. I don't want to have to punish you." He had a wicked look in his eye, and I could feel myself getting wet just from his words.

Before I knew what was happening, he had spun me around and put my hands up on the wall of the shower. He had obviously turned on some kind of steam feature in the enclosed shower because the glass had completely fogged up and it was getting very warm. I felt amazing as the heat swirled around me, but I also felt a little vulnerable up against the wall.

"I think it's time for a little payback for my delightful torture session from earlier, and there are some areas on your sexy body that I have had yet to explore." He whispered in my ear, then took his teeth and nipped my earlobe, swirling the area with his tongue to lessen the sting. I was starting to realize that Luke just might know a something about the pleasure of a little pain. My limited experience caused me to be a bit nervous, but I was also intrigued. Luke was somewhat intimidating, but strangely, I felt safe with him.

"Close your eyes and just relax," he said softly. He moved away for a second, and I heard him doing something behind me. The next thing I felt were his soapy hands massaging my neck; then they were circling around the front, massaging my breasts. He pinched my nipples, and I felt a tight pain that shot straight to my core. He hands gentled, massaging me and causing the pain to become an ache. I heard little sounds bouncing off the walls of the shower, and I realized it was me, moaning. My cheeks flamed in embarrassment, but it quickly evaporated as his hands moved to my back, traveling downward, massaging my ass cheeks gently.

"Now, here is an area I have been wanting to get more intimate with," Luke growled quietly as his fingers probed gently into my most private region. I squirmed. This was totally foreign territory; sex with Joe had been very vanilla, and I was nervous, unsure. Luke must have sensed my trepidation because his fingers changed course and reached around to the front, sliding into my wet slit. I groaned, feeling feverish from all the attention, my hands slick against the condensation on the walls. Luke's hands traveled back up, cupping the underside of my breasts, which were feeling heavy and full.

Luke leaned in, pressing his body against the back of mine, his cock pressing against me. My legs turned to jelly as he leaned in to whisper in my ear. "So, am I to assume that having someone lavish attention on that gorgeous round ass is not something you've experienced often?"

"Try never," I whispered nervously.

"That is a stunning oversight." He laughed softly. I felt the sound rumble against me, and it was oddly reassuring. "I hope you trust me to love every part of you. If not today, then eventually, I would like to make sure nothing is left unexplored."

His fingers had resumed exploring, and I gasped as he slid two fingers into my tight passage and began to move them in and out. I nodded in response to his comment about future explorations and moaned as he assaulted me with his fingers, his lips on the back of my neck and his slick body pressed against me. He rubbed his cock along my ass crack, which felt dangerous and oddly thrilling. Suddenly, he dropped down to his knees, dropping kisses down my back on his way. His hands were back on my ass, and he was pinching and rubbing, dropping kisses on the skin that burned from the pinches. The unusual attention made my whole body throb, and I moaned and pressed my cheek against the wall. His tongue slid slowing along my crack, and I gasped—it just felt so . . . As I was trying to adjust to the new sensations, he grabbed my hips and turned my body so my back was against the wall. I let out a breath, not sure if I was relieved or disappointed to be in a more familiar position. I didn't have time to consider my emotions because Luke immediately began to shower attention between my legs. He was licking and sucking, and his fingers were everywhere. I felt shivers racing up and down my spine, and I knew my orgasm was close.

"Luke, I am so, so . . . close."

Luke moaned softly, seemingly lost in his task. I threw my head back, and my legs stiffened as I felt the first wave. I was so caught up, I didn't realize one of his fingers had moved and was breaching my other very tight hole and the sensation was…arousing. I felt my whole body flush as my orgasm ripped through me, and I grabbed his shoulders to keep my balance. I couldn't help myself as I let out a shout, moaning his name.

I had never before felt so out of control. My whole body trembled, and I heard myself whimpering. Luke slid up my body and carefully wrapped me in his arms. The shower was still incredibly warm, and I let myself fall into his embrace. God, he felt so big and strong, and I felt so . . . good. Luke covered my face with kisses.

"Oh, Charlie, you are so amazing. I just love how you respond to me." He cupped my face in his hands and forced me to look up at him. "Are you okay, baby?"

I smiled, feeling self-conscious, but oh-so-satisfied, as I nodded and leaned in to kiss him. I looked down at his cock throbbing against my leg. "But I think you may need a little attention." He grabbed my hand as I went to reach down in between us.

"No worries, firecracker; he'll be fine. Just very happy to have satisfied you. Let's really get cleaned up this time and go have a midnight snack. I could go for that sandwich." He kissed me, smiling as he did, and reached behind him to once again grab the soap.

Thirty minutes later, I was wrapped in Luke's robe while he wore only sweatpants hanging just low enough on his hips to leave a little to my imagination. I once again sat at his island, feeling incredibly satisfied and just a little indulgent as I moaned my way through a delicious piece of coconut cake. Sadie, having decided I was a welcome addition, was lying contentedly at my feet.

"Please explain to me, Luke, how it is you have an entire coconut cake from Peninsula Grill in your refrigerator."

"Well," he said, reaching over to stroke my hair, "when you're as good at your job as I am, clients give you amazing and delectable gifts." He reached over with his fork to steal a bite. I knocked his fork away with mine.

"You have a whole cake in there; get your own!" I gave him my fiercest face to discourage another sneak attack on my dessert.

"Yes, but the calories don't count when I eat it from your plate." He laughed and managed to score a quick bite when he distracted me by rubbing a finger along my cheek.

Bastard, I thought, *already using his sexy moves to distract me*.

I looked over at him, my heart doing a weird flutter. His hair was rumpled and fell across his forehead, making him look younger than thirty-one. His face had a shadow from a day or two of beard growth, and I was fascinated to see that while his hair was blond, his beard was reddish brown, which matched his . . . well, his . . . oh, shit, don't even go there.

He caught me staring and raised an eyebrow, smirking. "Whatcha thinking about, firecracker? I'd offer you a penny, but all I have is a ten in my wallet."

I laughed self-consciously. "I'm just marveling over the fact that I'm here in your kitchen. It's kind of strange."

He looked worried. "Please tell me we're not going down the boulevard of regrets again." He ran his hand through his hair.

"Actually, Mr. Coleman, I have no complaints about our evening. I just can't believe how quickly you broke down my defenses. Clearly, I am like many of the single ladies in Charleston, unable to resist your charms." He threw back his head and laughed, and I was amazed at how awake I felt; it had to be after 1:00 a.m.

"I never know what's going to come out of that pretty mouth of yours, firecracker," Luke said, shaking his head and grinning.

He swiped my empty plate and put it in the dishwasher. *He's nothing if not neat*, I thought. He walked around the island, reached down, and scooped me off my stool. I couldn't help myself as I giggled uncontrollably, wrapping my arms around his strong neck, and he carried me back to the bedroom. Boy, this night had sure turned out differently than I had expected. As Luke dropped feathery kisses on my neck and I felt butterflies in my stomach, I realized that no matter how things turned out, this night would go down in the books as one the best in my life.

Chapter 11

LUKE

*Life just doesn't hand you things. You have to get out there
and make things happen. that's the exciting part.*
—Emeril Lagasse

I had texted Ethan early in the morning to push back our regular Saturday gym date to the ten thirty class. It was strange, but I was seriously in no rush for Charlie to leave. *So many firsts with this girl*, I thought as I walked to CrossFit. I reflected on the events from the night before, and even though I had lost count of how many times we'd had sex, I found myself getting aroused just thinking about her. She had caught me by surprise, and I still wasn't sure how I felt about it. The sex had been amazing, and even though I could tell she was inexperienced, it didn't matter at all. I had to admit, I found her innocence stimulating. She was so sweet and open, but still adventurous and ready to try anything. I had found myself warmed by her trust.

I pounded my thigh as I walked, trying to beat out this feeling of . . . need. Damn it, never had I felt like I really needed to be with a woman. She had left me not much more than an hour ago, and I was already wondering when I could see her again. My life had always centered around striving for success, growing my business to be the best, and acquiring the things I had never had as a child. The only people who were important to me were my brothers and my small circle of close guy friends.

Women had always been in the periphery—available to hang on my arm for an important social function or an occasional one-night fuck. The longest I could remember dating anyone was maybe a few weeks. The moment they started to get even a little clingy or demanding, I was gone. A few times last night, I could feel Charlie pulling away, and it made me unhappy. That was a new emotion for me, and I wasn't sure how I felt about it. Maybe Ethan could help me sort through it; after all, he had been married, and while he hadn't seemed to have much interest in dating since his wife died three years ago, he at least had experience with commitment. *Wait, what am I even thinking? Commitment? What the Hell?*

"Jesus, Luke, I don't think I've ever seen you so distracted during a workout. I'm surprised you made it through without dropping that bar on your head," Ethan said, mopping his sweaty face.

"Since you mentioned it, I was hoping maybe we could shower and then grab a couple beers because I need some advice, brother," I responded, grabbing my gym bag and heading to the locker rooms.

"Lucky for you, I brought a change of clothes," Ethan said, patting me on the back. "I can't wait to hear what has the great Luke Coleman so preoccupied."

It was Saturday, early in the afternoon, and as usual, the Charleston bars were hopping. It never ceased to amaze me that such a small city had so many bars and restaurants, and they were always buzzing with people. I guess that's what happened when the big travel magazines kept naming you the top tourist destination in the USA. When I first moved to Charleston after college, about ten years ago, it was easy to drop in to the best restaurants and get a table or a couple seats at the bar. These days, it required advanced planning and, God forbid, a reservation to enjoy some of my favorites. Luckily, I wasn't too proud to use my connections to get in when I needed to impress a date last minute. It wasn't always a necessity, but it never hurt to enjoy a great meal while paving the way to getting laid.

Ethan and I decided on one of the more casual spots close to my house to grab some burgers and beers. We had already ordered our food and were halfway through our second beer before our small talk turned more personal.

"So, what's got you so off your game, buddy?" Ethan turned to me with a smirk.

I ran my hand through my hair, trying to think about how to broach the subject of Charlie. I knew Ethan wouldn't be thrilled that I had already hopped in the sack with the owner of our newly hired interior design firm, but I decided to cut to the chase. "It seems I have found myself rather, ah, involved with a very intriguing young lady," I said.

Ethan choked on his beer. "Rather involved? Intriguing? Young lady? What the hell, Luke, this must be serious. I rarely hear you mention the women you're boning, and I don't think I've ever seen you lose focus in the gym over any of them. So, who is this mysterious woman of intrigue?" He was laughing at me, and I wasn't feeling it, so I forgot about being sensitive to his potential reaction.

"It's Charlotte Finley - You know, our *interior designer.*"

He slammed down his beer and glared at me. "What?! After what happened between me and Everleigh, we agreed it was a bad idea to get involved with any women in the workplace, dude. What are you thinking?"

I laughed a little self-consciously. "Honestly, at the time, I wasn't really thinking. I was just incredibly attracted to her and figured I would work it out later. You know . . . like now. That's why I needed to talk to you. You're much better with these types of situations."

"Clearly, I am not!" he practically shouted. "Look what happened with Everleigh. She quit, left real estate, and is making muffins on Sullivan's Island. It seems we both have bad judgment in this department. One would think with your love-'em-and-leave-'em track record, you wouldn't mess with Charlie, especially when we're starting the biggest project of our career with her. She is critical to our success, Luke." He sighed, looking frustrated.

Fortunately, I had a minute to gather my thoughts because the bartender delivered our food as I was about to answer. We both took a couple bites, with Ethan giving me the evil eye as he chewed aggressively on his burger. I took a large swallow of my beer.

"Listen, Ethan, I understand where you're coming from, and I'll be honest, I was actually interested in Charlie before I realized who she was."

Ethan looked at me, puzzled. "I didn't know you had met her before the night at the inn?"

"I hadn't, but something happened that night, and I may have, well... kissed her."

Ethan's eyebrows shot up and he nearly choked on his beer again. "You kissed her? In the room where I found you? The first time you met her? That's fast even for you, stud."

"Jesus, Ethan, I didn't plan to kiss her. It just sort of happened, spontaneously. We hadn't even exchanged names. She was ummm... sexy and kind of a spitfire, and I was moved in the moment."

Ethan looked very confused as he rubbed his beard. "Moved in the moment? Who are you?"

I pointed my fork at him. "Exactly. This is why I need your help. I'm feeling off my game here, and I need you to set me straight."

"So, it was just a kiss? Big deal. Just don't let it go any further—or wait until the project is done to explore things with her," he responded easily. My guilt was clearly written all over my face because Ethan dropped his fork and started rubbing his face again. "It wasn't just a kiss. You've seen her since. You've slept with her, haven't you?"

I nodded. "Yep, I'm afraid that ship has sailed . . . over and over again."

"Damn it, Luke, why'd you have to go and do that? How did she feel when you snuck off afterward?"

"That's the thing, Ethan. I couldn't sneak off because she was in my bed . . . until this morning when she left."

Ethan sat back in the barstool. His eyebrows had disappeared under his hair again. "You're telling me that you invited her back to your house, where she spent the entire night with you? Have I landed in some weird alternate universe?"

I couldn't help but laugh at his confusion, and I couldn't blame him for being nearly as shaken up as I was. This was far from my usual behavior. "This is why I need your advice, Ethan. I have no idea how to proceed. I'm not really sure how I feel about it all. I mean, I actually think I like her, and I'm planning how I can see her again . . . soon. She is obviously clued in to my reputation, and I get the feeling she's nervous about getting involved."

I could see that Ethan was trying to muster up some sympathy. He realized that me coming to him for romantic advice was a first, so clearly, I needed his help. "Luke, you know I'm not a fan of you sleeping with our interior designer, and your track record has me especially concerned that this will all end in disaster." He held up his hand as I started to interrupt. "That being said, you are my best friend, and I can see this is new territory for you, so let me just say this: Charlie is not like the other women you've dated. She's not the kind of girl you fuck a few times and move on. She's the kind of girl you settle down with, you have babies with—she's that girl. Hell, she's been married before, and from what I hear, he cheated on her with his secretary. I think it's understandable that Charlie may have some concerns about getting involved with the playboy of Charleston."

I scowled at him. "I am hardly the playboy of Charleston, Ethan. I'm merely more interested in my business than getting tangled up in a relationship."

Ethan's expression was sad, and I felt terrible for being an insensitive ass. I was sure he would give anything to still be "tangled up" with Jill.

"Listen, buddy," he said more gently, "having more than a one- or two-night engagement does require a little more time and effort, but believe me when I tell you, it is so worth the trouble. What I had with Jill . . . well, it was everything, man. I would give anything to have her back, but sometimes we only get one shot at that kind of partnership. If you like Charlie, don't fuck it up. Stay the course; be patient with her. If she's worth the trouble, you'll have no regrets in the end. Unfortunately, I think you may have an uphill climb. There's some baggage there with her, and, like it or not, your reputation is not going to help. Whatever happens, try and keep things at work professional. We need her, Luke, and I will kill you if you mess that up."

I let him finish and nodded to let him know I understood. I still wasn't sure how I felt about pursuing something long-term with Charlie, but I knew one thing: I really wanted to see her again—and soon.

Chapter 12

CHARLIE

You cannot swim for new horizons until you
have courage to lose sight of the shore.
—William Faulkner

I managed to convince Chase to come out to Sullivan's Island to hang out with me and Everleigh. It was always a battle to get Chase to leave downtown, especially on a Saturday night, but I knew if we went into the city, Chase would constantly be distracted by all the friends he ran into while we were out.

"Come on, Chase," I begged. "We haven't been to Mex 1 in ages, and I really need some uninterrupted time with you and Ever."

"Charlie, Minero downtown has the best margaritas, and Josh is working at the bar tonight," Chase responded, as expected.

"Seriously, Chase, I want a night out without constantly fending off your fan club. You can crash at our place; that way you can drink yourself into oblivion and not have to drive. I'll even treat you to brunch at Obstinate Daughter." I knew that was his favorite and he hadn't been there in ages.

"You drive a hard bargain, bitch, but how can I resist. Besides, I know you're going to share some juicy gossip. I can hear it in your voice." Chase was practically giddy as he chattered on. "Also, I want to hear the scoop you got from Luke on Friday about our new job; I'm almost bursting with anticipation."

I laughed at him and inwardly I cringed at the mention of Luke. Hopefully, Chase wouldn't freak out when he heard I had crossed the line with our new client. Yikes.

Mex 1 was crowded when we got there at 7:00 p.m. None of us were surprised, considering it had been a beautiful day at the beach and Sullivan's was full of tourists on their spring break or whatever. These days, Charleston and the surrounding islands seemed to always be "in season." I knew it was great for business, but as a local, it kind of sucked. We managed to score a high-top by the bar, which was ideal for gossiping and proximity to drink refills. Chase was full of energy, a continual blur of movement, as Everleigh and I settled into our seats at the table. Rather than wait for our server, he hopped over to the bar to grab a round of drinks. He had to make two trips; he was clearly planning on cutting loose, returning with tequila shots and margaritas for each of us.

"What the F, Chase," Everleigh exclaimed. "I'm supposed to open tomorrow, holy hell!"

"Calm down, sugar plum, the waitress is bringing over some queso dip and waters. You can sober up later; the night is young," he said, raising his shot glass. "Here's to Whimsical

Designs's new client, Coleman Grant, and Charlie's delicious secret, which she is finally going to share."

I tried not to choke on my tequila as I threw it back and then bit down on a juicy lime.

Everleigh, despite her complaining, had buried her shot and was already at work on her margarita. "All right, Charlie, fess up. What's going on with you? You didn't come home last night, soooo not normal, and you've been avoiding my text messages all day. Give us the scoop. Who is it?"

Chase jumped in, piling on before I could get a word out. "Fuck me sideways, Charlie, you didn't come home last night? An all-nighter! When has this ever happened? He must be *hot*. Details, girl!"

I laughed at the two of them as they leaned toward me dramatically. "Good Lord, you two are acting like the city is on fire or we have a new mayor or something. It's not all that big of a deal. Calm down."

"If it's not a big deal, why are you hedging, Charlie?" Everleigh asked, taking another big swig of her margarita. *I guess Bob will be opening alone tomorrow morning*, I thought, watching as she slurped happily.

I chose my words carefully, trying to keep my tone light and noncommittal. "Okay, so, yes, I did have a very interesting evening last night. And Chase, I need you to remain calm."

Chase looked puzzled by my comment. "Why? Did you fuck an NFL quarterback? Don't even tell me, I will be so jealous, Charles," he said, getting excited.

"No, dipshit, but I did fuck Luke Coleman last night," I said, dropping the mic.

The table got instantly silent, and Chase lifted his glass and took a deliberate drink, staring me down as he did so. I gave him a silly smile, trying to break the tension while Everleigh snickered next to me.

"Come on Chase, I know you have something to say," I said, fidgeting in my seat under his gaze.

"Actually, Charlie, I am speechless right now," he responded.

Everleigh giggled, and I noticed she had finished her margarita. Apparently, the waitress also noticed, since she chose that moment to descend upon us with waters and queso. Everleigh raised her glass. "Refill, please?"

I gave her a questioning look. "I thought you had an early day tomorrow?"

"Already texted Bob, and he said Lisa would love some more hours, so I'm covered," she said, reaching to take a sip of my margarita. "Anyway, stop trying to deflect. I'm dying to hear how you went from swearing off Luke Coleman to jumping in bed with him."

"Yes," said Chase drily, "I'm very interested in how this all came about myself. Especially considering I thought you had just met him a week ago at the inn."

I decided now was a good time to make some progress on my margarita, so I snatched it back from Everleigh and took a fortifying sip before answering. "Listen, Chase, I never mentioned the fact that Luke and I shared a kiss at the inn's grand opening because I really thought that was the end of it." Chase started sputtering as I pushed on. "It was a weird little encounter, and I only told Everleigh because I knew she wouldn't get all worked up over it. Luke and I went to lunch and sort of smoothed things over, he offered us the King Street job, and we agreed to be professional. I thought that would be the end of it. And it was the end of it, until Luke invited me for drinks to talk about the project last night."

Chase gave me a sarcastic look. "Girl, please," he said grumpily.

I tried to look remorseful. "I know, I know, that's why I tried to get you to meet us. I was honestly nervous to be alone with him. I thought I could handle it. I mean, I thought I should handle it."

Everleigh and Chase were both staring at me expectantly, waiting for me to finish my story, so I continued. The words flowed, and I felt a surge of relief to be able to share my feelings with my two best friends. The two people in the world who knew me best. Chase was on edge at first, obviously worried about our business relationship with Luke, but as usual, he was unable to resist any sort of romance. As I talked, leaving out some of the more intimate details, Chase rested his cheek on his hand and gave me his best swoony eyes. He sighed when I had finished, and Everleigh, finishing her second margarita, started to giggle again.

"Charlie," he began, "first of all, I can't even be mad at you. It's been so long since I've seen that look on your face, and it makes me so happy. I'm not going to lie, I am nervous about how this will affect us professionally, but I trust your judgement, and I'm confident you wouldn't deliberately jeopardize our business. I only know the Luke I hear about from the gossip hounds, but he is a yummy dish, and I can't blame you for jumping all over that, girl." He laughed, happy-go-lucky Chase once again.

Everleigh waved at our waitress, ready for another round, and she grinned over at me. "Charlie, you left out the most important detail. Did Luke live up to his tasty reputation? I need a little vicarious satisfaction."

"Well, let me put it this way, Ever, I never realized until last night what I was missing. If nothing else, it was a night I'm sure I will relive in my mind for quite a while."

Now we were all giggling; it was probably the tequila, but who cares, it was great, and for once, I was going to live in the moment.

The next morning, I really did not feel like living in the moment. I had a splitting headache, and my dry mouth was desperately in need of hydration. Everleigh and I both stumbled out of our bedrooms at the same time. Chase was still crashed out on the couch, but I got him a glass and two ibuprofens, knowing he would likely need it.

Everleigh nodded at the glass I had filled up for Chase as she gulped hers down. "You know, that dick probably won't even be hungover even though he drank us under the table."

"Ugh, I know," I said. "It must be a guy thing; Joe hardly ever had a hangover. It used to piss me off every time."

"Don't forget, you promised Chase OD for brunch. You'd better call ahead for a table; they're bound to be busy," Everleigh advised me.

"I know, I figured I would let him sleep a little longer and then wake him up to get cleaned up before we head over.

"What about you? Do you want to join us?" I asked.

"I wish I could, but I really should get over to the bakery and check on Bob and Lisa. I think they might be sleeping together, and I'm hoping they're actually working and not making out in the back room. What are your plans for the rest of the day?" She looked at me knowingly. "You gonna check in with your hot hookup from Friday night?"

I shook my head. "I really think we should take a little time. I mean, I had a great night, but I'm not sure it was anything more than that."

"Charlie, it may have been a great night for Luke, but I've never known you to have a one-night stand. I know it was more than that for you. Maybe give the guy a chance—he might surprise you. He knew how you felt about keeping things professional. I'd be surprised if he brought you home knowing that all he wanted was a one-night stand. That would be incredibly awkward."

I knew Everleigh was trying to be logical, but I waffled between trying to convince myself that it was no big deal and a great way to alleviate some sexual frustration in my life and trying not to freak out because I couldn't stop thinking about the guy and wanted to see him again.

It turned out that I wasn't the only one thinking about Friday night. When I got back to my room and checked my phone, I had several messages from Luke.

"Hey, firecracker. I've been thinking about you. I woke up this morning imagining all that silky red hair spread out on my pillow."

"Okay, maybe that was a cheesy line, but I did have a great time Friday night, and I kinda miss you."

"You're not answering, so I hope this doesn't mean you don't miss me . . . even a little."

I picked up my phone to respond, and another message came through:

"All right, I'm feeling a little insecure here, and I'm not enjoying the feeling. How do you feel about getting together later? Pretty please?"

"Calm down, big boy, I was in the other room, trying to hydrate after too many margaritas last night. Friday night was definitely a highlight of my week, but maybe we should cool it for a few days. See how we feel about things next week. Thoughts?"

"I may be okay with that, but Sadie is pretty upset. She was hoping you would come over and go for a walk with us."

"Now that is tempting, because I REALLY miss Sadie, but maybe we can revisit that idea after work on Monday."

"Sigh. (sad face emoji) I guess I will just be alone with my fantasies until Monday then. I wouldn't mind seeing you after too much tequila. Loose Charlie sounds fun. Bye Firecracker."

"Bye, Luke, say hi to Sadie. (smiley face emoji)"

I mean, seriously, who would have ever thought Luke would send a text message with an emoji? I shook my head as I got undressed to jump in the shower. Chase was already getting cleaned up, but I wasn't worried—that guy took longer to get ready than any girl. I found myself looking forward to brunch with Chase. We never got around to talking about King Street, and today would be the perfect time to fill him in on the details and start preparing for how we would budget the job. As I washed my hair, I did allow myself a minute to remember my shower with Luke. I quickly changed my train of thought, realizing that my shower would end up being a little too long if I continued down that road. It wasn't meant to be that kind of a shower.

Chapter 13

LUKE

Love is friendship that has caught fire. It is quiet understanding, mutual confidence, sharing and forgiving. It is loyalty through good and bad times. It settles for less than perfection and makes allowances for human weaknesses.
—Ann Landers

It turned out that I didn't get to see Charlie on Monday or Tuesday. She wanted to get everything done for our King Street project before we saw each other again "socially." I didn't know what was more aggravating, having to wait to see her or realizing how badly I wanted to see her. Ethan seemed to be relishing my discomfort and managed to find ways to bring up Charlie as often as possible. This did not help my gloomy mood.

On Wednesday morning, he popped his head into my office with a shit-eating grin on his face. "Hey, grumpy ass, I thought I'd let you know that Whimsical Designs will be in this afternoon to go over their bid. I wanted to make sure you would be available at 3:00 p.m."

I tried to control my sudden change of mood; I hated to give him the satisfaction. Instead, I gave him a scowl and threw back, "I'm sure I can free up my schedule."

He was already headed back down the hall, but I could hear his laughter as he went back to his office.

My spirits lifted, knowing I was going to be in the same room with Charlie later today. I hoped I could convince her to lift her social interaction ban, provided everything went well at the meeting. I had barely been able to sleep since Friday. I was amazed at how often she made me feel like a horny teenager. Cold showers didn't even cut it and I had to relieve myself three times over the weekend just remembering our night together.

Fuck. I really needed something to distract me for a few hours, so I decided to head over to King Street and walk through the building.

Just as I was about to leave, Crystal's voice came over the intercom: "Hey, Luke, I have Mrs. Winston on the line. She says it's urgent."

I scratched my head. Martha Winston? What could she possibly want from me? I had run into her and her daughter, Sasha? Sherry? Whatever her name was, at the inn, but for the life of me, I couldn't recall what we had talked about. I did remember she was on Charleston's architectural review board, so I figured I better be nice to her or Ethan would kill me.

"Hello, Mrs. Winston, how are you on this lovely day?" I said into the phone.

"Hello, my darling Luke, it is so nice to talk with you. Susan and I loved seeing you at the Southern Lady Inn a couple of weeks ago, and my dear girl is so looking forward to you accompanying her to the MUSC Cancer Benefit on Saturday. It was so kind of you to take our extra ticket and go with us at the last minute. It is such a wonderful cause. We don't see you out and about often enough, and I am looking forward to introducing you to some of our friends at the benefit."

I was trying not to have a heart attack as she continued on. "Susan's father and I were quite appalled at how her young man, Jackson, had ended things between them so abruptly, but you swooped in like a knight in shining armor, so she wouldn't have to face one of the year's bigger social events alone."

I still hadn't spoken, trying to remember our conversation at the inn. I did remember hearing about a breakup and feeling very uncomfortable that they felt like it was okay to share such personal details. Had I agreed to be Susan's date for the benefit?

Martha continued talking, clearly unperturbed at my lack of response. "I figured since we had not heard from you to finalize the arrangements, I should call directly to work things out. Were you planning to pick Susan up at the house, or should we all meet you at the hotel?"

I realized I needed to say something, so I responded in the only way I could, "I think it would be best if I meet you there because I didn't realize when we originally spoke that I have a work obligation earlier in the day. You know how it is with the real estate business . . . seven days a week." I laughed, trying to sound unruffled. "I would hate to cause Susan to be late, but I'll get there as soon as I am able to, certainly before we are seated for dinner." My mind was spinning, trying to think of a way to gracefully bow out, but with the benefit only a few days away, I knew the Winstons would be most unhappy if I bailed, and I needed Martha Winston in my corner for the King Street project.

"Very well, Luke, we will leave your ticket at the entrance and look forward to seeing you Saturday evening. I'm sure you are already aware, but the event is black tie."

"Of course, Mrs. Winston, I am looking forward to spending the evening with you and your family. I will see you then, goodbye."

I hung up the phone before she had even finished saying goodbye, my mood having plummeted by several degrees. How in the world could I have completely forgotten that I had agreed to attend the MUSC Cancer Benefit with Susan Winston? I struggled to remember what she even looked like. I seemed to remember a thin, attractive blonde, a carbon copy of most of the young women in Charleston's old-money elite. I usually tried to avoid those kinds of entanglements unless it was very clear that they were just looking for a fun diversion. Spending the evening with one of those girls and her parents did not sound at all like something I would have agreed to, but it looked like I was over a barrel in this case. Damn it, that was the last thing I wanted to do on a Saturday night, but I guessed it couldn't be helped.

A few hours later, I returned to the office after walking the buildings on King Street. My mood had lifted considerably. My juices were flowing after spending some time walking around our project, envisioning how it would look when we were done.

I must have been grinning like a fool because Crystal gave me a big smile when I walked in. I felt my smile get even wider when I noticed Chase and Charlie sitting in the reception area. I looked back at Crystal. "Does Ethan know they're here?"

Chase stood. "It's fine. We're early, please, take your time."

I walked over and shook his hand as Crystal responded, "Ethan is setting up the conference room and told me to send them back in five, so I was just about to take them back."

"Well, follow me then," I said, walking over to Charlie, smiling, as she also stood up. My heart skipped a beat as she smiled warmly back at me. I took her hand; I couldn't resist the need to touch her. "I am really glad to see you, Charlie." I turned to Chase, feeling a little awkward. "I mean, it's great to see you both."

Chase's eyes twinkled, and I could tell he wanted to say something mischievous, but he held back. "It's great to see you too, Luke."

Shit, I thought, *I guess the cat is out of the bag. I wonder if this is going to be uncomfortable.*

I needn't have worried because Charlie was nothing if not professional. And while I could see that Chase had it in him to cut loose, he was all business once we were all seated in the conference room. I was impressed, and I could tell that Ethan was too, as Charlie and Chase laid out their plan for King Street. At the previous meeting, Charlie had run the show, and it was clear that while she was the creative side of Whimsical Designs, Chase was the financial side. He concisely laid out all the costs and details of their portion of the job. It seemed as if no stone had been left unturned, and their plans were unique yet elegant, quirky and cool.

They seemed to be able to keep costs down while still providing quality finishes that I knew would help sell our condos. I was surprised to find myself inspired even more by their ideas, and the budget was even better than I had anticipated.

When they finished, I looked over at Ethan, who was nodding and smiling. He looked back and forth between Charlie and Chase before smacking one of his big hands down on the table. Charlie jumped, and Chase rocked back in his chair, unsure of what to make of his reaction.

Ethan looked at me. "So, buddy, are you going to thank me now for bringing these two in on this project or what?"

I looked over at Charlie and Chase, who had concluded that Ethan's reaction was a good one and were both smiling broadly. "I feel comfortable speaking for both of us when I say this proposal exceeds expectations. I think the pricing is fair, and while I am sure there will be changes along the way, it seems we're all on the same page. Congratulations. We'll draw up the contract and get it over to you tomorrow," I said, relieved that things were turning out so well.

Chase jumped out of his chair and ran over to me, grabbing my hand and pumping it up and down. "Thank you so much, Luke . . . and Ethan." He ran over to Ethan, practically dislocating his shoulder in his enthusiasm. I looked over at Charlie, who had a happy smile on her face; I wanted to go over and scoop her in my arms and kiss her senseless. I couldn't recall ever feeling so happy.

Chase was still babbling, "This is going to be an amazing project. I just can't wait to get started. Thank you both again for the opportunity. This is EPIC."

Charlie stood up and went over to fetch Chase, who was hopping around like a jackrabbit, causing Ethan to scratch his head in confusion. She was laughing now. "Chase, I think they get it. Let's get our things and head back to the office."

He looked at the three of us. "But wait, we should celebrate! It's five o'clock, let's go have a toast to our new partnership. Come on, guys, let's do it!"

Charlie was still laughing as she responded, "Geez, Chase, I'm sure these guys have better things to do."

I shook my head at them. "Nope, a happy-hour celebration sounds perfect. Ethan, you in?"

"You bet, I never turn down an after-work cocktail, and I definitely feel like celebrating. Should we text Seb and see if he wants to join us?" he asked.

"Let's do it." I looked at Charlie and Chase. "So, where should we go?"

Chase didn't hesitate. "It's a beautiful evening, let's go over to the rooftop at Stars."

"Sounds great, man, lead the way," I responded, gesturing to the door.

A few minutes later, we were seated at a table near the bar on the rooftop of Stars, overlooking the city. Ethan and Chase had gone ahead of us, so I managed to sneak Charlie's hand in mine as we walked. I was afraid she would protest, but she just gave me a little smile, and I could feel the air heat up between us. She let go of my hand when we got to the bar, and that was okay, but I was determined to try and get her alone later.

As soon as our server had delivered our drinks, Chase raised his glass. "Here's to a wildly successful and very profitable collaboration," he said happily.

"Hear, hear!" we all agreed, clinking glasses. Chase talked animatedly to Ethan, who smiled indulgently and nodded every so often.

I leaned in to Charlie, who was sitting next to me. "Is he always like this?" I asked softly.

"As long as I've known him, going on ten years," she answered.

I put my hand on her knee, wanting to feel her warm bare skin. I watched her cheeks turn pink, and I took it as a sign of encouragement. I leaned over and whispered in her ear, "After this drink, can I talk you into dinner at my place?"

She looked me in the eye. "That sounds like trouble."

"Only the best kind." I smiled at her. "Besides, Sadie keeps asking about you."

"Your dog is asking about me?" she responded sarcastically. "I highly doubt it."

"Hey, what's with the whispering over there?" Chase interrupted. "You two are looking mighty cozy."

"Yeah, I would have to agree," said Ethan, raising an eyebrow suggestively.

"If you must know, I was just asking Charlie here if she would like to go with me to take Sadie for her evening walk through Hampton Park," I said pointedly.

"Oh, so you weren't planning to invite the whole group?" Ethan asked, smirking now.

I finished the rest of my drink, dropped the empty glass on the table, grabbed Charlie's hand and stood up. She gasped as I said, "Nope, but I'm sure you two can find your own trouble to get into."

She laughed as I threw some money at Ethan, who was also laughing, and I pulled her toward the elevator without a backward glance at our friends.

"I would say that was mighty presumptuous of you, Mr. Coleman," Charlie said to me, still smiling.

"Sometimes, in order to get what you want, you have to take control of the situation, Ms. Finley." I said as we got on the elevator. The door had barely closed before I pushed her against the wall and grabbed her lips with mine in a searing kiss. "Oh, yes," I moaned against her, "I have been wanting to do this for days."

A moment later, the elevator stopped, and she pulled away, but her eyes were warm as she looked up at me. "Wow, that felt really nice," she said.

My arms were still around her when the door opened, and as we walked out, I caught the eye of one of my least favorite people, who was at that moment seated at the bar, scowling in our direction. I guess Charlie saw him too because she let go of my arm and started to step away from me.

"Well, what do we have here?" sneered Tad Winthrop as he sauntered toward us from the bar. I pulled Charlie in closer to me as she tried to scoot away. "I'm starting to understand what it takes to get your attention, Charlie," he continued. "Clearly a high-profile project is just the ticket."

"Shut the fuck up, Winthrop," I growled at him. "You have no idea what you're talking about." I could see Charlie's eyes widen and her face get pale, but I also felt her stand up straighter and her wide eyes were piercing as she looked Tad in the eye.

"You are out of line, Tad, Chase and I had already commit-ted to Luke and Ethan when you contacted us about working with you. We're a small firm, and we can't handle more than one large project at a time."

Tad looked pointedly at my arm around Charlie's waist. "It seems that your services extend outside of just decorating these days. I'm sorry to have to miss out on working with you." He laughed. "Maybe next time."

I wanted to punch him right there in the bar, wipe that sneer off his face. Charlie must have sensed my feelings because she grabbed my arm as I balled my hand into a fist. Charlie smiled at Tad, but it didn't reach her eyes, as she responded before I had the chance: "I'm sure Britt would be interested to hear about your desire to work with me, Tad. She and I are overdue for a lunch date. Maybe I'll give her a ring tomorrow. Oh, and let me tell you this, there is no job, no matter how big or high profile, that would entice me to work with you. But I'm sure there are plenty of other designers happy to step in. Call them." She smiled up at me and reached up to stroke my cheek. "Come on, Luke, I'm ready to get out of here."

I turned my back on Tad and steered her toward the door.

Charlie looked up at me as we walked out onto the side-walk. "I guess the rumors about you and Tad are true. He doesn't seem to be your biggest fan," she said.

I laughed ruefully. "He didn't take it too well when we stole a few big listings out from under him. He seems to be a rather competitive sort who doesn't play well in the sandbox with oth-ers. Unless, of course, they're fellow native Charlestonians." I looked down at her. "He also seems to have a bit of a thing for you. Some history I should know about, firecracker?"

She shook her head. "Nothing worth talking about. I turned down his advances in high school. . Despite the fact that he and Britt have been together off and on since high school, once Joe and I split up, he seemed to want to revisit the idea of us becoming an item. I thought I'd heard that he and Britt had finally gotten engaged, but maybe I'm wrong."

I shook my head. "No, not wrong. They are definitely engaged, but clearly, he's less than devoted. Hopefully you scared him off with your threat to call Britt. Although I can't believe she's not clued in to his indiscretions; he's not exactly subtle from what I can see."

She sighed. "It seems to be par for the course with that crowd. I mean, Britt isn't my favorite person, but nobody deserves to be treated with such little respect. I'm sure Tad knows that I'm not likely to meet Britt for lunch and that was just an empty threat, but I was just so angry. Truly, though, he's not worth worrying about. Right now, he's the last person I would want to work for." She looked at me, smiling. "Besides, I think I'll have my hands full for the next year or so."

I pulled her close as we started walking back to my office. "You're damn right you will. I intend to keep you very busy, starting tonight. My place? There's a pit bull that's just dying to see you."

She laughed, and my chest warmed at the sound. "All right, all right. Let me just text Everleigh that I'll be home late."

"Or maybe not at all," I responded.

She just shook her head as she pulled out her phone.

Chapter 14

CHARLIE

But when a woman decides to sleep with a man, there
is no wall she will not scale, no fortress she will not
destroy, no moral consideration she will not ignore at its
very root: there is no God worth worrying about.
—*Gabriel García Márquez,* Love in the Time of Cholera

I checked myself to see if it felt weird to be back at Luke's, but
I actually felt comfortable and glad to be there. He also seemed
happy to have me, and his demeanor had softened considerably
since we had left the bar. Chase had sent me some funny text
messages and suggestive emojis, which I chose to ignore, after
responding that I would see him tomorrow at work. Everleigh
hadn't responded to my text, but she was likely in the midst of
closing up and not looking at her phone. I expected something
similar to Chase's texts once she did finally answer.

I was sitting in the living room while Luke took Sadie for a quick walk. I was wearing heels (not prepared for a walk through the park), so he'd told me to get comfortable and he would be back shortly. He had taken the time to pour me a glass of wine, so I had my feet curled up on his couch, feeling quite relaxed when he returned. He stopped as he entered the room, and his eyes warmed up when he saw me snuggled on his cozy couch.

"I never would have guessed that you were so into comfort when it came to your furnishings," I said.

He shrugged. "I work long hours, and when I come home, I want to be relaxed. I guess I consider my home to be my sanctuary. Besides, dog friendly is also important to me. I like nice things, but fussy is of no interest."

He walked over and sat next to me, reaching for my wine glass and taking a sip. "How about you? I'm sure your place is decorated beautifully."

I laughed. "You would think so, but aside from a few family pieces, I haven't had much time to decorate my own place. I left most of the furniture with Joe when we got divorced. I really didn't want to keep anything that would remind me of him at the time. Now, I wish I had a few things that I really loved and I kind of miss, but there's no point in dwelling on regrets, I guess."

I felt myself getting a little sad, and Luke must have noticed because his expression was soft as he listened to me talk. "I hate the thought of you hurting," he said finally. "But I want to know more about you. I feel like we've done things a little backward, but our attraction was a bit, ahem, overwhelming."

I nodded in agreement as he reached over to play with my hair. I had pulled it up in a twist, and our walk from the bar had caused pieces to fall out. He seemed fascinated by the tendrils, twisting them through his fingers as he watched me. "Will you tell me about your marriage?" he asked quietly.

I hesitated. The last thing I thought I wanted was to talk about Joe, but I found myself opening up anyway. What was it about this man that made me feel safe enough to talk about even my most uncomfortable memories? "Joe was my first love," I began.

I must have talked for over an hour, and as I talked, Luke moved us into the kitchen, where he effortlessly put together dinner for two. He cut up a rotisserie chicken and put it on a bed of greens with fresh vegetables. It was nice to watch him moving around his beautiful kitchen, chopping and plating our food. He was attentive to my wine glass, refilling it the minute it started to get low. I found myself relaxing, and it was cathartic to share my history with Luke, who listened quietly. Every so often, he would reach over and pat my hand or stroke my cheek, and I couldn't ever remember feeling more comfortable with a man. It was difficult talking about Joe's infidelity, but I felt it was important that Luke understand my insecurities about embarking on a new relationship. Not that we were necessarily headed in that direction, but it seemed important that he understood what he might be getting into.

I could feel his anger when I told him about walking in on Joe and Michelle in our bedroom. I laughed and was surprised to be the one comforting him when he got upset on my behalf. "Luke, it's been over two years, I have mostly moved on. I'm not sad or angry anymore, but I can't deny that his cheating left a mark. I just didn't see it coming and I guess that is what has me doubting myself the most. How can you be in a marriage with someone, thinking that everything is great and be so misguided? It makes me question my intuition at every turn, especially when it comes to men."

He laid down the knife he had been using to cut a tomato and walked around the island to my side. "Charlie, you should never doubt that you are deserving of love. I know we've only known each other a couple of weeks, but I already know that you are a wonderful, interesting and very sexy woman. Any man would be a fool to allow you to get away, much less cheat on you. I have to believe Joe is just messed up with his own problems and you are certainly wrong to blame yourself for failing to see the signs." He gently stroked my cheek before walking back around to finish preparing our meal. I had to hold back a swoony sigh from his words as he put our plates down on the table and sat across from me.

"Wow," I said, "this looks incredible. You're pretty domestic for a single guy."

"You should see how I dazzle in front of a grill; this is nothing. Seriously, a guy can't live on takeout alone. It gets old real fast. How about you? Do you like to cook?" he asked.

"Yes, I really do, but since I moved in with Everleigh, I don't do it as much as I would like. We both spend so much time working; plus, she brings food home from the bakery all the time." I patted my thighs. "It's not great for my figure."

He reached over and put his hand on top of mine. "You have no complaints from me in that department. I love your appetite, and your figure is all I have been able to think about this week. It's very distracting."

I looked back at him. During his dinner prep, he had unbuttoned his shirt and rolled up his sleeves, and I couldn't help but admire his hand on mine and the golden hair on his strong forearm. He was all man, and he was mouth-watering.

I finished up my salad and grabbed our empty plates before he had a chance. "So, I feel like all I've done is talk about myself. What about you? Do you have any crazy ex-wives in your past? How about siblings?" I felt like there was so much I didn't know about Luke Coleman. His professional life was well documented, but I knew very little about his personal life. I had tried pumping Everleigh for information, thinking she might have intel from her time working for him, but she didn't know much. She did tell me that he and Ethan went way back and had been roommates in college.

"There's really not much to tell," he said. "I have two older brothers who both still live in Maryland, close to where I grew up. My oldest brother is married with two kids and my middle brother is an adventure junkie who travels constantly when he isn't working. He has a girlfriend, but I'm amazed that she continues to put up with him. He's never met a mountain he didn't want to ski or climb. He has his pilot's license and also loves to race cars for fun. He's nuts. He drove my parents crazy when we were younger, and I keep waiting for the phone call that he's finally fallen off a cliff somewhere."

"How do your parents handle his antics now?" I asked.

"Unfortunately, they both died when I was in college, so they no longer have to stay up nights worrying," he responded, looking a little sad.

"Oh, I am so sorry. I had no idea," I said quickly.

"Of course you didn't," he said, walking over to me and taking the plate out of my hand, then drying it off with the towel he had slung over his shoulder earlier. "It was a long time ago, and at the time, it was devastating. They were killed by a truck that ran a stop sign. They were on the way home from a date night. I was in my last year of college, so the timing was also terrible. If it weren't for Ethan and my brothers, I don't know how I would have graduated on time."

I put a hand on his shoulder. "I'm sure you had to grow up really fast. It couldn't have been easy, Luke."

"It helped that I was the baby of the family and in South Carolina at the time. Jack and Bryce did all the heavy lifting. I went up after the accident and again for the funeral, but they dealt with my parents' affairs, the sale of their house, etc. It's funny, we never had much growing up, but Mom and Dad were very frugal and had managed to save for their retirement and pay off our house. After everything was sold and settled, they were able to leave me and my brothers each a nest egg that allowed us to do things we wouldn't otherwise have been able to do. I used that money to start Coleman Grant with Ethan. I think they would have been really happy to know they did that for us."

"They sound like amazing parents, and it's obvious you loved them deeply," I said.

"They really were great. We didn't have a lot, but I always felt loved, and I could see how much they loved each other. They set a great example for us." He was intense as he looked me in the eye. "I have always wanted to find what my parents had; I just thought maybe it wasn't in the cards for me."

I nodded thoughtfully. "I get it. My parents are still disgustingly in love after more than thirty years. When I married Joe, I thought I was going to have the same thing. It never occurred to me that he wouldn't always feel the same way. But we can only control our own feelings; loving someone is always a risk."

He pulled me into his arms then. "I think it's time to set aside the talking and do a little more of this." He bent down and kissed me slowly. His kiss caught me by surprise, but it wasn't forceful, just asking to be let in. I didn't feel pressured, and it felt natural.

With his mouth on mine, all other thoughts flew out of my head. His lips were firm, his tongue seeking entrance into my mouth, swirling against mine. I felt like I was drowning in his kiss, and I held on to his shoulders like they were a life preserver. His muscles flexed under my hands as he moved his arms up and back down, stroking my back and squeezing my ass cheeks as he pulled me closer. I could feel his desire against my stomach, and I heard myself groan in response.

He pulled away, breathing heavily, and tucked my hair behind my ear, smiling at me. "I have fantasized all week about having you back in my bed again. Would you let me show you how much I've missed you, my little firecracker?"

I felt a little self-conscious, but I couldn't imagine anything I wanted more. I nodded, and he put his hand on the back of my neck and led me toward his bedroom. My thighs clenched in anticipation. I was still getting used to the way he took control, but my body clearly responded to his dominance.

"I've thought about taking this dress off of you from the moment I saw you in our lobby. I want to take my time and enjoy undressing you. Is that okay, Charlie?" he asked me in a low, husky voice.

"Yes," I whispered as I felt my nipples getting hard inside my lace bra. I may have gotten dressed this morning knowing I would see Luke, and maybe I had hoped he would see what was underneath my clothes and appreciate the effort. I wasn't wrong, and it was so worth it when I saw his face as he slowly peeled off my dress, revealing my prettiest black lace bra and matching teeny-tiny panties.

"Jesus, Charlie. You're going to break me." He was peppering me with kisses as he spoke and continued working his way down toward his hands, which were cupping my breasts, his thumbs massaging my nipples through the lace. We were still standing, and I was going crazy, wanting to see him naked.

"You have too many clothes on," I said, tugging at his buttons.

"That's kind of how I like it right now," he said, grabbing my hands and pulling them over my head as he pulled down my bra with his other hand and began sucking my nipple. I moaned, feeling helpless as he bit my nipple and then stroked it with his tongue. I felt tiny bursts of pain followed by unbelievable pleasure as he held me captive while he assaulted me. I was nearly naked; he unhooked my bra and tossed it aside, his mouth never leaving my neck and chest. I felt vulnerable as he took control of me, remaining fully clothed.

Unlike our first time together, he seemed to keep his emotions in check, enjoying his dominance over me as I fell apart under his attention. I gasped as he pulled my panties, ripping them off of me. He began to tell me all the things he wanted to do to my body in great detail. Before I even had a chance to be intimidated, his fingers probed my wet opening, and any potential protests left my lips as I begged him to fuck me with his fingers.

"Is this what you want?" he asked. His voice was steely in my ear, and I quaked with desire as he ruled my body. "Tell me what you like Charlie, I want to please you. Harder? Softer?"

"Yes Luke, so good, harder." I murmured. I was having trouble expressing my thoughts, I was so wrapped up in the feeling of losing control. He chuckled softly as he released my hands at last and moved me over to the bed, his fingers still massaging my clit. He slid me onto the bed.

"Roll over onto your stomach," he commanded.

I whimpered but did as he asked. I wondered when he would take off his clothes; my fingers itched to touch him. I felt his hand run down my back and I shivered, wanting him to make me come. He leaned over and took my earlobe in his mouth, and I wondered if it was possible to come just from that.

"Charlie has anyone ever spanked you?"

I jerked my head to look at his face. His eyes were warm and gentle, and I felt a surge of juices between my legs as he searched my face, waiting for an answer. "No, never," I said softly.

"Do you trust me?" he asked.

"Yes," I said, realizing it was true.

"Okay, just relax. I promise I would never hurt you," he said, his voice breaking just a little. He leaned back, and I felt his hands running down my back. He probed into my now-sopping hole with one hand, and I felt a sharp sting as his other palm landed on my ass cheek. His hand rubbed softly where it had landed, and I felt my whole body get hot as the brief pain exploded in pleasure. His finger began to massage my swollen clit as he hit my other cheek, and I felt my orgasm beginning. He continued to smack me, always following it up with a soothing massage or open mouth kisses on the area. I could barely form a coherent thought; I felt my body start to explode.

Just as I was starting to come, he grabbed my hips and raised me up in the air, dropping his mouth between my legs and sucking hard. I fell apart, screaming out as my orgasm tore through me, turning my limbs to jelly. I could feel my ass throbbing, and every part of my body burned in the best way as I continued to moan and whimper, coming down from the best orgasm of my life.

I wasn't sure how to feel as Luke gently rolled me onto my back. I wanted to hide my face; I expected him to look smug when I rolled over and looked up at him, still fully clothed. But I saw something I didn't expect. He was looking down at me so seriously, his eyes a little fearful, like he wasn't sure what to expect. "Was that okay?" he asked. "I didn't hurt you?"

Chapter 15

LUKE

*Do you want to be safe and good, or do you
want to take a chance and be great?*
—Jimmy Johnson

Charlie and I were lying naked, side by side in my bed, both of us covered in sweat. We were exhausted after exploring every inch of each other for the past two hours. I had surprised myself earlier when I had spanked Charlie. Not to say I hadn't explored that side of me with the occasional willing partner, but it wasn't something I had thought about doing with Charlie. It just sort of happened in the moment.

I wondered if we should talk about it. *Damn*, I thought, *where is my mind going?* It was rare for me to hang around very long after sex, and I had certainly never considered talking about it afterward. There was something about Charlie that made me want to check in, make sure she was okay and we were good.

"Hey," I said, looking over at her. "It seems we keep finding ourselves here." I gestured to our naked bodies, keeping my tone light, testing the waters.

She looked at me shyly. "Yes, I can't say I mind. Do you?"

Oh, shit, I thought. It felt like a loaded question.

"I can't think of anywhere else I'd rather be right now," I said as I gently ran my fingers along her ribcage. "I hope I didn't overwhelm you with my, ahhh, enthusiasm." I was glad when she laughed lightly, putting her hand on mine as I continued to stroke her.

"You are definitely raising the bar as far as my sexual experiences go, and I'm not about to complain." She stretched out her toes as she continued, "I can't remember ever being so satisfied, Luke. I didn't even know I could have that many orgasms in one go-round. You clearly know your way around the female anatomy."

I wasn't sure how to take her comment; it was obviously a dig at my previous track record, and I hated the idea of her thinking about me that way. *Why do I even care?* I thought. It had never bothered me before when other women knew they were not exclusive in my life. In fact, I preferred it that way— better that everyone understood the game. I could feel something shifting, and while it wasn't entirely unwelcome, I was still trying wrap my head around it.

I rolled over to my side, so I could see her face more clearly, and I gently tugged her hip so she would do the same. "Charlie, I hope you know that you bring out a side of me I have never explored." I paused, trying to choose my words carefully. "I know what you think of my history, and you're not wrong, but, well, I don't know . . . what we're doing feels a little different. I find that I want to please you. It's important to me that you feel good and to be clear, I'm not interested in seeing anyone else." I could see her turning my words over in her mind. I wanted her to know she was different, but I still hadn't figured out what it all meant. I only knew that I liked her being here, in my home, in my bed and I was not interested in sharing her with anyone else.

She grinned. "Thank you for saying that, Luke. It means a lot to me. My heart is still fragile after what happened with Joe. I'm not asking for a major commitment, but I'm not the girl who sleeps with more than one person at a time. My dating experience is limited, but I am a one-man woman, for sure."

She suddenly sat up in the bed, excited. "Do you have any plans on Friday?" She looked both nervous and eager as she asked me.

I tried not to be distracted by the bouncing of her voluptuous boobs as she wriggled on the bed next to me. I shook my head. "None that I can recall right now. Why?"

"My parents are having their annual garden party at the inn Friday evening. I know social events aren't your thing, but this is just close friends and family. Everleigh and Chase will be there, and I was thinking about inviting Ethan. I know he and Everleigh are a bit uncomfortable around each other, but she's my best friend and he's yours, and if we're going to be seeing each other . . . " She shrugged, looking at me hopefully. "Also, I would really like you to meet my parents." She said this quietly, clearly uncertain about my reaction.

"I would love to come." I smiled, rubbing her shoulder, trying to get her to relax. To my surprise, I realized that I really did want to go. "Besides, I have a rather fond memory of that red guestroom, and I would love to have you give me a personal tour."

She giggled. "You're ridiculous, Luke. My parents block off this weekend for their friends from all over the States to come and visit. I'm sure that room is booked. However, I'm happy to give you a tour of the gardens. They're very romantic." She laid her hand on my chest as she said this, curling her fingers in my chest hair. I felt my cock stir against my leg, and I was amazed to realize how easily she turned me on.

"Oh, and also," she continued, stroking my chest, "if you could talk to Ethan and tell him to go easy on Everleigh. I'm really hoping we can all be friends." She leaned down and kissed me, sliding her body on top of mine.

I groaned against her lips. "Of course, whatever you want," I murmured.

I failed to talk Charlie into spending the night with me, and I found myself feeling disappointed not to be waking up with her in the bed next to me. But she insisted she wanted to go home. She didn't want to have to drive home in the morning to get ready for work. I did convince her to let me drive her home since it was so late. I invited her (and Chase) to our walk-through of the King Street property tomorrow with Sebastian; that way, I could pick her up tomorrow morning and we could go straight there. It was an easy sell since her car was still parked at her office.

When I stopped in front of her house, she stayed in the car a few extra minutes, letting me kiss her. It gave my ego a boost to realize that she didn't want to leave me either. I was comforted knowing I would be back to pick her up in just a few hours. I realized that I was starting to fall hard for this girl and I wasn't yet sure how to feel about it.

Thursday and Friday flew by as Ethan and I worked with Charlie and Chase to finalize our vision for King Street. We had yet to come up with a name, and Sebastian pressured us, saying we needed an official property name to file with the city. After much debate, we decided on Revival on King. Everyone felt it was a great description of what we were trying to do with the old tired apartments. It also described the location on Upper King, which was rapidly becoming the hot spot of restaurants and bars downtown. What had previously been a fairly rundown area now had renovations aplenty, starting at Calhoun and continuing a good distance uptown.

Ethan quickly had a classy sign made for the front of the property that said, "Coming Soon, Revival on King, Condos from the 500s." Watching the sign being installed was a huge moment for the two of us, and it was all we could do not to high-five each other right there on the street.

"This is the beginning, man," Ethan said, shaking his head in disbelief. "You always believed, Luke, you never gave up on our dreams."

"Well, it never would have happened without you, buddy," I said, feeling a little emotional myself. "If you hadn't hauled my depressed ass to graduation and then followed me to Charleston . . . " I grabbed him in an awkward side hug.

He punched me in the shoulder, lightening the mood. "Forget it. We would both be a shitshow without each other." He laughed.

"So, listen," I said, changing the subject. "I know you mentioned you were going to the garden party at the Southern Lady Inn tonight, and I thought we could, ahh, talk about it for a minute." Having grown up in a house full of brothers, conversation outside of football stats and hot chicks was rare and usually uncomfortable. This was no exception; Ethan looked at me inquisitively.

"Sure, man, what's up?" he asked

"You see, Charlie asked me to talk with you, and I told her I would, so, well . . . " I ran my hand through my hair, trying to figure out the right thing to say without getting punched or laughed at.

Ethan was getting impatient. "Spit it out, Luke. What's the deal?"

"Apparently, it's important to Charlie, with Everleigh being her best friend and all, that we all sort of, you know, get along," I concluded lamely.

Naturally, Ethan started to laugh. I guessed I was happy I didn't get punched. "Fuck, Coleman, it hasn't taken that girl long to whip you into shape." He laughed harder, and I began to wish he had just punched me.

"Listen, asshole, I know about your history with Everleigh, and it seems like you never really closed the book on all that. I'm just asking you to try and not make things awkward for the rest of us. She is really important to Charlie, and I guess, Charlie is sort of important to me," I said, pushing my finger into his chest.

"Holy batshit, Robin," Ethan said in amazement. "I never thought I would see the day that the mighty Luke Coleman would fall for a woman—and a mere mortal, at that." He was still choking back laughter even though I was sure he could sense my rising irritation. "All right, calm down, brother. I hear what you're saying, and to be perfectly honest, I'm getting right sick of tiptoeing around Everleigh. There's no reason why we shouldn't be friends. In fact, I really liked the girl before I mucked it all up by going and sleeping with her." He smacked me on the shoulder. "No worries, I've got this, and we will all have a rip-roarin' good time tonight. After all, we have a lot to celebrate, including Luke Coleman's balls in a vice." With that comment, he turned around to walk back to the office, his laughter still floating back as he turned the corner.

I wanted to drive Charlie to the party, but she insisted on riding with Everleigh. I decided to focus my energy instead on getting her to come home with me after. Ethan came over to my house, and we each enjoyed a glass of scotch before heading over to the inn together. It was a short drive; if Charlie came home with me, Ethan could easily get an Uber home.

According to Charlie, the party was a casual affair, but Ethan and I both wore button-up shirts and lightweight slacks rather than jeans. It was nearly April and already warm in Charleston, but with the sun going down, the air had cooled—perfect weather for an outdoor party. There was a sign in the front yard inviting guests to follow the path around back, so Ethan and I headed toward the sound of music and laughter behind the inn.

I had spent very little time in the gardens during my two visits to Southern Lady, and I was looking forward to letting Charlie show me around. The Finleys had installed a large tent over the grassy area of the yard, and I could hear music coming from that direction, so I assumed they had hired a band.

"Classy," Ethan commented as we entered the gardens, strategically lit by spotlights and thousands of twinkle lights strung overhead.

I searched the small crowd, looking for red hair and sweet curves, and it wasn't long before I saw Charlie over near the waterfall, talking with Everleigh and Chase. I noticed a hand-some, dark-skinned man standing close to Chase and assumed they were together. Ethan and I headed toward their group as Charlie turned and caught my eye. I marveled at how the little thrill of excitement I felt every time I saw her never seemed to dim, despite having seen her earlier in the day. I admired how the blue knit dress she wore hugged her in all the right plac-es—it was so sexy, and paired with cowboy boots, it didn't take itself too seriously. Charlie's sense of style continued to take me by surprise in the best possible way.

Her hair hung in waves down her back, and I couldn't resist stroking my hand down the back of her head as I bent down to kiss her cheek. She looked relaxed and happy, smiling up at me.

"Hi there, handsome," she said, putting her hand on my arm. It was a possessive gesture, and I was surprised to discover I liked it.

I heard laughter coming from Everleigh who was stand-ing with Chase and his friend. She nodded towards me and Charlie. "Is it just me, or did it suddenly get a whole lot warmer out here? Geez, the heat coming off the two of you is ridiculous. I'd tell you to get a room, but I heard the inn is all booked up," she said, walking over to us, smiling at me and ignoring Ethan. "Nice to see you again, Luke."

Charlie lightly punched her arm. "Thanks for making things awkward, my very obnoxious friend."

"Not at all, she's actually quite charming and very astute," I responded, raising an eyebrow at Charlie.

"Hello, Everleigh," Ethan said gruffly. "It's nice to see you again."

Chase and his friend walked over, relieving some of the tension between Everleigh and Ethan. "Hi, boys," he said. "This is my friend, Marc. Marc, this is Ethan and Luke."

He reached out and shook my hand and then Ethan's. "Nice to meet you both. I can see that Chase has very good-looking friends." He spoke with a slight Hispanic accent, and he had blindingly white teeth when he smiled.

Charlie spoke up, "Marc is on a business trip from Miami, and Chase talked him into coming to the party and staying for the weekend."

"Yes," Marc said, "I haven't had nearly enough time to enjoy all the recreation your beautiful city has to offer." He winked at Chase. I was amused to see the normally self-possessed Chase get a little flustered at his suggestive remark.

Charlie hooked her arm through mine. "Why don't I get you a drink? Clearly we're a bit ahead of you in that department." She rolled her eyes at Everleigh and Chase.

"Girl, I think I need a refill," said Chase, shaking his glass and following behind.

Out of the corner of my eye, I saw Ethan lean in and say something to Everleigh. She nodded, and he looked over at me. "Hey, we'll catch up with you guys in a minute," he said over his shoulder as they headed for a more secluded part of the yard.

Charlie looked at me curiously. "Did you have something to do with that?" she asked.

"I may have suggested that it would be more enjoyable for the rest of us if Ethan and Everleigh could put their history behind them and get back to being friends."

She looked pleased and laughed. "Hopefully that's what's happening and they both return unscathed."

I got a drink for Ethan as well as myself, and we moved our group under the tent in search of Charlie's parents. The bar was just outside the tent, and across from the bar was a buffet set up with appetizers and desserts. Charlie explained that later they would trade out the apps for the family's favorite, Smoke BBQ. Wings, hash, pulled pork, and brisket sounded great to me.

Under the tent, several tables and chairs were scattered as well as high-tops. The remaining garden was dotted with cozy nooks and seating areas, allowing for plenty of opportunity for the guests to spread out and have some privacy, if that's what they wanted. Unable to find the Finleys, we sipped our drinks and waited for Everleigh and Ethan to return. Feeling hungry, I suggested we head over to the buffet. Charlie grabbed a plate and started to pile food onto it. I realized I hadn't eaten since breakfast, and the food looked delicious. I was reaching for a plate when I heard a deep voice behind me.

"There's my favorite daughter. I was starting to think I had to do another remodeling project so I could see your pretty face." I turned around to see Charlie fling her arms around a tall, handsome, imposing man with gray hair at his temples and a short military haircut. His eyes were steady on mine as Charlie grabbed my arm.

"Daddy, this is my friend, Luke Coleman. Chase and I are working with him and Ethan on the King Street condo project I told you about," she said.

His expression was deliberate as he looked at Charlie's hand on my arm, but he smiled at me and reached out to shake my hand. "Very nice to meet you, young man. I've heard a good bit about the renovation you're undertaking; it sounds like a challenging project. That ARB can be a bear to work with, but I'm sure you have experience with that under your belt already."

"Yes, sir," I responded. "We're hoping to have enough fans on the board to keep it from being too much of a headache, and our architect has a good bit of experience with historical preservation."

"Please, Luke, call me Don," he said as he was joined by a slightly older and equally beautiful version of Charlie.

"Hello there, sweetie pie," she said to Charlie. "I just saw Chase under the tent with Ethan, Everleigh, and another handsome young man, so I figured you were around here somewhere." She turned to me, and I felt the full force of her personality as she smiled broadly, her eyes practically dancing.

Now this is a person who knows how to enjoy life, I thought as I found myself returning her smile. I reached out my hand.

"You are obviously Charlie's mom, but you look more like her slightly older sister," I said.

She took my hand in hers, laughing. "Aren't you just the charmer," she responded.

Charlie was laughing as she introduced us. "Luke, this is my mom, Judy. Mom, this is Luke Coleman."

"It's very nice to meet you, Luke," she said. "I understand you're partners with Ethan. We could not have been happier with the work he and Sebastian put into our inn. It turned out beautifully. I also understand you've been spending time with Charlie outside of the project you're working on together."

Uh oh, I thought, *clearly she's a straight shooter too.*

"Mom!" Charlie exclaimed, glaring at her. "Was that really necessary?"

I laughed and found I didn't mind the inquisition. I put my arm around Charlie to reassure her. "I have been thoroughly enjoying the time I'm spending with your daughter both personally and professionally." I smiled down at her. "She is a wonderful woman."

Charlie's dad looked on quietly, but I could almost hear her mom sigh in relief. She looked at Charlie. "I know I shouldn't butt in, dear, but it's been a long time since you brought a young man around, and I'm quite pleased." She looked back at me, patting my arm as her eyes twinkled. "And he is certainly a handsome one."

At that, her husband took her by the arm. "It was very nice to meet you, Luke. We'll catch up with you both later. Have fun with your friends," he said, steering his wife back toward the tent.

I could see that Charlie wanted to say something, but just then, I noticed our friends waving and laughing as they headed our way. I realized that Ethan and Everleigh, while not hand in hand, were smiling and appeared more relaxed around each other.

"I saw you over here with Don and Judy," Ethan commented with a raised eyebrow. "How did that go?"

I had just bit down on a cracker, so I waved at Charlie to respond. "It was just fine," she said, making a face. "My mother was over the top, as usual."

"I thought she was adorable," I said. "She's a mirror image of you, just a bit more relaxed."

She frowned at me. "I'm relaxed. In fact, I'm usually the life of the party. Right, guys?" she said, turning to her friends.

"Oh, yeah," they all said, nodding emphatically. I noticed even Marc was joining in, despite having just met Charlie.

I laughed as I ran a hand down her back. "Well, I'm looking forward to seeing this party-animal side of you. Bring it on."

She looked at me with a sexy pout. "Be careful what you wish for, Coleman."

I can hardly wait, I thought.

It turned out that Charlie outside of work and in a group was quite the social butterfly. She was clearly in her comfort zone, surrounded by close friends and family, and I enjoyed seeing her this way. She was bubbly and fun, laughing and joking with everyone. She also made sure to check in on me frequently, making sure I had enough food and booze and that I was having a good time. I couldn't get enough of Charlie one on one, but this was nice too. I couldn't remember attending a party with a woman where I felt so relaxed and in no rush to leave.

It also appeared that Charlie had a rather large fan club. The owner of Smoke BBQ was at the party setting up the food, and Charlie ran over to give him a hug. "Hi, Ronnie," she said. "How's the new baby? I can't believe you're here and not at home snuggling with your sweet little bundle."

He laughed, hugging her. "I wouldn't have missed the chance to be at your family's annual garden party for at least a few minutes. Did you see I brought your favorite hash and grits this year?"

"Yes!" she squealed. "And I'm hoping to have leftovers to take home. Everleigh and I don't do much cooking these days—too busy."

She grabbed my hand to pull me over. "Ronnie, you have to meet my new friend, Luke."

I could see she was a little tipsy, and I was amused.

He reached over to shake my hand. "I hope you're being good to our girl here. She's quite special."

"I wouldn't disagree," I said seriously. "She also has great taste in barbeque."

He laughed at that, looking back at Charlie. "This one's all right, Charlie. You should keep him around."

An hour later, after Charlie had dragged me over to the band to dance with her under the tent, I managed to get her alone. I found us a little alcove away from the party with a wooden bench next to an enormous hydrangea plant overflowing with purple flowers. I dragged her into my lap, kissing the soft skin on her neck.

"Mmmmm," she moaned softly, turning her face and seeking my lips.

I pulled away, knowing once we started down that road, it would be difficult to hold back, and I wasn't about to get caught by her parents making out with their daughter.

"How about I take you back to my place?" I asked. "I would really like to see you in these cowboy boots and nothing else."

She giggled as she twisted her fingers in my hair, pulling me toward her to try and get to my lips. "That sounds like fun, but I'm not prepared for a sleepover," she answered, frowning.

"That's no problem, firecracker, you won't need any PJs, and I have an extra toothbrush that you used last time. I can drive you home in the morning after I feed you pancakes."

"You drive a hard bargain, Mr. Coleman, and how can I resist this?" she said, wriggling in my lap, referring to my lengthening erection.

I nipped her bottom lip with my teeth. "What do you expect? You could hardly keep your hands off of me all night," I responded, giving her an arrogant smile.

She sighed, pressing her lips to mine. "Well, you are quite irresistible."

I lifted her off my lap and onto her feet. "Give me a second," I grumbled. "I need to make myself presentable to say goodbye to your parents."

We said our goodbyes to Charlie's parents and the rest of the guests that remained and headed over to our rowdy group of friends by the bar.

Chase grabbed Charlie. "We're headed over to Dudley's for karaoke. You two need to come. Marc promised me some Ricky Martin or Enrique Iglesias."

Charlie shook her head, laughing. "That sounds amazing, but I think we're going to head back to Luke's. He needs to . . . ummm . . . let the dog out."

"Oh yeah, let the dog out," Ethan said knowingly. "I'll just bet he does."

Everyone laughed as Charlie blushed, but I didn't care. I was just happy she had agreed to come home with me. It had been a great evening, but I was looking forward to being alone with her for the rest of the night. I looked over at Ethan as we headed for my car. "Ten thirty tomorrow?" I asked.

He smirked at me. "Sure, buddy, whatever works for you."

Chapter 16

CHARLIE

Any fool knows men and women think differently at times, but the biggest difference is this. Men forget, but never forgive; women forgive, but never forget.
—*Robert Jordan*

I convinced Luke to let me take an Uber home Saturday morning. He had planned to drive me back to Sullivan's, but me taking an Uber allowed us another forty-five minutes in bed before he had to meet Ethan at the gym, so in the end, it wasn't a difficult sell. Really, all I had to do was snuggle backward against him as he spooned me; he immediately got hard as I wiggled suggestively.

I was still amazed at how strong our desire was for each other. Even in our teen years, I couldn't remember Joe and I being so passionate. I kept waiting for Luke to grow tired of us being together, but if anything, he seemed anxious to know when we would see each other again. Anytime I felt uncertainty niggling in the corner of my mind, I tramped it down, instead focusing on how his eyes warmed up to a deep teal when he looked at me.

This morning, I insisted on making the pancakes, feeling like it was my turn to cook for him. Of course, he was right there alongside me since I had no idea where he kept anything in his kitchen. I found myself enjoying the mundane task of preparing breakfast with Luke. It felt normal and cozy, and he seemed to make everything more fun.

After breakfast, I prepared to leave, and I was surprised Luke didn't mention getting together later today. I was fine with not seeming him because my parents always bought a table at the annual MUSC Cancer Benefit, and I was expected to attend. It was part of the reason they had the garden party on Friday night. Several of their friends came into town for the benefit, so years ago, they'd decided to extend the festivities throughout the weekend. Things were new with Luke, and our table was full, so I hadn't bothered to mention it.

We stood on Luke's circular drive, and he leaned in for a kiss that started out as a gentle peck and, as usual, began to grow in intensity. "How about brunch on Sunday out your way and an afternoon walk on the beach?" he asked.

"I'm supposed to have brunch with my parents and their friends at the inn, but I might be coerced into changing my plans," I murmured against his lips.

"So, brunch and a beach walk with me aren't incentive enough?" he asked, chuckling. "I'm sure we can find some additional ways to burn off the brunch calories. Maybe you could give me a tour of your bedroom?"

I put my hands on either side of his face, pulling away to look into his eyes. "I think that sounds wonderful. I'll make a reservation at Obstinate Daughter. Just text me what time you want to meet." At that moment, my Uber pulled up, and I stepped away to slide into the car.

For the first time in quite a while, I found myself with no plans for the day. I was meeting my parents at their house so we could all share an Uber to the benefit tonight, but I didn't need to be there until five o'clock. We were just a few minutes away, and the cocktail reception started at five thirty, followed by a seated dinner at six thirty. I was already missing Luke, but I was looking forward to catching up with my parents and their friends since I had spent most of my time with Luke at the party the night before. I was sure I would get some ribbing from Mom and Dad for that, but it was so worth it.

Before Joe had torpedoed our life and lit fire to everything I believed in, I had been a very optimistic person. I guess it's easy to be optimistic when you feel like you have everything you ever wanted at twenty-two years old. I was still nervous about getting too caught up in Luke, but I was trying to live in the moment, get back a little of what I had lost. I was beginning to understand that what I'd had with Joe had maybe been built up in my mind. I had ignored the things that weren't great and had romanticized what we had. Just these few short weeks with Luke made me realize how much I had been missing. More than the great sex, he made me feel alive and vibrant. It was as if everything around me had been faded and washed out, and suddenly, the world was filled with bright and beautiful color. Ugh, I was really getting sappy.

I decided to spend the afternoon pampering myself. I started with a leisurely soak in Everleigh's amazing clawfoot tub. Then I put on a face mask and painted my toes while it dried. For fun, I decided to straighten my usually wavy hair and loved how sleek and shiny it looked. I had originally planned to wear a floor-length dress, but after doing my hair, I decided I was in the mood for a short, beaded sheath dress in kelly green that almost perfectly matched my eyes. I wore a thick gold cuff and simple gold hoops. I was tempted to wear a necklace, but the sparkly dress seemed like enough, and for once, I decided that less was more. I added my favorite pair of gold strappy sandals to complete the look. My makeup was very simple except for my lips, which were a dark, rich burgundy. I felt sophisticated and elegant, and for a second, I wished I was seeing Luke. I couldn't help but wonder what he would think of this look.

My dad whistled when he saw me, and for the first time in a while, I felt sexy and confident going out on the town. It was amazing to realize how Joe's infidelity had affected my self-esteem. I wished Everleigh had come with me tonight, but she had begged off when I'd invited her. I understood why—it wasn't really her scene. My mom was on the community board of the hospital, and it was important to her that I come; otherwise, it wasn't my cup of tea either. I knew it would be a lot of old money and society types. I expected I would run into Tad and Britt and some of their snobby friends, but that was okay, because nothing could dampen my spirits. Besides, I had a date with Luke tomorrow to look forward to.

My parents found their friends, and I stayed with their group, managing to avoid Tad, who was eyeballing me from across the room. Joe had always attended this event with us, and I briefly wondered if he had bought tickets this year. He knew my parents would have a table, so I didn't expect he would come. Our divorce had been final for a year and a half, but I still didn't want to have to make small talk with him and Michelle. *Ewww.*

I heard a bell chiming, announcing that dinner would be served, and the servers began to usher the crowd into the main ballroom. The MUSC Cancer Benefit was always held at the Charleston Place Hotel. It was beautiful and elegant, and the event attracted hundreds of well-heeled Charlestonians who ponied up $250 for a ticket. There was also a silent auction to raise additional money for the oncology wing. It was their largest fundraiser of the year. There were dozens of ten-top tables scattered around the room, and at one end was a dance floor and a stage. A string quartet was playing, and I imagined they would be replaced by a band after dinner had been served.

My mom led our group to our table near the dance floor. I enjoy dancing, but I couldn't imagine there was anyone here I wanted to dance with. However, I liked the idea of being able to watch couples on the dance floor; people-watching was always a plus. I sat next to one of my mom's rowdier single friends, and it was obvious she was already enjoying herself. As our server kept her wine glass full, she regaled me with hilarious stories about her adventures, and her commentary on the attendees of the benefit was at times jaw-dropping and wildly entertaining.

We had finished dessert, and my parents and a few friends had gone over to bid on the silent auction. I stayed at our table, watching the couples that had started to fill up the dance floor, and enjoyed an after-dinner drink. Suddenly, my heart seemed to drop to my feet. Not thirty feet from me was none other than Luke Coleman, dancing with a skinny blonde. Even worse, I recognized said blonde as Susan Winston, daughter of one of Charleston's oldest families and a professional social climber. It was no secret that her mother was on a mission to get her daughter married off to any available wealthy bachelor. Her prowess in that department was legendary. I immediately felt sick to my stomach. No wonder Luke hadn't mentioned seeing each other tonight—and how ironic that he had also failed to mention his date with another woman!

I knew that we had not exactly come right out and agreed to be exclusive, but I had really thought that we were on the same page. I had assumed it was implied when we both said we weren't interested in seeing other people. What a fool I was. I felt my face getting hot, and I had a lump in my throat as I stood up from my chair. At that exact moment, Luke saw me, and our eyes locked. He looked confused and then stricken as he whispered in Susan's ear. I didn't stay to see what happened next; I had already turned and fled the room.

I thought for sure that tears would come, but mostly, I felt an empty anger. Logically, I knew this wasn't the same as walking in on Joe and Michelle, but emotionally, it felt the same. More than that, I felt like I had made a huge mistake by trusting Luke. My brain had kept telling me to tread lightly, but my heart hadn't listened. I had wanted to believe it when he'd said I was different; I had wanted to believe I wasn't like the others.

I walked quickly down a hallway, looking for somewhere I could catch my breath. I needed to be alone and pull myself together. My heart was pounding, and I felt hot and cold at the same time, but my eyes remained dry. I saw a door and reached for the handle to see if it was unlocked. It was. I went inside the dark room, and as my eyes adjusted, I realized it was a small classroom with tables and chairs set up facing a large screen. Some low lights near the front kept it from being pitch black. I walked over to the closest table, rested my hands on the cool surface, and looked up at the ceiling, wondering how I could have made such a huge mistake.

As I began to berate myself, I heard the click of the door latch and spun around. I saw the outline of a tall man with broad shoulders wearing a tuxedo standing in the open door-way. I barely had time to register how incredibly handsome he looked in his formal wear before he entered the room and shut the door behind him.

He was in front of me almost before I had a chance to register his presence. "Charlie, please let me explain," he said as I held up my hands to keep him from coming closer.

"No," I said, "I don't want to hear it." My anger was rising. "I don't know why I'm so shocked," I said, and I could hear the bitterness in my voice. "I kept telling myself not to get caught up. I knew who you were." I took a deep breath, all the feel-ings from the moment I'd walked in on Joe flooding back to me. Deep down, I knew it was unfair to compare this to Joe's betrayal, but I couldn't seem to separate the two. My anger came from a deep place that I had put away in order to cope and move on.

"I realize what I am to you, Luke." I saw him shaking his head in the room's low light, but I kept going. "I wanted to believe you when you said I was different and that you weren't interested in seeing anyone else. I had hoped what we had was special to you." I grabbed his lapels and pulled him in closer, and I felt my anger raging inside me as I realized that despite everything, I still wanted him. As his body pressed against mine, I burned for him. In that moment, I couldn't think about anything else but my physical desire. "It's obvious what you want out of this," I said, gesturing to the two of us, "so take it." I put one hand on the back of his neck and tangled the fingers of my other hand in his hair as I pulled him angrily toward me. I could feel him stiffen, and I sensed his confusion, but as I pushed my lips against his in a bruising kiss, a moan tore from his lips.

He tried to pull away. "Charlie, just let me...," he said, growling, and I could hear the frustration in his voice.

"No, no talking. Just this . . . " And I pulled him in again as I reached down to put my hand on his cock. I could feel him straining against his pants, and he plundered my mouth as I felt him losing control. Our lips tore at each other in a frenzy I had never before experienced. "Fuck me, Luke. I know you want to, and I want you inside me now," I said, realizing it was true. My body was on fire and I ached for him.

His hands were all over me, and our tongues lashed together as we fought each other for dominance. Suddenly, he spun me around, and I caught myself against the table. I was leaned over, palms on the table, as I panted, so filled with lust I could hardly catch my breath. I felt him pressed against my back as his hand slid up my thigh, jerking my dress up above my waist. He groaned loudly as he realized I was naked underneath. He didn't waste any time; my heart thumped in my chest as I heard the sound of his zipper.

"Hurry, I need to feel you. Come on, Luke. Time to do what you do best."

I felt him hesitate, and I was afraid I had gone too far, but at that moment, he reached between my legs and felt my juices running down my leg. In almost the same instant, I felt him thrust inside me in one powerful stroke that nearly took my breath away. He slid all the way in—and not gently. I could feel his anger growing and desire coming off of him in waves, and I didn't care. I pushed back hard against him, and he grunted, meeting me stroke for stroke. He put a hand on the back of my neck, squeezing, in an effort to let me know he was in control, but I pushed back again, enjoying the sound of our bodies slapping together. His hand fisted in my hair, and he pulled my head back. His lips were on my neck, biting and sucking as he pounded into me.

"Is this what you want, Charlie? I never heard any complaints from you the many times I made you come. So, tell me, how do I make you feel now?"

"Shut up, Luke, and just fuck me," I said in response. Talking was the last thing I wanted to do, and I turned my head so I could shut him up with a kiss, which he readily returned, swallowing my moans just as I heard muffled voices outside the room. I realized the door was unlocked and we could be discovered at any moment, but I didn't care. My only focus was on my body as it tightened up and I felt the waves beginning low in my stomach. Luke took his hand off my waist—God, he knew me—and reached around for my clit. I expected him to rub it like he usually did, but instead, I felt a sharp pain as he pinched it between his thumb and forefinger. The pain immediately exploded into a euphoric pleasure that took over my entire body as my orgasm soared through me. I barely registered the fact that Luke also seemed to be losing control, thrusting wildly as he bit my shoulder to keep from shouting out as he emptied himself inside me. His hands gripped my waist so hard, I knew I would have bruises.

As Luke pulled away from me, I felt hollow and suddenly cold. I didn't turn around as I heard him zip up his pants. I waited for him to say something, but instead, I heard the click of the door opening and closing. Slowly, I pulled down my dress, turned around, and sat on the edge of the table. My eyes, which up until now had remained dry, were hot with tears. My anger had evaporated, and suddenly, I felt empty and very much alone. I wondered if I would ever find someone who would love me, someone I could trust, someone to share my life with. Why was it that the small taste of happiness I had had with Luke made me yearn for more?

I managed to pull myself together, but I didn't fool my parents, who made their excuses and said their goodbyes the minute they saw me. The car ride back to the inn was quiet, my parents waiting for me to volunteer what had caused my sudden change in mood. I just couldn't. But I did ask if I could sleep in their guest room tonight; I just wasn't up to driving myself home. As I lay in bed staring at the ceiling, there was something nagging at me. My mind went over the events of the evening, starting with seeing Luke on the dance floor and finishing with the sound of the door shutting as he left without a word. My stomach dropped as it suddenly hit me.

After the first night Luke and I were together, I had planned to see my doctor about getting back on the pill. But I hadn't gotten around to it, and I wasn't too concerned because Luke and I were always very careful. Until tonight.

Chapter 17

LUKE

Our lives improve only when we take chances—and the first and most difficult risk we can take is to be honest with ourselves.
—Walter Anderson

Ever since my parents died, I trained myself to shut off my feelings and focus on whatever was important at the time. First, it was finishing college, and then it was building my "real estate empire." So, after I turned my back on Charlie and left the room following our insane encounter, it was easy to go back to Susan and her family and pretend everything was fine. I assumed that Charlie's parents were also at the benefit, so when I returned to the ballroom, I discreetly looked for them. I managed to locate them quickly and stayed out of their line of sight until they left a short time later. Susan was incredibly annoying, hanging all over me and stifling me with her presence. I sent Ethan a quick text begging him to call and bail me out so I had an excuse to leave. I was relieved when my phone rang, and after leaving the room, I returned to tell Susan I had a personal emergency and had to cut the evening short. I could see she was disappointed; she had dropped several hints about going back to her place, and I was relieved to have avoided that conversation. I managed to extricate myself from her, thanking her for a pleasant evening and promising to catch up soon. Not a chance.

I couldn't get home and out of my tuxedo fast enough. Even poor Sadie didn't get more than a trip to the backyard because I just wanted to take a hot shower and climb in bed. Finally, as I lay under my cool sheets staring at the ceiling, I allowed my mind to drift to thoughts of Charlie. I wanted to stay angry at her for jumping to conclusions. Why didn't she trust me? But I knew why, and I was devastated that I had made such a massive miscalculation by not telling her about Susan. I tried to tell myself that I simply hadn't thought it was a big deal, but I knew that wasn't true. I didn't want to deal with explaining to her why I was going to the benefit with another woman. I didn't want to face the disappointment and the uncertainty that had finally started to disappear from her eyes. But this. This was so much worse.

I thought about the hurt and anger I saw on her face when she saw me dancing with Susan. Even worse, she looked humiliated. I managed to make an excuse to Susan and followed Charlie as she ran from the ballroom. I was barely thinking rationally as I followed her into the room she had disappeared into. I just wanted to explain, to wipe the hurt from her eyes. But nothing went as I'd planned. She was angry; she didn't want to hear what I had to say. I had never seen her that way, and I had to admit, the way her eyes blazed and the sight of her flushed skin in that short tight dress did things to me. I started to feel out of control.

When she pulled me in for that kiss and pressed her soft curves against me, I was lost. She was frantic, pouring herself into me and begging me to fuck her. I wanted to say no, but there was no way I could. It was amazing in the moment; I loved the feeling of owning her and having her fight me for dominance. It was unlike any sexual experience I had ever had, and in the end, she broke me. I left because I didn't know what to say. I had wanted to tell her my true feelings. That I loved her, that there was only her. But I knew she was angry and it wasn't the time. But there would only be one outcome. I loved Charlie, and I would make her understand. We were meant to be together. I had found her, and I wasn't going to let her go.

The next morning, I texted Ethan first thing. I knew he wouldn't be happy with how I'd handled things last night, but I was going to invoke the best friend card. I needed his advice ASAP. As I thought about it, I realized that maybe I should call in reinforcements. This was too important of a play to rely on just Ethan. I also texted Sebastian and Austin, offering Bloody Marys, omelets, and donuts from Glazed Bakery as bribery. Being dudes who were ruled by their stomachs, it was an easy close, and an hour later, I was whipping up omelets while Ethan was mixing Zing Zang and vodka.

"Not that I am in any way complaining, but what's with the impromptu bro brunch?" asked Sebastian.

"I, for one, am happy to be spending the day here at your palatial pad, versus doing chores around my own place on my only day off," said my friend Austin. Austin owned a landscaping business with his brothers and worked harder than anyone I knew. "But I do agree with Seb that this is not how you normally roll, so something must be up," he continued.

Ethan was quiet as he made our Bloody Marys, but of all my friends, he knew me best, and I was sure he had an inkling that I had fucked things up with Charlie.

I cleared my throat, trying to decide where to start. "Well, ummm, as you may or may not know, I've been seeing someone for the last several weeks."

"Wait," said Austin, "the same someone? Not multiple someones? This IS big news."

"I assume this mysterious woman is Charlie Finley," added Sebastian. "I noticed a little tension between you two at our meetings. It's nice to know there's someone who can bring down the mighty Luke Coleman," he said, laughing.

"All right, geez, I didn't think my reputation was quite so obnoxious. I just wasn't interested in getting serious with anyone; I was too busy building Coleman Grant to focus on a relationship. But lately, it seems I am starting to feel a bit more . . . ahhh . . . domestic. I've fallen hard for this girl, and unfortunately, I may have fucked things up royally," I finished.

"I knew it!" Ethan exclaimed, slapping a hand on the counter before sliding my drink down the bar toward me. "You couldn't keep it in your pants, and now you've gone and broken her heart. I figured it was only a matter of time. Goddamn it, Luke."

Sebastian and Austin both busied themselves with their drinks, looking uncomfortably from me to Ethan.

"Now, wait a second, Ethan," I said, trying to calm him down. "I made a stupid mistake, but I didn't sleep with anyone else. God Damn it, I'm in love with the girl. I have no interest in any other women." Suddenly, the room was dead silent as three pairs of eyes turned to me in astonishment.

Sebastian looked at Austin. "Did you hear what I just heard?" he asked.

Austin was shaking his head. "I wouldn't have believed it was possible," he said, his voice filled with awe.

"Give me a fucking break, guys," I said, feeling aggravated. "This isn't the apocalypse, but I do need some help here because I think Charlie is really mad at me, and I'm not sure how to fix things. I need some advice. That's why I invited you over. You've got help me figure out how to convince her that I'm in this for real."

Ethan had gotten quiet again as he looked at me intently. "This is really it for you, isn't it?" he finally said softly.

"Yeah, man," I answered him. "Unfortunately, she saw me last night at the cancer benefit with Susan Whitman, and she thinks that everything she feared about me is true. I've always prided myself on being honest with women about my intentions, but the one time I want to commit myself to one woman, she thinks I'm too much of a player to be taken seriously." I ran my hand through my hair in frustration. "I'm at a loss as to what to do to fix it."

Austin was looking at me with interest. His dark eyes were always serious, and this morning was no different. He was my most intense friend, having spent four years with the Army Special Forces in the Middle East, he came back a different man. I hadn't known him before he left, but he and Sebastian grew up together. Austin had gone to college after leaving the military, and he and Sebastian had roomed together at Clemson after Ethan and I had graduated. Sebastian was also good friends with Austin's younger brother, Noah, so they had hung around each other since childhood. Apparently, in his younger days, Austin was pretty wild, and his parents decided a stint in the military might do him good.

Austin approached the Army in the same manner he approached cutting loose in high school. His fierce dedication and amazing physical abilities sent him soaring straight to the top, and he was the youngest recruit to join special forces. According to Noah and Sebastian, his shooting skills were legendary. But something happened to Austin overseas, and he came back changed. His dad had wanted him to join the family landscaping business, but he wanted to get a college degree first. After graduating, he did go to work with his dad and brother, and his talent and creativity, along with his dedication, helped grow their business to another level of success. He added pool construction to their already booming landscaping services, and his unique and beautiful designs were the talk of the Southeast.

Austin was usually quiet, so when he spoke, people tended to listen. The room was silent as he spoke to me, his words deliberate. "It's rare to find someone who makes you feel that level of intensity, Luke. And sometimes, when you find it, you don't have much time to enjoy it." I saw Ethan nodding out of the corner of my eye as Austin went on. "If what you feel for Charlie is the real thing, you need to do whatever it takes to make it right. It's time to make the big moves. Show her what she means to you. Don't let misunderstandings get in the way of you guys having something real and lasting." He took a sip of his Bloody Mary, and I waited for him to say more, but he just shrugged and looked away like he was embarrassed.

I went over and smacked him on the shoulder. "Hey, thanks, McDonnell. I appreciate the advice." He just nodded, still looking out the window as I walked over to the stove to start the omelets. "Well, if anyone has any more specific ideas on how to make my big move, I'm open to all suggestions," I said.

Ethan looked thoughtful. "From what I know about Charlie, I think you're going to have to try something new: a little patience. She got rolled over pretty bad by her first husband, and I think she's super skittish in the romance department. But from her reaction to seeing you with Susan, I think she's got it bad for you too, my friend. She's just afraid of getting hurt, and your history isn't helping your case. You're going to have to do some old-fashioned wooing, the kind that involves flowers and hand-holding and walks in the park." He laughed. "It's going to be an uphill climb, and I, for one, cannot wait to watch you win her back."

With that, Sebastian raised his glass. "Hear, hear!" he shouted. Even Austin was nodding and smiling.

"This is just fucking great," I said. "Next thing, you'll all be placing bets on how long it takes me to get her back."

Sebastian and Ethan looked at each other and high-fived. "Great idea!" they both exclaimed.

My impromptu brunch with my friends turned out to be just what I'd needed to get my head on straight. After we ate, we decided to continue the party out on the water. Luckily, I had moved my boat out to my lift, and it was no problem to drop it in the water and head out. We spent the afternoon listening to music, drinking beer, and talking about women. It had been too long since I had spent that kind of time with these guys, and it really helped to get my mind off of Charlie for a while.

After hanging on the water for a few hours, we drove the boat over to Shem Creek and met up with Austin's brother, Noah; Sebastian's sister, Lily, and a few other friends. It turned into a regular party at Red's Icehouse as we watched the sunset from the upper deck while eating nachos and buffalo shrimp and drinking margaritas.

I found myself alone for a minute, enjoying the view of the creek and the marsh. My mind naturally started to drift to thoughts of Charlie when Seb's sister, Lily, plopped down on the seat next to me. I didn't know Lily well, but we had interacted a few times at parties, and I knew Sebastian adored her. She had spent most of the last ten years traveling the world as a fashion model and had only recently decided to return home and settle down at the ripe old age of twenty-five. I had heard from Sebastian that she was starting a fashion line and had plans to open a store on King Street. It was impossible not to notice how beautiful she was, with her long legs and perfect cheekbones. She had a long, straight nose that kept her features from being too perfect and yet somehow made her even more attractive. Her most arresting feature, though, were her eyes. Large and turquoise, they gave her an innocence that made you want to scoop her up and protect her.

Today, she had her long, strawberry blond hair pulled into a ponytail, which made her look even younger. Free of makeup, her skin was golden, and as she smiled mischievously, I couldn't help but feel relief that I didn't have a little sister. Sebastian was constantly grumbling about her choice of boyfriends, and I couldn't imagine how much I would want to kill anyone who came near her. She bumped me with her shoulder, smiling up at me. "So, I heard the boys talking earlier, and it seems hearts are breaking all over Charleston these days," she said.

"What do you mean, you little troublemaker?" I said, bumping her back.

"It seems that Luke Coleman has finally lost his heart to a lucky lady, of course," she answered, looking at me with wide eyes.

I couldn't help but laugh at her expression; she was trying so hard to be serious, but the twinkle in her eyes gave her away. "I know you're teasing me, Lily, but I'm afraid the only heart that may get broken is mine. I'm not sure the lady returns my feelings," I responded.

She looked stunned and put her hand on her heart in a dramatic gesture. *Boy, this girl is a handful*, I thought.

"There is not a chance in hell that this woman, whomever she may be, will be able to resist your charms, Luke Coleman. You just need to transfer some of that intensity you pour into your work and get serious about winning her heart." She leaned into me eagerly as she said this, and the force of her personality took me by surprise.

I laughed again. "This is what everyone seems to be telling me, but I have to warn you, Lily, this woman will not be swayed by superficial gestures. She can see through bullshit from a mile away. I intend to put together a full-scale plan of attack, and I'm still not sure it will be enough. For me, she's the one, but I'm not sure she knows that I'm the one for her." I sighed, swirled the ice in my glass and tossed back the remnants of my Patron on the rocks.

She reached over, gave my arm a squeeze, and smiled encouragingly. "Luke, if you love her, she must be special, and a girl like that is worth fighting for. Don't give up on her. She'll figure out eventually what a great catch you are. I'm only sorry that I never had a go at you," she said as she moved her hand up my arm to squeeze my bicep. I must have looked shocked because she threw her head back and laughed at my expression. "Don't worry, Sebastian threatened me with all kinds of torture if I even considered making a play for you. I'm not sure which one of us he was trying to protect, but he had nothing to worry about. While I think you're super-hot, you aren't really my type. I prefer them more stubborn and broody." I watched as her eyes drifted across the bar and landed on . . . Austin? She leaned over and kissed my cheek. "I think you've got this, Luke. My money is on you getting the girl." She waved to Sebastian, who was glaring over at us, and got up to leave. "Come join us at the bar. The night is young, and Sebastian was about to buy a round of shots. You can plan your strategy for romantic domination tomorrow." She held out her hand, and with a sudden feeling of optimism, I grabbed it and followed her over to my friends at the bar.

Chapter 18

CHARLIE

Friends show their love in times of trouble, not in happiness.
—Euripides

I managed to beg off of the brunch with my parents' friends after reassuring them that everything was fine, I was just exhausted. When I got back to the cottage, Everleigh was drinking a mimosa on the back deck. I dropped into the chair next to her and stretched out my legs with a sigh. After ten years of friendship, Everleigh didn't miss much, and she gently reached a hand over to stroke my arm.

"So, what happened last night? You seemed in good spirits when you stopped by the bakery on your way into town, and you certainly looked drop dead gorgeous," she added.

I sighed again, this time feeling tears bubbling to the surface. "I think I may have made the biggest mistake of my life, Ever," I responded.

She moved her chair to face me and pulled it closer. "What in God's name are you talking about, Charlie? Everything has been going so well. What could have possibly happened?" she asked.

"Luke was at the benefit with another woman, and they were dancing, and I got upset and ran out of the room, and he followed me, and, and . . . " I realized I was babbling, but I didn't care. I had been holding everything in for over twelve hours, and it just sort of flowed out like a river, all over my best friend. She was quiet as I told her the whole story, leaving out a few of the racier details. I vented and I cried, and finally I finished, dropping my face into my hands as I tried to pull myself together.

Everleigh reached over and put her arms around me as I sniffled into my palms. "Charlie," she began, "this is not the end of the world. This is not the same as what happened with Joe, and frankly, Luke isn't anything like Joe. I'm sure there's more to the story than you realize. I can see the way Luke looks at you—he's not interested in other women. You need to give him a chance to explain. The two of you have something good. You can't let fear keep you from exploring it further."

"I know, Everleigh, but he walked out on me without a word," I responded. "Why would he do that? Besides, I'm not sure I'm ready to give him my heart. I don't trust him, and where can we go without trust?" I looked out at the water and the sun was sparkling off of the surface; it was beautiful, and I barely noticed. Suddenly, I felt so lost. I wondered if Joe had ruined me—maybe I could never love someone again.

Everleigh blew out a breath and grabbed my hands. "Look at me, Charlie." I did as she asked, and her eyes were troubled.

"I know what Joe did to you was life-changing, but it had nothing to do with you. You gave him all of yourself, and he didn't cherish that like he should have. But not everyone is like Joe, and in order to have that kind of love again, you have to let go and allow yourself to fall.

"I know I've never talked about what happened between me and Ethan because part of me just wanted to put it away and pretend it never happened, but maybe that was wrong. I fell hard for him, Charlie, and he still wasn't over his wife. I pushed and pushed, and he gave in. I knew he was damaged, and I didn't care because I had it bad for him. I thought I could fix him and that if we were together, everything would be okay. I tried to force things, and I was the one who ended up with a broken heart. Maybe if I had waited and let him come to me, things would have been different. I guess I'll never know," she shook her head as she continued.

"You and Luke can be different. Don't let what happened in your past get in the way of finding happiness with Luke, or anyone else, for that matter. If you push him away, Charlie, he may not come back. Is that what you really want?"

I leaned back in my chair to think about what she had said. "I don't know what I want," I said softly. And I realized I didn't. I had been happy these last few weeks with Luke, but I wasn't sure I had really faced my feelings. The sex was amazing, the best I'd ever had, but what about the rest? I had tried to ignore my unease, my fear that he would hurt me. The moment I saw an indication that he may have betrayed me, I wanted to run.

I looked at Everleigh, and I wanted to be strong. "I think I just need some space, Everleigh. I need to think about really facing what Joe did to me and how I can truly move on. I threw myself so fully into starting a new business that I never faced my pain; I just ignored it. I realized last night how much my self-confidence has suffered since that day. I'm not the same person I was before Joe. I don't know if I'll ever get back to that, but I shouldn't need a man to get me there. I need to find myself on my own terms. I just have to hope that Luke will wait for me."

Everleigh nodded, and I knew she understood. She held onto my hand as we both leaned back in our chairs and lost ourselves in the view of the ocean.

After chilling out with Everleigh on the deck and thinking about what to do, I came to the decision that I needed space from Luke to figure things out. I thought about calling him, but I knew if I heard his voice, it would be more difficult to hold my ground. I decided to text him instead. I hadn't looked at my phone all morning, and when I pulled it out, I saw that he had sent me a few text messages.

> **"Good morning, Charlie. I assume we're off for brunch, but I hope you know I'm thinking about you."**
> **"I want us to talk. I need a chance to explain . . ."**
> **"I miss you, and I want to fix this."**
> **"Please give me a chance."**

My heart broke a little reading his messages, but my resolve stayed strong, and I knew what I needed to do.

"Luke, I'm sorry about what happened last night. I'm not sure what came over me, but it is not who I am. I was angry and emotional, and I just lost control."

"It's okay, baby. Let's just get together and talk so we can make things right again. I need to tell you how I feel."

"I can't right now. I need time to think. I need to figure some things out on my own. I'm not angry, I just need space. I hope you can understand."

"Are you sure that's the best thing? We should talk it out."

"I need to figure out where my head is at right now. It's unfair for me to be with you until I do that. Please, I need you not to push me. I want you to know that the time we've spent together has been special, and I haven't forgotten that; I just realized I need to work some stuff out.

"Chase is going to handle the interactions with King Street for now. He will keep me in the loop, and I will be involved with any and all decisions. This will not affect our business relationship in any way."

"Okay, Charlie, if that's what you need. Please call me if you decide you want to talk."

I wasn't surprised by his response; I knew he would respect my wishes. But a small part of me wished he would drive over and force himself on me. My mind drifted, and I started to fantasize about how that might play out. I hadn't forgotten the feel of his lips on mine last night. I could still feel the anger pulsating off of him in waves, and it only made me hungrier for him. Our encounter last night was not something I wanted to think about, but I knew I had to. I needed to come to terms with what had driven me to respond that way when he'd chased me down. It was more than just my physical reaction to him. I wanted to punish him and to punish myself.

After I walked in on Joe, I had shut down emotionally. I knew there was no going back for me, so I severed my ties to him as quickly and efficiently as possible and never stopped to examine my feelings. Sure, family and friends had tried to talk to me and comfort me, but I was like a robot. That part of my life no longer existed, and I poured everything I had into work and my friends. Eventually, I tried dating, but the men I went out with didn't excite me, and I couldn't bring myself to move past one or two dates.

It was different with Luke. He challenged me, and I couldn't wait to be with him. I didn't want to fall for him, and I tried to keep him at arm's length, but he broke through my defenses. Seeing him with Susan had raised all my insecurities to the surface, and I was angry at him for the betrayal and at myself for caring. So, when he showed up in the room and I had all those buried emotions bubbling up, I just responded. I let my emotions rule, and it resulted in crazy, dirty, amazing sex. Did I regret it? Hmmm, no, I didn't regret it. I felt a little foolish, and I worried about the outcome of not using protection, but regret? Nope. In fact, thinking about Luke's angry hands squeezing and frantic all over my body made me uncomfortably hot, so I decided to finish my thoughts on the beach.

After I texted Luke, I called Chase to fill him in on the latest. He was kinder than I expected, barely commenting on how this might affect our business dealings with Coleman Grant. We talked about how we could divide up the workload and keep my interactions with Luke to a minimum for now.

"Are you sure this is the best thing for you, Charlie?" Chase asked. "It feels like you're avoiding dealing with the situation."

I sighed. "Yes, Chase, I've thought about it a lot, and I need time to work through my own issues without the influence of Luke. It's not permanent."

"Whatever you think is best—as long as I don't lose my ray of sunshine. It's been so bright and happy around here since one Luke Coleman entered our lives. Just sayin'," he responded.

I laughed. "I'll keep that in mind and try to not let the sunshine dim. And thanks for being a good friend and not saying I told you so. I will figure this out, and we will still crush this project together," I said with enthusiasm.

"All right, girlfriend, I will see you bright and early tomorrow so we can do some more planning. Get a good night's sleep so you aren't grumpy. Ciao for now," he said before hanging up.

I wondered if I was doing the right thing by steering clear of Luke. Everyone seemed to have concerns, but I guessed I should listen to my gut, and my gut was saying I needed a breather, so I was determined to listen, no matter how hard it was. Considering I could hardly keep my thoughts off of the man, it was going to be an uphill battle, but I was determined.

Avoiding Luke proved easier than I expected. The Charleston Architectural Review Board had approved the plans for Revival on King, and Coleman Grant was ready to start moving on the project. Luke was busy with the financing and marketing side of things while Ethan, Sebastian, Chase, and I focused on finalizing the plans and preparing for demolition. I guessed I should be happy that Luke was so accommodating about letting Chase know when he would be at a meeting so I could avoid him if I chose to. And I did. I knew if I saw Luke, it would be harder to stick to my commitment to give us both some space. Even though I was happy, a part of me still wished he would fight to see me.

The first couple of weeks, Chase and I worked with Sebastian to finalize the lobby design. The blueprints had been approved by the city, allowing for a certain number of revisions. Our goal was to finish up the lobby so Ethan could get in and start demo. Eventually, Luke would hire a sales team to sell the eighty units, and they would use the lobby as the sales office, so it was priority number one. There were three different condo units: a one-bedroom, a two-bedroom, and a three-bedroom. There would be models for each floorplan, and once we had finalized plans for the lobby, we would move onto finishing up the designs for each unit.

It was all new and exciting for Chase and me, and Sebastian did a great job walking us through everything on paper. A few times a week, we would also meet him and Ethan on-site to walk the various areas to get a better conceptual grasp of the space. Sometimes Luke wanted to come to the walk-throughs to get an update, and in those instances, I let Chase handle it without me. He always took great notes, and things on our end continued to run smoothly.

I had started to hear some strange rumblings in the community, and my dad even asked me one day how things were progressing. He mentioned that he had heard some complaints from the environmental community about the demolition. They were worried about runoff of hazardous materials. With the age of the building, there was concern about lead paint, asbestos, and other potential contaminants. I knew for a fact that Ethan had been diligent in his handling of the removal of anything that could be a danger to the environment, and I told my dad as much.

"I don't doubt Ethan's abilities, Charlie, I just wanted to let you know that a few people are making a fuss in the community. It's always best to stay ahead of the naysayers," my dad said to me patiently.

I filed away his advice to discuss with Ethan, and I couldn't help but wonder how Luke was handling any bad publicity. I felt a tug to call him, but I wasn't ready to open that can of worms. It had been nearly three weeks since the benefit, and I realized I missed Luke, but I was still struggling to find my footing. I was probably being dramatic, but I needed a little more time before we talked. Even still, I thought about him several times a day, and when I let my mind wander to our more intimate moments, my skin got hot and tingly, and I actually yearned for him. Ugh, I still had it bad for the guy—no doubt about it.

It was Friday, and I had plans to meet up with my friends downtown. Chase wanted to hit up happy hour at his favorite raw bar before oyster season ended. I was looking forward to spending time as part of my favorite threesome—it had been a while since we had all been together—but oysters were not at the top of my list. I had been feeling a little under the weather the last few days, and I much preferred the idea of something a little less fishy. Of course, The Ordinary had a few other options, so I decided to be agreeable. At five o'clock, we had three prime stools at the bar.

Chase didn't waste any time before ordering a dozen oysters and a gimlet. The thought of alcohol was not very appealing, so I ordered a white wine spritzer and met with the raised eyebrows of my friends.

"Since when does the lady order a wine spritzer to kick off a Friday night?" Chase asked in a mocking tone.

"Since this lady started feeling kind of queasy. And be sure to keep those oysters far away from me—my nose can't take it," I responded.

Everleigh looked at me with concern. "You didn't mention you hadn't been feeling well. How long has this been going on, Charlie?" she asked.

"I started feeling a little tired a few days ago. I think I may be fighting off that spring flu that's going around," I answered. "It's really not a big deal; I don't feel that bad."

"Just don't bail on us early, girl. It has been way too long since our little clique has partied on a Friday night," Chase said, frowning at me.

I laughed at his pouty face. "No way, handsome. I've been looking forward to this all week. I feel like I've been a hermit since that shit went down at the benefit, and I'm ready to get back in the swing of life. Just get me a bread basket so I have something besides shellfish to soak up this wine. I've hardly had a drink for weeks, and I'm sure I'll be a total lightweight."

"Since you are ready to get back in the swing of things does that mean you're ready to talk with Luke and maybe work things out?" Everleigh asked. "It hurts my heart to see you so down. You can't hide that mopey face from your two besties; we see right through it."

I shook my head. "I haven't decided when I'm going to talk with him. Sometimes it's all I can do not to pick up the phone and call. He sends me an occasional text, but he's been good about giving me my space like I asked. I just don't want to rush into anything. I know once I see him, it will be harder for me to think straight."

"Charlie, I don't understand why seeing him is a bad thing. That chemistry between the two of you is what makes you so great together. And from what I can see, he's living like more of a hermit than you. He doesn't do anything but work long hours and walk his dog, or so my sources tell me," said Chase with a wink.

Everleigh nodded in agreement. "Yeah, Charles, how are we supposed to live vicariously through your sexcapades when you aren't having any?"

I gave them both a punch on the arm as the bartender dropped a basket of bread in front of me. "Ugh, you guys aren't going to make this easy. It's more than just about the sex, but thanks for reminding me. I'm really starting to fall for the guy, and I'm not sure he's ready for much more than a fling. I don't think we're on the same page."

"But, Charlie, isn't that the point of talking it out?" said Everleigh, getting frustrated. "You're miserable without him, so at least find out where he stands before closing the door on being with him at all."

"Ever, it's not that I don't want to be with him; I just need to find a way to get back to being me before I go down any type of road with Luke or anyone else. It's hard for me to do that when he's giving me hot looks with those baby blues. It's actually quite distracting," I replied.

Chase sighed, putting his elbow on the bar and resting his chin on his hand. "Tell me more about his baby blues, and also about his abs, and his pecs . . . please, Charlie, tell us more."

I smacked him again harder. "Chase, you are a fucking nightmare. Go find your own hot guy. Speaking of which, how about that Marco, the hot Latin guy you brought to my parents' garden party? Have you heard from him?"

He shook his head as he slurped down his sixth oyster. "I sense that you're trying to deflect, my dear, but no, my hot little Latin lover is back in Miami, and my love life has sadly dried up since he left. I'm meeting up with some friends tomorrow night, and they're bringing a cute boy they want me to meet, so I'm hoping things are looking up." I thought I saw a look of sadness flicker across his face, but maybe I imagined it because he quickly raised his glass in a toast. "Here's to finding love," he looked at Everleigh, "fixing love," he raised an eyebrow in my direction, "or just having a warm body in your bed to love." He smiled wickedly at us.

"Cheers to that," we both said, raising our glasses and laughing.

Just as I was thinking about how lucky I was to have the two most awesome friends, I saw someone heading in our direction. I realized unhappily that it was a former member of our very tight circle, my ex-husband, Joe. It had been months since I had spoken to him and two years since our divorce. So how was it I still felt an uncomfortable mix of emotions as I watched him walk over? He still had the tousled look of someone who didn't really care that much about their appearance, his too-long brown hair falling forward into his eyes, like I always remembered. He smiled and looked happy to see us, but his eyes were nervous, unsure of how he would be greeted.

He stood awkwardly in front of me, shoving his hair nervously off his forehead, his brown eyes scanning my face intently. "Hi, Charlie, fancy meeting you here," he said, trying to keep his voice light. "How have you been?" He nodded at Everleigh and Chase, who were openly shooting daggers at him with their eyes.

"I'm doing great, Joe, keeping busy. How's Michelle?" I asked, trying to make him uncomfortable. He didn't take the bait.

"Michelle is fine; she just started a new job, so she's trying to get her legs under her. You know how it is."

I nodded, not even cracking a smile. "Oh, yes, I know exactly what that's like, Joe."

"Listen, Charlie, I just wanted to come over and say hi. We have so much history, and I was really hoping someday we could get back to being friends, you know, we were always good as friends… " I tried not to scowl at him as he continued, "I also heard through the rumor mill that you're working on the new King Street project with Coleman Grant. I thought I should warn you that things aren't looking good for those guys. There is a lot of resistance in the city and concerns about the environmental impact of such a massive undertaking. I wouldn't get your heart set on it going through."

I took a deep breath to try and compose myself, but my tone was icy. "I appreciate your concern for me, Joe, I really do, but I can take care of my business. I happen to know that Ethan and Luke have all the bases covered and this project is moving forward. They have already started demo with the city's approval. Instead of worrying about me, I suggest you focus your concerns on making sure your *new* wife is able to hold down *this* job." I knew I was being catty, but I didn't care. His audacity was amazing.

He looked sad as he nodded. "I hope you're right, Charlie, I really do and I hope you know I just want the best for you?" The last part came out as a question, and I wanted to throw my drink in his face, but he seemed oblivious because he continued on. "I also heard you're involved with Luke Coleman, which was quite a surprise. He certainly doesn't seem like some someone who's in your lane."

I held my arm in front of Chase as he made a move to grab Joe. I reached over and patted my ex-husband's cheek. "Joe, I'm afraid you gave up the right to have any opinion on my personal or professional life when you slipped your wick into another woman while you were married to me. Whether or not Luke fits into my 'lane' is none of your business, but I'll tell you this, he is twice the man you will ever be. Now go back home to Michelle and stop worrying about my life. I am no longer your concern. And for the record, I realize that you did us both a favor when you cheated, because I may never have known what it was like to be with a real man if you hadn't."

Joe tilted his head to the side; I could see him deliberating on what to say, but I never gave him the chance. I turned my back on him and gestured to the bartender as Chase turned to him and waved him away. I saw him shrug out of the corner of my eye before he headed to the back of the restaurant with his head down. I felt sad and a little numb. It finally hit me that a chapter of my life was truly over. The four of us had been the best of friends. Joe had been my boyfriend, my lover, and eventually my husband. We had all grown up together, always having one another's backs, wading through the murky swamp of high school as a unit. As angry as I wanted to be, my heart broke a little for what once was. Joe had once been my family and now I felt like I hardly knew him.

The mood had changed, and I sensed Everleigh trying to pull us back to our happy place, but I wasn't sure my heart was in it. And much to my annoyance, my stomach had started to act up again, and I actually felt like I may get sick. I pushed back my stool and grabbed my purse. "I need to go to the ladies' room. I think I'm going to throw up."

Everleigh's face was stricken as she followed me to the bathroom. "Charlie, are you going to be okay? I hope Joe wasn't the one to make you feel worse," she said, holding the door for me as I ran for a stall.

I leaned against the open stall door as I held my stomach, trying to get control of my nausea. I rubbed my forehead and tried to smile. "No, I actually think that was a long time coming, and I feel better having unloaded on him a little. I never really let him have it outside of the day I found them together, and even then, I was so knocked off balance I didn't say much. I just ran to my parents and shut the door on that part of my life as quickly as I could. I never faced my anger and hurt." I nodded at her. "No, it's good, I feel better. I think I'm just fighting a flu."

She looked at me, a little puzzled, clearly working something out in her mind. "Charlie, you don't think there's a chance you could be pregnant, is there?"

I stared back at her as my thoughts drifted back to the night of the benefit. I had chosen to block out the fact that Luke and I had not used protection that night. If I didn't think about it, then nothing would come of that little slip-up. But suddenly, it was clear. I had been so exhausted these last few days, my breasts were tender, and I could hardly eat, my stomach was so sensitive. How could I have been so stupid not to realize it sooner? I should have done something the minute I realized we hadn't used protection. Maybe I was so upset about seeing Luke with Susan, that I hadn't thought about it at the time. Or maybe there was more to it? Maybe deep down I couldn't bring myself to destroy something Luke and I had created, even if it was in a moment of angry passion.

Everleigh must have seen the answer on my face because she came over and wrapped her arms around me. "It will be okay, Charlie. We just need to get you a pregnancy test and see if it's true. This doesn't have to be a bad thing."

I felt tears welling up as I looked at her. "How did my life become such a mess, Ever? I feel like things are so out of control, and I don't know how to fix it."

"It's okay, honey. Let's grab Chase, and we can head back to the cottage and have a slumber party. We can talk this through, and we will figure it out if we have to stay up all night. You have so many people that love you, Charlie, and I'm pretty confident that one of them is Luke, so everything will work itself out. You'll see."

Chapter 19

LUKE

You can't go through life protecting yourself from everything. You have to take chances. Because if you don't, then you might as well not be living.
—Unknown

It had been all I could do not to go running to Charlie's and demand that she talk to me. It was Ethan who convinced me to give her some time. "Buddy, I know you want to make a grand gesture, but I think if you just give her a little time, you'll get a better reception when you do," he offered. I felt like I had to heed his advice. After all, he had more experience in this area. I was completely out of my depth.

Fortunately, Revival on King was absorbing every spare minute, and this helped to keep me from wallowing in misery. I was actually surprised by how much I missed her. I had never before felt so alone in my house. It was amazing how everywhere I looked, I could imagine her there looking back at me, smiling with that mischievous twinkle in her eyes. I wanted to touch her, to kiss her, and most importantly, to tell her how I felt about her. It was a constant ache that never really seemed to go away no matter how busy I tried to stay.

My friends had been great, doing their part to keep me occupied with nights out, weekends on the boat, and endless poker games. But every time I walked into my bedroom, all I could see was the vision of her tousled hair on my pillow and the curve of her hip as I spooned her in my bed. I was kind of a mess, and I just wanted to make it stop. I wasn't used to being patient. If something needed fixing, I fixed it . . . immediately. The waiting game was killing me, but I didn't want to make things worse. So, I sent an occasional text to let her know I was thinking of her, and I let Charlie have her space.

A more unwelcome distraction to my Charlie obsession were the environmental groups making a fuss about the impact our demolition could have on the waterway. However, Sebastian and Ethan had been all over the city with details of the protective measures that were being taken during the course of construction. Despite a few squeaky wheels and one article in the local paper, it seemed that nothing would come of the fervor. I was especially annoyed to see that my old pal Tad had been quoted in the newspaper article, naturally trying to stir up the pot and make things more difficult for us. So far, the city seemed firmly in our corner, and local officials were pleased with how our plans would improve the curb appeal at our end of town.

Sebastian had really outdone himself, and even the press seemed to be leaning in our direction, publishing the beautiful rendering of our future buildings. We were already being inundated with calls from interested buyers asking to be put on a waiting list so they could purchase the units once they were released. As far as I was concerned, Tad could just go fuck himself. His petty commentary wasn't about to put a damper on our progress.

Despite Charlie remaining scarce, her vision was all over the plans that were taking shape. Both Ethan and Sebastian sang the praises of Whimsical Designs, and their input was invaluable as the blueprints for the interior were being finalized. Ethan was making good progress on the demolition, and they hoped to start reframing the interior soon. I wanted to call Charlie and tell her how much I loved her ideas, but I knew I wouldn't be able to leave it at that, so I satisfied myself by making sure Chase would pass along my praise.

Early Monday morning about three weeks since I had last seen Charlie, I was sitting at my desk, plotting how I might start working on winning her back, when my cell phone rang. It was only 7:00 a.m., and I was surprised to get a call so early, but I was less surprised when I saw it was Ethan. He liked to check out the job site first thing before coming to the office. "Hey, Eth, what's shaking?" I said, answering the phone.

"Nothing good, I'm afraid, partner. I am here with the city inspector, and it appears that someone sabotaged our construction site last night. Some of the contaminants were tampered with and spilled out into the street, and the city received an anonymous tip. When I got here a few minutes ago, they were waiting for me outside." He paused, and I felt my anger rising. "It's pretty obvious it was deliberate, and the inspector can see that, so it doesn't look like anything will come of it, but I thought you should know that someone is trying to rain on our parade, so to speak."

"Who do you think it might be?" I ground out.

"No idea, I was hoping you could shed some light on that," he responded.

"I'm thinking Tad may have had a hand it. Maybe he's disappointed that his trash talk didn't go anywhere, and he's decided to up the ante," I said.

"The city has offered to bring in the police to do an investigation, but I'm going to try and shut that down. It will just bring in more adverse publicity if word gets out, and I don't think we want that. I'll get the guys to clean it up as thoroughly as possible, and we will just press on. Hopefully that will satisfy the city," he concluded.

"Let's hope so. It seemed like we were finally making some progress and had shut all this down. Clearly, we have an enemy or two. I can't wait to get through this demo and start on the improvements. I think once everyone sees your beautiful renovations, things will quiet down," I surmised. "Thanks for the update, Ethan. Let me know if you find any clues as to who might be behind this. I'll stop by a little later to check out the progress."

"You've got it, man. See ya later."

I heard him talking to the inspector as he hung up the phone. His news sucked, but if anyone could smooth things over with the city, it was Ethan. He was not only a master builder, but a master politician, as well.

After answering a shit-ton of emails and working on some budgets, I decided to head over to see how things were going with the cleanup.

I was a little dismayed to see a news truck out front as I walked up to the building. A reporter scurried over to me as I headed for the front door. "Hello, Mr. Coleman," he said. He held a microphone out to me. "Can I get a statement regarding the alleged chemical leak on your job site?"

"It appears there was possible foul play, causing contaminants to spill onto the site and leak into the street. These contaminants had been appropriately stored and would have been disposed of today, but unfortunately, they were forcibly removed from their containers, causing the leakage. The city has already been apprised, and everything has been cleaned in a manner deemed appropriate by the city inspector," I responded calmly.

"Do you have an idea of who may be responsible for the foul play, Mr. Coleman?" he asked.

"At this time, we are doing an internal investigation, but I cannot speculate on who might be to blame. Thank you for your time. Please feel free to call my office with additional questions." I turned and walked inside, not giving him the chance to say anything more.

Once inside the building I found Ethan and several workers gathered around some barrels. A couple of the men were working on sealing them up, and they were so focused on their task that they didn't see me come in.

As I approached, Ethan looked up and gave me a nod. "Hey there, partner," he said drily.

I gave him a wry smile. "I just had the pleasure of being blindsided by a reporter out front. Hopefully, I gave him enough to keep them from beating down the doors of the city inspector's office, but I'm sure they will at least call to verify my statements."

"Well, you're always great on camera, so I'm sure your sincerity shone through. Also, you are quite pretty, so that should help." He laughed heartily at his own joke, and the other guys snickered. I shot him a dirty look, which he ignored, as he continued, "It seems unlikely that we'll be able to figure out who sabotaged our site. They didn't leave behind any evidence, and no one seems to have seen anyone lurking around. They likely came late at night. Maybe you should pay Tad a visit and see if you can shake anything out of him. If you lean on him a bit, he might back off," he suggested.

I scratched my head, contemplating what he had said. "So, you think Tad really would stoop this low?" I asked. "I know he's a slimy fuck, but this seems over the top even for him, don't ya think?"

"I don't know, Luke, but I can't imagine who else would be behind it. Tad has a lot of animosity toward you in particular, and your encounter with him at the bar with Charlie may have pushed him over the edge. I heard he's had a thing for her since high school," he responded.

"I guess it's worth a trip over to his office to see if I can rattle him. I'll head over there now and see if I can catch him at work. Are you guys done with the cleanup?" I asked as Ethan walked back to the front with me.

"Yep, it really wasn't too bad. The containers were sealed up tight, so it took a lot of effort to get them open and to spread things around. Most of the spillage was contained within the building, so there really isn't any cause for alarm. Fortunately, the inspector agreed and was pretty bent out of shape that someone would come here and try to cause harm. I think it actually worked in our favor that he was here before me. It was obvious someone had broken in and it wasn't just negligence on our part," he said. "I just hope this is the end of it. I can't understand why someone would go to such lengths to shut us down. This place is going to be beautiful when we're done, and it will only increase the value of everything around us. Geez."

I shook my head, feeling his frustration. "I'll let you know what I find out from Tad. Hopefully, this will be the last of it," I said, heading out the door and in the direction of Winthrop Real Estate.

I walked into the posh lobby of Winthrop and approached the perky blonde behind the reception desk. She looked like a Southern debutante fresh out of the sorority house, and I tried not to roll my eyes. I guessed it was rude to assume Tad was probably sleeping with her behind Britt's back.

"Hello, I'm here to see Tad Winthrop," I said in my most authoritative voice.

It must have worked because she seemed intimidated as she asked, "Is Tad expecting you?"

"If he isn't, he should be, and it's imperative that I see him immediately," I responded.

"Okay." She looked unsure. "Head on back. His office is the last one on the left."

"Thank you." I gave her a slight nod and headed down the hall.

When I got to Tad's office, the door was open, so I walked right in. A pretty blonde was sitting on the corner of his desk;

they were deep in conversation, and it seemed a little heated. She turned as she heard me walk in, and I flashed her my best panty-melting smile just to irritate Tad.

"Hi, Britt, how've you been?" I asked.

"If it isn't the illustrious Luke Coleman. I haven't seen your handsome face since the MUSC benefit. How's Susan?"

"I wouldn't know," I answered, giving her another cheesy smile. "I escorted her as a favor, and I haven't seen her since."

"Wait, Britt, you haven't heard? Luke is dating Charlie Finley," Tad interrupted with a sneer. "I saw them making out in the elevator at Stars. That is, unless you've moved on from her. I know you like playing the field, so it wouldn't surprise me if you've already tossed her aside—poor girl. But I'm sure you didn't come here to talk about your love life, so what brings you by without an appointment, Coleman?"

Britt got up from the desk and walked over to me, brushing her lips against my cheek before heading for the door. I was amused by the gesture because I sensed she did it for the sole purpose of pissing off Tad.

"I hope to see you around town, Luke, with or without Charlie." She gave me a wink and kept walking.

I looked back at Tad as the door shut behind Britt, and he looked like he had just sucked on a lemon. I tried not to smirk.

"I'm here about the trouble you're causing out at my job site on King Street. This mess was amateur at best and has your name written all over it," I said, feeling my anger rising as I looked at his pompous face.

"So what? I talked to the paper. They called me for my thoughts on your shitty little condos, and I gave an honest expert opinion. Sorry if it wasn't what you wanted to hear, Coleman."

"That's not what I'm talking about, Winthrop, and you know it. Just cut the shit and admit it, and we can move on from here. Otherwise, when we find whatever evidence your inept crony left behind, I will nail your ass to the wall."

He sat back in his chair, a look of confusion on his face. "Luke, seriously, man, I have no idea what you're talking about. What happened?"

"Some asshole broke into our building last night, pried open the containers of waste from our cleanup, and spilled it on the floor, and some ran out into the street. Then they made an anonymous call to the city to report it. Real bullshit," I said angrily.

His eyes were wide and he started to shake his head. "Listen, Coleman, I know we don't like each other and I hate to miss an opportunity to get a dig in, but I would never stoop to vandalism. I'd rather one-up you fair and square. That kind of shit is not cool in my book. I swear I had nothing to do with it," he said emphatically.

My heart sank because I actually believed him, which meant I had no idea who was responsible. I looked him in the eye, and his gaze didn't waver as he looked back at me, shrugging his shoulders. "This really sucks because now I have no idea who would do something like this," I responded.

He couldn't resist smirking at me. "Clearly you and Grant have more enemies than you realized. Way to win over the locals, Coleman. I guess you need to get out and grease more palms." He chuckled, clearly enjoying my frustration. "And

REVIVAL ON KING STREET

don't worry, if the newspaper comes calling about your latest scandal, I'll be sure to express my outrage over your sabotage."

"Wow, thanks, Tad. You're a real pal. Just do me a favor: focus on your own shit and stay out of my business. There's plenty out there for both of us. Oh, and also, lay off of Charlie. As far as you're concerned, she's off limits. It seems like you need to spend more time worrying about your own girlfriend. I noticed her getting pretty close to your friend, Chad at the benefit." Without giving him a chance to respond, I turned on my heel and left his office. I breezed to the front of the lobby, turning to smile at the receptionist. I gave her a wink and chuckled to myself as she blushed. "Have a good day, little lady," I said as I headed out the door.

I called Ethan and gave him an update on Tad. He was surprised to hear that I believed Tad was not involved, but he trusted my gut. Of course, this brought us right back to square one with who was responsible. On the bright side, until getting into it with Tad, I hadn't thought about Charlie for several hours. I was annoyed he so easily awoke my inner caveman and now all I could think about was her. I just needed to figure out how to get her back. Fuck, this was getting ridiculous. I needed to see Charlie and look at her face and get a read on how she was feeling about me. I decided to take a chance and go to her office.

Since the Whimsical Designs office was only a few blocks from Tad's, I headed over on foot. I took my time so I could think about what I was going to say. It was cloudy today, but the April temperature was warm, and the streets of Charleston were bustling with both locals and tourists on their way to lunch. On a whim, I went into a sandwich shop to get Charlie and Chase something for lunch. I wasn't sure what Chase liked, so I bought several different things and carried out a giant shopping bag of food.

I started to feel uncertain as I got closer. I hoped that Charlie would at least hear me out. But I just couldn't wait any longer. I at least needed to tell her how I felt and let the chips fall where they may.

Chapter 20

CHARLIE

I believe in being strong when everything seems to be going wrong. I believe that happy girls are the prettiest girls. I believe that tomorrow is another day, and I believe in miracles.
—*Audrey Hepburn*

I wasn't sure how I kept it together through the weekend, but by Sunday night, I was actually starting to feel hopeful. There was nothing like a crisis to bring into stark relief who in your life you could count on. I learned that first when Joe had cheated on me and my perfect little world imploded instantaneously. My parents could not have been more supportive. They had loved Joe like a son, but not for one second did they try to make excuses for him or come to his defense. Their entire focus was on me and what I needed. My dad immediately offered up their condo for me to use as long as I needed it, and he and Chase helped me move my things out of my and Joe's house.

Everleigh and Chase were also the best friends a person could ask for. Joe had been one of their closest friends, but in the end, their loyalty was to me, and they made that perfectly clear. I knew Chase had it out with Joe, but he never told me exactly what went down, and I never asked. He and Ever both cut Joe out of their lives and focused on helping me put my shit back together. Everleigh saw that I was lonely in my parents' condo and invited me to live with her at the beach. She refused to let me wallow in self-pity, and even though she was nursing her own broken heart, she pushed it all aside to be my friend and champion. The two of them and my parents were like four legs to a chair, and whenever I felt overwhelmed, I just took a seat, and they helped to make things right again.

On Friday, as I cried in the bathroom on Everleigh's shoulder, I decided that while I would take comfort from my loved ones, I needed to take control of my situation. We left the restaurant and headed back to the house, stopping at Walgreens to grab a few pregnancy tests. As we drove home, I thought about what I would do if I really was pregnant. I wasn't sure how Luke felt about a relationship; I couldn't even fathom his reaction to a baby. Things were going so well with my business, and this would certainly throw a wrench into things. It wasn't like I hadn't thought about children. Joe and I had discussed starting a family, and I expected if we had stayed together, I might have been pregnant by now. But since our breakup, having a child hadn't even entered my mind, so this possibility was rocking my world.

Everleigh patted my knee, and I realized we had pulled into the driveway. She gave me an encouraging smile as the three of us got out of the car and headed inside. I decided there was no point in delaying the inevitable, so I headed straight for the bathroom. I looked at my friends over my shoulder. "You might as well pour us some drinks. Make two for me—a sparkling water and a glass of something stronger. I guess the outcome will determine which one I drink," I said.

A few minutes later, the three of us sat pressed together on our comfy sofa, leaning over the little stick on the coffee table. I blew out a breath as the plus sign appeared. "I guess that settles it. This girl appears to be knocked up." Unbelievably, I started to laugh.

Chase and Everleigh were looking at me, their eyes wide and mouths agape as I doubled over. "Ummm, Charlie, are you okay?" Everleigh asked, rubbing my back.

I leaned my head back on the sofa and wiped my eyes, wet from laughter. "Here's the thing, guys," I said, struggling to regain control. "I have spent the last three years working so hard to get control over every aspect of my life, and in just a couple of months, Luke Coleman strode into it and blew it all out of the water. I thought this opportunity for Whimsical Designs would change everything for us, and boy, did it. It looks like I got more than I bargained for." Everleigh looked stricken as I dissolved into laughter once again.

Chase gave her a shrug as he grabbed my arm to get my attention. "You're right, Charlie, your life is definitely going to change, but it's not necessarily a bad thing. You have no idea how Luke's going to feel about this until you talk to him. I think you need to give him a chance to do the right thing. Either way, you have so much to offer a child. Your parents are the best, and I know they will be over the moon about having a grandchild. Sitting on either side of you, you have two of the world's best babysitters. God knows Ever had some experience babysitting her little brother, Conner when we were in high school. Not to mention half of the babies and toddlers in Mount Pleasant. And me? Babies are naturally drawn to me. I was constantly beating them off with a stick at the hotel." He smiled at me then, and I couldn't help but smile back.

"I know you're right, Chase, and I love living here with you, Everleigh, but I can certainly afford to get my own place," I said with a small sigh. "It's not the end of the world, but telling Luke is going to be so hard. I need some time to mentally prepare for that conversation. I know he has feelings for me, and I can hardly stop thinking about him, but this is a whole new level. I think I should tell my parents first; it will make it easier if I get one difficult conversation out of the way. I also think I should go to the doctor and get everything checked out before I tell Luke. No use getting him all worked up if the test is wrong."

Everleigh nodded, looking more relaxed now that I had stopping giggling. "Charles, I am here for whatever you need. You can stay here after the baby is born; your room is plenty big enough for a bassinet. There's no need to rush into getting your own place. And Chase is right, I am a master babysitter, and I love babies . . . bring on the poopy diapers."

I laughed as she pumped her fist in the air. What a nut.

"I appreciate everything, you two, but I think it's time I took ownership of my choices. You have been the best these last two years—you made it so much easier for me to get over Joe. But this time, I need to face things on my own, whatever the outcome may be with Luke. And you know what, I feel like I can do that. Having a baby at twenty-seven is not the worst thing that can happen, and I have to think a baby Luke is gonna be damn cute," I said, smiling.

Chase nodded emphatically. "You can say that again!" Chase stood and grabbed our drinks (mine was the sparking water). "Another toast to our girl. Your future is gonna be bright, and we are going to have so much fun turning this baby into a fashionista."

At that, the three of us dissolved into more laughter, and I couldn't help but believe everything would be okay.

Telling my parents I was pregnant was easier than I thought it would be. Everleigh had offered to come as moral support, but I thought it was best if I handled this on my own. Before heading over to their place, I spent about five minutes thinking about options besides keeping the baby. But I knew in my heart that if all was well with the pregnancy, I wanted this child.

I had invited myself over for dinner on Saturday night. My parents had help at the inn and tried to take Saturday and Sunday off most of the time, so they were thrilled to have me over for a visit. I had finally told them about seeing Luke with another woman at the benefit, so they knew things were rocky between us, and I guess they figured I needed to take my mind off of him. They seemed happy to entertain and feed me.

We had finished eating Mom's homemade enchiladas (Mexican food was my favorite), and we were sipping coffee

(Mom and Dad) and tea (me). My mom had put cookies from a local bakery on the table, and I nibbled on one, marveling over the fact that the enchiladas hadn't made me nauseous.

"So, Charlie, how are things going with your King Street project?" my dad asked. "I ran into Ethan at the hardware store, and he said they were nearly finished with the interior demolition."

I nodded. "Yes, Chase and I have been working long hours collaborating with Sebastian and Ethan on what types of finishes need to be ordered. Fortunately, most of the windows are in good shape, and we were able to track down similar antique windows for the few that needed replacing. Chase is a master at finding almost anything."

My mom smiled. "I recall some of Chase's amazing finds," she said. "We get comments on our beautiful, enormous fans almost daily from guests. But more importantly, sweetheart, how are you doing?"

This was my opening, and I decided to take it. I let out a small sigh and looked at both my parents, who were looking back at me with concern in their eyes. "It's funny you should ask, Mom. I wanted to come here tonight to share some rather, ummm . . . unexpected news." They looked at each other and then back at me as I continued, "I've been feeling under the weather the last several days. Initially, I thought I was suffering from the flu or a stomach bug." My dad still looked confused, but I saw understanding dawn on my mother almost immediately. I pressed on. "Everleigh thought it might be something else, and she convinced me to take a home pregnancy test." My dad's mouth was open, and I saw him trying to gather his emotions. "The test showed that I'm pregnant. I just took it last night, so I haven't been to the doctor, but based on my symptoms, I think it's probably accurate." I finished, waiting nervously for their reaction.

My mom jumped up from her chair and threw her arms around me, tears flooding her eyes. "Oh, honey, this is not bad news. A baby is never anything but a blessing," she exclaimed. "Oh my gosh, Don, we're going to be grandparents!" She was smiling at my dad through her tears, and my heart lifted, but I was still uncertain as I looked over at my dad, my rock. Until this moment, I hadn't realized how important his reaction was to me, and I held my breath, waiting.

He smiled, and I saw tears glistening in his eyes as well. "Charlie, I hope you are not considering anything except keeping this baby because I know you will be an amazing mother, and I cannot wait to be a granddad. I know things are up in the air with you and Luke, and we can talk about all that, but this is wonderful news. I'm going to be a grandfather," he said softly, awe in his voice.

He and my mom were beaming at each other, and I knew in my heart that everything was going to work out. *Maybe, just maybe,* said a little voice in my head, *things will be okay with Luke too.*

It was close to lunchtime on Monday, and Chase and I had been going over the plans for Revival on King for several hours. We were making a list of the items that needed to be ordered based on Ethan's construction update from Friday. Chase was very detail-oriented, and he had laid out a timeline and a to-do list. We had already been busy contacting suppliers to identify lead times for the fixtures we needed to order, but now that installation was imminent, we needed to get back on the phone and start scheduling the deliveries. There were a few things on our wish list that we were initially unable to find, but Chase was excellent at locating the most obscure items, and he was practically rubbing his hands together in anticipation of the hunt.

He was about to start a new list of the items we still needed to locate when his phone rang. He looked down, jumped out of his seat, and headed toward the door of the conference room. "This is Sebastian. I better take it in case he has made any recent changes to the plans. I'll talk in my office, and then we can decide on where to go for lunch. I need a break." He walked out the door, answering his phone at the same time. "Hey, Seb," I heard him say before his door closed, cutting off any further conversation.

I considered going to my office to wait for him, but I knew if I did that, I would get caught up in emails and it would be harder to break away for lunch. I was feeling pretty hungry, and my nausea from early that morning had faded away. I was already learning to eat around my morning or evening sickness, since feeling sick was not just limited to the early hours of the day. As I was thinking about options for lunch and what appealed to my picky stomach, the conference room door opened again. I looked up, expecting Chase, but was surprised to see none other than Luke Coleman standing in the doorway.

I noticed his eyes light up when he saw me, and I couldn't help but feel a jolt at how they warmed as he looked me over from head to toe. I could sense that he was nervous. I felt sad that we were in this place of uncertainty, and I knew I was mostly to blame. I wanted to reach out and reassure him that we could be good again, but I wasn't sure how. I had never been in this position before. My experience was limited to Joe, and when things were good, we rarely fought, and when we ended, I had no interest in patching things up.

Luke walked toward me, and I felt my heart rate speed up as he got closer. "Hi, Charlie," he said simply. "I've missed you."

I felt my mouth open, but no words came out, and I felt at a loss as to what to say. I wanted to jump up and throw my arms around him. To tell him that I missed him too and we were going to have a baby. But, of course, I didn't do any of that; I just sat there looking at him.

He held out a bag. "I brought you lunch," he said somewhat awkwardly.

My brain finally sent some appropriate signals to my limbs, and I stood to face him, nearly eye-level in my heels. "Luke, wow, I wasn't expecting you, and lunch—I am actually hungry, and Chase and I were talking about going out. Wow, so thoughtful of you . . . " I realized I was babbling, but I guessed that was better than just sitting in my chair like an idiot.

He came closer and set the bag down behind me on the table. I was reminded of the night in the inn when he had set the plate of strawberries on the bed. The night he had kissed me for the first time. Suddenly, I was desperate for him to kiss me again. I just wanted to remember what his lips felt like against mine.

He must have read my thoughts because he brought his fingers up to my lips and stroked them softly. My heart was racing now, and I was embarrassed to realize I had moaned softly when he touched me. His eyes lit up again at the sound, and he leaned in and put his lips gently where his fingers had been. Even though his kiss was just a whisper of a connection, I felt an electric charge surge through me from my lips down to my toes. He was murmuring something against my lips, but my mind couldn't focus on his words. I just wanted to feel him against me. I moved in closer, pressing my body against his, pressing into him urgently and tilting my head to increase the pressure of our kiss.

It must have been the invitation he had been waiting for because his arms circled around me and his tongue surged into my mouth, seeking mine. My hands were in his hair and on the back of his neck, stroking his shoulders and clinging to him.

"Charlie," he said between kisses. "I have been dreaming about this, missing you so much. I didn't know what to do to make it right between us. I just needed to tell you . . . " He moaned as I grabbed him to pull him tighter against me, feeling his growing erection and delighting in the power I had over him. "I just need you in my life," he said, trying to pull away to look me in the eye.

I wanted to hear what he had to say, but I also just wanted him to hold me. Being in his arms again felt so good, and I hated to let it end. He pressed his forehead to mine and looked at me so earnestly that I felt warm from his gaze.

"Please, Charlie, will you hear me out?" He said it softly, but I could hear the emotion in his voice.

I nodded. "Yes," I said, but I reached for his lips one more time, needing the reminder of what I had been missing all these weeks. I felt him chuckle as he kissed me back and then slowly pulled away and moved us toward the chairs.

As I sat, I saw Chase in the doorway over Luke's shoulder. He made a motion asking whether he should stay. I shook my head, and he nodded, pointing back to his office, letting me know he was there should I need him. I felt some comfort, and I smiled as he walked away.

Luke noticed my distraction and looked toward the door to see Chase's retreating back. He smiled at me. "I see your friends have your back. I guess I should tread carefully," he said.

I laughed. "I think you can rest easy. They're a little over-protective but compared to Joe's antics . . . " I shook my head. "No worries."

He smiled again and reached for my hand, turning it over and stroking my palm. Impulsively, he brought it to his lips and kissed it, closing his eyes as his lips touched my skin. I quivered. He had such an effect on me; I still marveled at our chemistry. He lifted his head to look at me seriously, his eyes a vivid blue, and I wanted to let go and lose myself in him, but I managed to pull it together as he spoke.

"I have so many regrets, Charlie," he began hesitantly. "Foremost is not telling you about taking Susan to the benefit. Her mother cornered me at the inn, the night we met, and asked me to do their family a favor by escorting Susan. She had been dumped by her boyfriend. They had an extra ticket, and she didn't want to go alone. I had completely forgotten about it until she called me a couple days before to iron out the details. Selfishly, even though I didn't want to go, I also didn't want to rock the boat because her mom is on the Architectural Review

Board and I need her endorsement for Revival on King. It was stupid of me to go, considering where you and I were in our relationship, and I was an even bigger idiot not to have told you. Looking back, I realize I was too chickenshit to bring it up because I knew it would likely bring about a bigger conversation that I didn't know how to have with you." He paused briefly and held his hand up to stop me as I started to speak.

"Charlie, I've thought about this every day for the last three and a half weeks. I need to get it out, and then you can have your way with me—give me whatever you think I deserve. Just let me say this." I nodded, giving him what I hoped was an encouraging smile. The explanation about Susan wasn't a big surprise—Ethan had already told Chase, who had passed it on to me. He looked away for a second, and then he looked back at me. I noticed he hadn't shaved, and he had a short beard and mustache. How had I missed that when he was kissing me? I wanted him to kiss me again so I could focus on what it felt like against my cheek.

He reached his hand up to my face, wanting to make sure he had my full attention. I felt my breath catch at the intensity of his expression. "Charlie, the thing I regret the most is not telling you how I really feel. It was all so new for me and, frankly, unexpected. I didn't know how to handle it. I was a fool. But the thing is, Charlie, I love you." I couldn't help it—I gasped when he said it. I had expected him to tell me I was important to him or that he cared about me, but to hear the words . . . my heart leapt into my throat. His eyes got big in response to my reaction, and I quickly reached out to grab his hand. "I'm sorry," he said. "I know this seems sudden, but these past weeks have been torture. Every day, I wanted to call you and just lay my feelings at your feet, but I was afraid of scaring you away."

His eyes were pleading as he looked at me, and I felt a surge of happiness. Luke loved me; he really loved me. I felt my eyes well up with tears. I wanted to tell him about the baby, but I needed to be sure that everything was okay with the pregnancy. But hearing his words made it all seem so much better. Telling him was no longer so intimidating. I reached out to touch is scruffy face. "Luke, can you do me a favor?" I asked.

"Anything," he responded, still so serious.

"Please, will you say it again? Tell me again that you love me," I begged through my tears.

His face broke out into a grin, and suddenly, he looked so much younger. "Charlie, sweetheart . . . I love you. So very much." He leaned in to kiss me, and I let him because I wanted to feel the roughness of his beard, the realness of his lips against mine. I had things to say too and apologies to make, but right now, I just wanted him to kiss me and tell me again that he loved me.

Chapter 21

LUKE

You know you're in love when you can't fall asleep
because reality is finally better than your dreams.
—Dr. Seuss

I was both relieved and filled with the kind of happiness I had not even known possible after telling Charlie how I felt about her. The feel of her in my arms was like a drug, and I didn't want to let her go. I could tell she felt the same because she kept smiling and touching the beard I had grown out due to laziness, leaning in for more kisses as we talked. I wanted her to tell me that she loved me too, but for now, her shining eyes and soft kisses were enough. I knew in my heart that she felt the same way, and I was willing to wait for as long as it took to hear her say the words.

After a few more minutes, Charlie went to get Chase so we could share the lunch I'd brought. They laughed at the fact that

I had bought so much; not knowing what Chase liked, I had made sure to have plenty of options. We spent most of lunch talking excitedly about King Street. Sebastian had called Chase and told him about the vandalism, so that was discussed briefly, but I hated to have anything kill my mood, so I brushed it off and focused on the progress we were making. I hadn't talked directly with Charlie about work in the last several weeks, and it was fun to hear her plans.

After we finished lunch, Chase excused himself again to make some phone calls. Charlie looked at me shyly and smiled, and I wanted to scoop her up and take her home.

"Will you come to my house tonight so we can talk some more?" I asked her hopefully.

She nodded. "I think that would be great." She studied me thoughtfully. "I've missed you, Luke. I'm really glad you came today." She stood and gathered the leftover sandwiches. "Do you want to take these back for Ethan?" she asked.

"Great idea, I'm sure he'll be happy to demolish them. That guy can eat like no one I've ever seen," I responded.

"How about if I meet you at your house around six? Chase and I have to finish up our plans for the week, and then I can head over. Is that cool?" she asked.

"That's perfect," I answered, getting up to leave.

She walked me over to the doorway and laid a hand on my chest. Leaning in, she gave me a soft kiss, and I immediately wanted more, but she pulled away, probably sensing my desire. She gave my chest a pat and smiled. "I'll see you soon."

I winked at her. "I'm looking forward to it," I answered and headed out.

I planned to stop by the office before going home. I was hoping Ethan would be back from the job site so I could get an update on the cleanup and the schedule for this week. Frankly, even though it wasn't very manly, I also wanted to tell him about making up with Charlie. As I walked the few blocks from Whimsical Designs to our office, I found I was actually enjoying my stroll through downtown. I noticed the details of the historic buildings and the one-of-a-kind architecture like I never had before. I found the uneven sidewalks and occasional cobblestone street that usually annoyed me (because they slowed my progress) suddenly quaint and charming. I shook my head and smiled, marveling at how much Charlie influenced my entire mood. I noticed people smiling at me as I walked past, and I realized I was still smiling as I thought about her.

I was practically whistling as I walked through the front door, and our receptionist, Crystal, looked at me strangely as I bounced into the lobby, smiling broadly. I held up the bag of leftover sandwiches. "I know it's getting late for lunch, but if you're hungry, I have a delicious array of sandwiches that I'll leave in the kitchen. First come, first served, so I'll distract Ethan if you want to get at them."

She was still looking at me like I had two heads. "Okay," she said. "Thanks."

"No problem. It's really a beautiful day today. You should leave early and enjoy the sunshine. Rain is in the forecast for tomorrow," I said. I could feel her staring at me as I headed down the hall to the kitchen and Ethan's office.

Ethan's door was cracked, so I walked in without knocking to find him on the phone. I started to leave, but he waved me toward a chair as he wrapped up his call. I could tell by his tone that the call was not business-related. "Okay, baby, I'll see you later tonight. Yes, I love that restaurant. It sounds great. Yep, seven o'clock is perfect. I'm excited to see you too. Bye, sweetie." He grinned at me sheepishly as he hung up the phone.

I looked at him with raised eyebrows. "Baby? Sweetie? What are my ears hearing coming out of your mouth?" I asked, smirking.

"Okay, okay, lay off, asshat. It's only been a couple of weeks, but I'm seeing someone new, and maybe it's moving a little faster than expected. But honestly, man, I'm ready to get off the merry-go-round and just enjoy one person for a while. These one-night stands are for the birds. There's no fun in it anymore." He scratched his head and gave me a knowing look. "I think you get where I'm coming from."

"I completely get it, Ethan, and I want to hear all about this new lady in your life, but before we get into that, I have some good news," I said, smiling.

"I'm hoping you figured out who's trying to sabotage our renovation," he said drily.

I shook my head. "Still working on that one. With Tad off the table, I'm at a loss. But I did decide to swing by Whimsical Designs after my visit with him."

He looked at me in surprise. "And how did that go over?" he asked with a raised eyebrow.

"Well, it did help that I came bearing lots of sandwiches— the leftovers are in the kitchen for you, by the way," I said, still smiling and feeling just a little smug. "Also, Charlie is coming over this evening so we can talk and work things out. I may be jumping the gun, but she seems to have forgiven me."

"Now there is a bit of good news," he said. "I hope this means we've seen the last of your depressed, mopey ass. Sad-sack Luke has been a lot to put up with these last several weeks. I much prefer freshly laid Luke."

I laughed. "From your mouth to Charlie's ears. I am definitely looking forward to reacquainting myself with—"

Ethan held up his hand. "I don't need the dirty details. Let's just agree that we're both happy your love life is back on track."

"Speaking of love lives, tell me about this hot babe you've been seeing. I assume she must be smokin', the way she had you talking on the phone," I said.

"To be honest, man, she seems too good to be true. I met her a couple weeks ago when I was out with the guys. Her friend was climbing all over Austin, no surprise, and she was just laughing as he tried to fend her off. She seemed quiet and sweet, and we ended up talking until the bar closed. All our friends left, and I eventually drove her home. She teaches yoga and is working on her MBA. Her name is Elizabeth Rutledge—Liz—and I'm pretty sure she went to school with Charlie and Everleigh." He paused and rubbed his chin. "She has been very upfront about not rushing into anything, ahem, physical, and I'm trying to respect that." He smiled wryly. "You know, trying something new. I'm hoping I can introduce her to our group this weekend. Maybe you all can come to my place for a cookout on Saturday. Something laid-back and casual."

I looked at Ethan thoughtfully, my mind flashing back to happier times for him, when his wife, Jill, was still alive and they were expecting their first child. It was hard to believe it had already been over three years. Ethan had always been the most happy-go-lucky of our friends. He grew up not far from me, across the Potomac River in Northern Virginia, but we didn't meet until Clemson. He was a great athlete and played football, and while I didn't play a sport in college, I spent all my free time in the gym, and lots of my friends were athletes. After our freshman year, we decided to be roommates off campus, and our house was always party headquarters. Ethan loved to have a good time in college, and he had a new sorority girl hanging on his arm nearly every weekend. So, it was surprising that after we both moved to Charleston, he met Jill and fell head over heels.

Jill was a party planner, and we hired her to help us with our grand opening party for Coleman Grant. She was laid-back and fun to be around. Nothing seemed to rattle her. It was obvious she had Ethan's number from the start and managed to keep him at arm's length for quite a while. But not too many ladies could resist Ethan when he turned on the charm full blast, and Jill was no exception. The biggest shock was how quickly their relationship turned serious; within six months, they got married. Marriage to Jill suited Ethan, and it was rare to meet a happier guy. When he told me that Jill was pregnant, I wasn't really surprised, and his joy over impending fatherhood almost had me wishing I could find someone too.

But Ethan's world came crashing down just a couple months later when Jill was driving home from an event and was struck by a drunk driver. It was ironic that while Ethan had been the one to get me through college after my parents were killed in a car accident, now it was me who had to be there while he dealt with the loss of both his wife and unborn child. The first year after Jill's death was a dark time for Ethan. Our business was growing, and he buried himself in work. Everleigh joined our real estate team and was like a calm in his storm. He leaned on her friendship, but when things crossed the line, he shut down and pushed her away. For the last two years, he was happy to revert back to his college ways, enjoying the most beautiful women, but never for long, and never letting things get serious.

"I'd love to meet Liz and hang out at your place on Saturday. I'm happy that you're ready to think about settling down again, Ethan. If you think there's something there with Liz, I'm sure she will be worth waiting for. You deserve to have some happiness. I hope you know that," I said.

He looked sad for a minute but seemed to shake it off. "I know it will be worth the wait, but she's hot, and I'm thirty years old. I'm not really used to taking it slow. Hopefully I can encourage her to move things along tonight. She's agreed to come back to the house after dinner, so we'll see."

I chuckled and nodded. "It looks like we're both in the same boat tonight, brother. I'm hoping to talk Charlie back into my bed. I guess we have our work cut for us. I'm gonna spend some time at my desk. I'm sure I have a mountain of emails to respond to. Are we back on schedule with Revival? I know Charlie and Chase were working on a schedule for ordering and installing the finishes once you've completed the construction."

He nodded. "Yep, the cleanup this morning only set us back a couple of hours, thank God. We should be right back on track by the end of the week."

"That's good news," I said, heading for the door. "Don't forget about the sandwiches in the kitchen," I threw over my shoulder as I left his office and headed down the hall to my inevitable pile of messages.

Later that day, I walked in from my garage and was met by an enthusiastic Sadie. So there was no misunderstanding, she also had her leash between her teeth as she leapt around me. "Down, girl. Maybe we can go for a walk with Charlie when she gets here, but right now, I need to prep for dinner," I said, scratching her ears. "You'll have to settle for the backyard for now." I took the leash out of her mouth and let her out the back door. I had made a pit stop at the store to grab a few things to make lasagna. It was easy to make ahead, and Charlie and I could talk while it was cooking. I also had all the fixings for a beautiful salad. I had even stopped at a local bakery and grabbed a key lime pie. I wasn't foolish enough to attempt baking.

There was a knock at my door just as I slid the lasagna into the oven. As soon as I opened the door, Sadie came dashing over, assaulting Charlie with affection, her pit bull face frozen in her trademark smile.

Charlie bent down to return the love. "Hello, beautiful girl, I've missed you too," she said, smiling fondly and doting on Sadie.

I cleared my throat. "Excuse me, Sadie, do you mind if I get in here?" I said, nudging her away.

Charlie handed me a bottle of red wine, her green eyes sparkling just like I remembered. I took the wine and scooped her toward me with my other arm. I pulled her up against me almost possessively, desperate to feel her in my arms.

She laughed, her voice husky. "I see Sadie isn't the only one who's missed me." She tilted her head up, and I brought mine down for a kiss. The feel of her lips against mine was like bright sunshine after a dreary winter, and I couldn't get enough. Her laughter quickly turned to moans as she returned my kisses with equal passion. She reached her hands up to stroke my hair and slid her tongue into my mouth, seizing control as I lost myself in the moment.

I managed to walk us back into the room and shut the door behind her. When I bumped into the island, I reached back and set down the wine. With two hands free, I explored her body, running my hands down her back and squeezing her firm, round ass, pulling her tight against my nearly painful erection. I considered taking off our clothes and having her right there on the floor, so urgent was my need to be inside of her, but reason took over, and I slowed down our embrace. I continued to kiss her softly, stroking her face and hair, all the while watching her. She followed my lead, and her eyes opened, slowly seeking mine, dark green with desire.

"I was starting to consider having appetizers right here on the floor, but I'm not sure that's how I want to reconnect with you," I said against her lips.

She leaned back and touched my face. "I've thought about being with you so often in the last several weeks, but it can never live up to the real thing." She sighed softly as she kissed my neck to emphasize her words.

I pulled away regretfully. "I thought we could have a glass of wine and then take Sadie for a short walk around Hampton Park. The lasagna will be cooking for about an hour, but I have some cheese and crackers if you're hungry now."

"I think I'm still full from the mountain of food you brought us for lunch, and normally I would love wine, but I've been feeling a little queasy for a couple days, so I think I'll just have sparkling water, if you have it. But I did bring this for you; it's my favorite cabernet," she said, reaching for the wine.

I went to the fridge to get her water and grabbed a lemon and the wine opener also. She'd been ill and I hadn't even known; it made me crazy that I had been shut out from her and hadn't been there to care for her if she needed it.

"Is everything okay? Have you seen a doctor?" I asked, feeling the unusual urge to tuck her into bed and tend to her every need.

She laughed self-consciously. "Not yet. I think it could be a touch of the flu, but I have an appointment on Wednesday if it doesn't go away." She fidgeted and appeared to be uncomfortable. "I'm sure it's no big deal."

I studied her as I poured her drink. Now that I was really looking at her, she did appear to be a little pale—and had she lost weight? Her curves were still in all the right places, but her face seemed a little more drawn, and the look in her eyes was . . . guarded. Was there something she was keeping from me? I handed her the water with a lemon wedge and poured myself a glass of wine. I took a sip and tipped the glass toward her. "You're right, this is delicious. Are you sure you don't want even a small glass?"

She shook her head. "Nope, this is just what I needed. Thanks."

I walked around the island to sit next to her at the bar. It felt so comfortable, and I had to admit, it felt great to have her back in my house. I opened my mouth to tell her so, but she beat me to it.

"I've missed this. Just hanging out here with you, enjoying your beautiful views," she said with a sigh.

"I've missed this view too," I said, smiling at her and stroking her hair.

She looked from the window back at me. Her expression was serious. "So, where do we stand, Luke?" The corners of her mouth turned up into a small smile. "Now that we've shared our feelings. What does it mean?"

I turned to face her and put my hands on her bare knees; they were warm under my hands, and I could swear I felt a small sizzle. "Charlie, I am navigating new territory here, and honestly, you probably have more experience with relationships than I do. I've never found the need to have more than just a casual fling, but now I find myself dreaming about having it all. I don't want to scare you, and it's more than a little terrifying for me, but I'm in this with you. I'm not interested in seeing anyone else, and I want you in my bed as often as you will be here. I was miserable every day we were apart, and I don't want to experience those feelings ever again. You are *it* for me, Charlie." I searched her face, imploring her, wanting her to feel what I felt.

She put her small hands on top of mine and ran them gently up my forearms; my spine tingled from her touch. "This feels so fast, Luke. I never expected to be in this place with you—or anyone, for that matter—in such a short period of time. But I feel the same way. I drove my friends crazy while we were apart, questioning everything and trying to get right with my feelings. Joe did a number on my head and nearly obliterated my heart. The idea of putting my emotions on the line that way again was too much. When I saw you with Susan . . . I just went right back there, and it wasn't fair. I was judging you based on what I knew of your past instead of how you had been with me. That combined with my own baggage, sent me off the rails. I reacted . . . badly." She squeezed my arms to emphasize her words. "I'm really so sorry, Luke."

I took her hands in both of mine and raised her palms to my lips one at a time. I wanted to kiss every square inch of her until the only thing she could see was how much I loved her. "I think we can agree to put our mutual mistakes in the rearview, my little firecracker. It seems we worked out our frustrations and anger the night of the benefit, and the only regret I have about that night was walking away. But to be completely honest, I think we both needed this time to put things in perspective. Maybe it inspired me to speak up a little sooner, and I know my feelings are crystal clear. I realized the very next day that I couldn't lose you and I would do anything to get us back to a good place. Now that we're here, I'm not going to fuck it up again." I smiled at her as I kissed the inside of her wrist, tasting her salty skin with my tongue and inhaling the scent of her, lavender with a hint of eucalyptus.

She sighed deeply and shuddered. "Luke, I think we better go for that walk now or we won't be leaving. You're killing me." She took my hand and stood. "Come on, Sadie girl, let's go for a walk." She headed for the door, and reluctantly, I followed. *Maybe a little fresh air is what I need*, I thought, adjusting my fly discreetly as I grabbed Sadie's leash and hooked it to her wriggling body.

Much to Sadie's disappointment, our walk was brief. The lasagna was nearly done, and we were both anxious to get back to the house for other reasons that didn't involve food. It was nice to see my best friend had missed Charlie too. She stayed up against her thigh anytime she wasn't off sniffing a bush or exploring the park.

We walked back into the house, and Charlie groaned. "Oh my God, that lasagna smells amazing. I am suddenly so hungry."

I laughed. "Well, that's good because I made enough to feed the entire Clemson football team. Since it is such a beautiful night, why don't we eat on the porch?"

Charlie got busy pulling out plates and utensils. "I'd love that," she said.

I was continually amazed by the amount of food Charlie could consume and still stay slim. We had both finished off two helpings of lasagna and a salad apiece, and we were relaxing side by side on my overstuffed loveseat looking out at the twinkling lights on the Ravenel Bridge. Charlie sighed and leaned her head back on my shoulder. I couldn't imagine feeling any more content than I did right now. I stroked her arm gently, enjoying the moment. She turned to look at me, and I took advantage of the proximity of her mouth and leaned in to capture her lips with my own. I chuckled as we both moaned, and I wrapped my hand around her neck and brought her closer.

"Maybe we should move this inside since I'm still waiting on the bed swing I ordered last week," I said against her lips.

She drew back in surprise. "You ordered one? How did you get the information?" she asked.

"Naturally, I asked Chase, who not only found the info, but picked out the bedding and placed the order for me. He's very efficient, that guy," I said, smiling. "I can't wait to have it installed and try it out." I wiggled my eyebrows suggestively. "But for now, I hope I can talk you into coming to bed with me." I cupped her face and kissed her softly, not wanting to push her, but needing her so badly. "I've missed you, and I want to show you how much."

She stood and reached for my hand. "What are we waiting for then?"

We were both suddenly filled with urgency as we reached for each other inside the bedroom, tearing at each other's clothes before we even made it to the bed. I kissed and sucked her neck, breathing in her scent. My hands were everywhere, stroking and pinching. Her head was thrown back as my tongue swept downward and encircled a rosy nipple, which hardened enticingly against my eager tongue. I pushed her roughly back on the bed, and she reached for me, her eyes dark green and glittering with desire. I was only wearing my boxer briefs. She put her hand on my cock, and impossibly, it grew even more as she stroked it. I wanted so badly to take things slow, but I didn't think I could hold back as she pulled me down on top of her and kissed me so deeply, I thought I would lose it as I rubbed against her soaked panties.

"Luke, I want you inside me. I can't wait. Please, I need you to take me . . . and don't go slow."

I felt a surge of heat as I ripped her panties off of her and she pulled down my briefs. I reached into my nightstand and grabbed a condom, ripping it open with my teeth and quickly sliding it onto my throbbing cock. Without another thought, I slid into her heat, and she wrapped her legs around me.

I felt her softness clenching me so tightly I nearly exploded right then.

"Woah, slow down, baby. I want us both to enjoy this, and you are making me crazy," I said to her as I rolled us on to our sides so we were facing each other.

I laid my forehead against hers and looked into her eyes as I slowed down my rhythm, pressing against her clit with each stroke. I pulled her top leg over mine pulling her closer to get a better angle, it felt amazing being so deep inside her. Her mouth opened slightly, and she closed her eyes. I could feel her tightening against me, and I knew she was close. I leaned in and kissed her, seeking her tongue with mine. She started to moan as I sped up, grabbing her buttocks and pulling her into me with each stroke. I felt her body start to shake as she frantically sucked on my tongue and drove her hips into mine. Unable to hold back, I slammed into her, matching her urgency with my own as I felt the telltale tingling up my spine. She grabbed my shoulders and arched into me, moaning with abandon and crying out my name as I exploded inside her.

I pulled out slowly, removing the condom and dropping it on the nightstand. As I pulled Charlie against me, feeling every inch of her curves against mine, I was amazed to see that I was still hard. She laughed in her husky voice, rubbing against me, clearly noticing the same thing. I smirked at her.

"I was hoping that might take the edge off, but I guess distance does make the heart—and other things—grow fonder. God Charlie, I just love you so much." I said and kissed her shoulder, still breathing her in and reveling in the moment of having her naked in my bed.

She smiled, her hand stroking my face and searching my eyes, apparently finding what she was looking for, because she let out a contented sigh. "Oh Luke, I love you too, so much."

"You know I won't let you leave," I said in response. "I can't let you out of my sight, I'm afraid I'll wake up and think this was all a dream."

"I'm afraid if I stay, I won't get any sleep tonight," she said, pulling my head up so she could see my face.

"What if I promise that I'll only keep you up a little longer if *you* promise to let me make love to you in the morning before work. I still have a toothbrush for you, and I'll even wash your hair for you before bed so you don't have to wash it in the morning. That will give you extra time to go home and change." She snuggled against me, and I felt my victory was imminent. "I don't want to pressure you, but maybe you could leave some toiletries and a few outfits here to make it easier when you stay over. Lord knows I have plenty of space." I tried not to sound too eager as my heart pounded in my chest.

Charlie looked at me, her face quite serious, and I could barely breathe as I waited for her response. Her fingers curled into my chest hair, and she kissed me softly before answering. "I would love to spend the night, and it would make things easier if I had a few of my things here ... if you're sure," she said, hesitating.

I kissed her deeply, filled with happiness, unable to believe my luck. "I have never been more sure of anything." I pulled back the covers and scooped her from the bed as she dissolved into a fit of laughter. "Now how about we try out the jets in my bathtub?"

Chapter 22

CHARLIE

On a day when the wind is perfect, the sail just needs to open and the world is full of beauty. Today is such a day.
—*Rumi*

I was having the most wonderful dream. I was lying under the softest sheets with a cool fan blowing overhead while firm hands gently caressed me. I felt warm lips on my neck and shoulder and then a tongue . . . My eyes flew open to see a rugged face smiling up at me as his lips worked their way toward my breasts, which, seemingly of their own volition, arched in the direction of that delicious tongue. Simultaneously, his large hands scooped them up, and I nearly lost myself as he sucked first one than the other nipple into his hot mouth. I couldn't contain my moans as he lavished attention on my heaving breasts, and I felt a rumble of approval in his chest.

He paused and looked up at me. "I promised to make love to you this morning, and I waited as long as I could for you to wake up, but I just couldn't wait another minute with you wiggling and snuggling next to me."

The only word I could seem to muster was "oh," as he immediately returned his attention to my flushed chest.

I wondered if I could have an orgasm just from him sucking and biting my nipples. It had never happened before, but I was so turned on, and my entire body tingled with need. "Please, I need more," I said, flush with heat.

He grunted and continued downward, and I nearly screamed as his mouth latched onto my hot, aching center. I was amazed at how quickly I went from groggy with sleep to wide awake and tingling from head to toe. His tongue lapped from back to front as he nipped my nib with his teeth. I squirmed frantically, wanting to slow things down, yet unable to contain the need for release. Almost as if he had read my mind, he slowed down and flicked his tongue against my clit, making me crazy. He teased me with gentle kisses, spreading my legs wide, his soft lips running along my thighs and dipping lower toward the tiny bud below my dripping passage.

I felt my cheeks flame with both embarrassment and wild passion as his tongue explored this tender place. His eyes locked onto mine as his wicked tongue continued its delicious torture. I was at once turned on by, and slightly self-conscious of, his intense gaze as he watched me respond to his skillful manipulation. His smile was cocky as his tongue set me on fire, and I was unable to think of anything except the orgasm begging to be liberated.

His fingers slowly massaged my clit as he lifted his head from between my ass cheeks. "Do you like that Charlie? I knew you could be a naughty girl. I love watching as you lose control, it makes me incredibly hard."

God, the dirty talk was almost as arousing as his talented mouth. I felt like I was on a roller coaster; he would first speed up, and as I began to feel an orgasm approaching, his ministrations would suddenly become languid and gentle. I heard myself begging and moaning, straining for the release he kept just out of reach. Just as I thought I couldn't take another minute of torment, he pulled away, giving me a crooked smile, his eyes still locked on mine. I tore my gaze from his and threw my head back as he slammed two large fingers inside of me and dropped his lips to my swollen and dripping cleft, sucking it hard into his mouth as his fingers worked in and out, curling against my G-spot and sending an orgasm spiraling through me unlike any other I had ever experienced. It seemed to go on forever, and I wasn't sure how much time had passed before I was able to focus once again on Luke. He was still gently sucking and licking me, the flicks of his tongue so tender, clearly aware of my sensitive flesh.

Once he realized I had returned to planet earth, he slowly slid his body up to cover mine. It was a delicious sensation, as his coarse chest hair rubbed against my thighs, stomach, and eventually pressed against my tender breasts, causing them to harden and ache. His tongue dove into my mouth, and I tasted myself on him as he whispered against my lips all the ways he wanted to pleasure me. I barely noticed as he slid a condom on his large erection, which was hot against my thigh. He slid one of my legs to the side and was buried inside me in seconds, my wetness making it easy for him. He moaned and dropped his face into my neck, his new facial hair tickling and scraping my tender skin in the best possible way. As he sucked and licked with abandon, he slid slowly and deliberately in and out of my dripping passage.

I had had missionary style sex dozens of times (if not more), but somehow this was more erotic, more intimate, than I had ever experienced. My heart swelled in my chest as our eyes locked and I saw the love emanating from his green eyes still dark and stormy with passion. He held himself up with one hand, and the other cupped my cheek as he showered me with kisses from my lips to my neck and down to my breasts and back again. He murmured my name as he kept up his sensual rhythm, allowing me to feel every inch of every stroke. My release built slowly this time, but I could tell it would be no less powerful, and I moaned in anticipation.

"Charlie," he said. "I can't wait much longer; it just feels too good. You are so wet and tight . . . " He groaned and seized my lips, once again swallowing my pants as I felt my body tightening around him. He picked up speed, sending shivers up my spine.

I heard screaming, and I realized it was me. So unlike me, but I had lost control, and the sensations were tearing through me, causing me to quiver and shake as I felt myself shatter. Luke drove into me with abandon, his hands tangled in my hair. I watched his face and reveled in the ecstasy I saw there. As I felt his body grow tense, I grabbed his muscular buttocks, pulling him tight against me, and he bent down, sinking his teeth softly into my shoulder as he moaned loudly. His body began to shudder, and he slid against me, spent, both of us slick with sweat.

"Oh my God. What you do to me, Charlie. I've never felt this way about anyone else. I love you so much," he moaned, his face still buried against my shoulder. I laughed as he propped himself up and dropped kisses on the mark his teeth had left there. "I'm so sorry. I hope I didn't hurt you; I just couldn't control myself. You make me feel like a horny teenager half the time. I have all of these plans to take it slow and make sweet love to you, and then, next thing I know, I am pounding uncontrollably and biting you." He looked at me sheepishly, and I couldn't help but laugh because, despite the sexy facial hair, he looked like a teenager in that moment. His face was unguarded and his messy hair fell across his forehead, his smile sheepish as he looked at me. My heart melted just a little as I looked at him.

I reached up and rubbed the rough fur on his face, smiling at him, my heart feeling full. For a moment, I thought about telling him about the pregnancy, but I really wanted to wait until after my appointment on Wednesday, and I didn't want to ruin this moment by opening up a whole new conversation when we were still in such a fragile place. Luke put his hand over mine, still stroking his beard.

"I know ... I can't believe I let this thing get away from me. I just didn't have any desire to shave, but I promise, it comes off today," he said firmly.

I reached up and kissed his soft lips as his mustache tickled my nose, the contrast not unwelcome. "I don't know. You can do what you want, but I kinda like it," I said, still stroking his beard. "It feels pretty nice, especially in the more sensitive areas."

He sat up, looking surprised. "In that case, it's not going anywhere until you give the word." He rubbed a hand down my side, stroking my hip, and I loved the feel of his callused skin against mine. He dropped another kiss on my lips and rolled out of bed. "As much as I want to stay in this bed and worship you all day, I think it's time I deliver on that shampoo-ing I promised last night," he said, heading into the bathroom.

I lay there for another minute, enjoying the sight of his broad muscular back, which curved down to a small waist and a tight round butt, as it retreated into the bathroom. I heard the water turn on. The hot spray of his luxurious steam shower was too much to resist, and I scampered after him, looking forward to an attentive scalp massage.

After going home to change and gather up some necessities to store at Luke's place, I headed into the office. I had just gotten comfortable behind my desk when Chase came barreling in.

"So, give me the 411. How did things go with Luke last night?" he asked, dropping into one of the chairs across from me.

"Good morning to you, too, Chase," I responded, chuck-ling at his eagerness.

"Come on, spill it. I want all the dirty details, including a full description of his hot bod," he teased.

"You know I rarely kiss and tell, but I will say, memories of the evening will keep me warm for many days. If there hadn't been such a huge pile on my desk, I would have been tempted to take the day off and continue the reconciliation," I said with a wink.

"So you're saying the makeup sex lived up to the hype? Hmmm, I can't say I've ever experienced that. I've never been in a relationship long enough to fight and make up. I am intrigued," he said.

"Let me put it this way: it was so fabulous, Luke offered me a drawer so I could spend the night more often," I said.

"A drawer? This is getting serious. Was that before or after you told him about his impending fatherhood?" he asked, raising a perfectly shaped eyebrow.

I sighed. "I nearly told him, but I really want to get confirmation from my doctor tomorrow, and I didn't think during the afterglow of amazing sex was the right moment. I plan to tell him Wednesday night. Oh, and by the way, we are meeting at Indaco after work. Do you feel like joining us? You can bring a date."

"Now that you mention it, a hockey player gave me his number the other night. He seemed nice—very hot and macho. Maybe you two can screen him for me. If he doesn't fit in with my buds, there's no use in pursuing anything more," he answered.

"Does this mean you're looking for something more serious?" I asked. "I can't remember you being concerned about your flings passing the friend test. Now I'm intrigued," I said archly.

"Let's not get carried away; I'm just trying to broaden my horizons. This guy seemed, well . . . normal. Normal, but still hot. And truthfully, we've met several times through mutual friends, and he was very nervous when he approached me. It was clear his friends don't know he's gay, and he definitely didn't want them to know. He cornered me in the bathroom, and to be honest, I hadn't even realized he was interested in playing for my team. It was kind of cute how apprehensive he was. I could be wrong, but I don't think he has much experience with men, and this is new territory for me. I haven't been with a newbie since high school. I'm not sure how I feel about taking that on, but he was pretty irresistible. What do you think?" he asked.

"Given what you've told me, are you sure he would want to go out with us? Maybe he would rather meet more on the downlow?" I pointed out.

"That's possible, but I think it would be easier to be around strangers who won't judge him. Also, I'm not sure I'm up for a secret relationship. Oh well, we'll just have to see what he says. I think I'll call him now," he said, standing. "By the way, you are positively glowing, girlfriend. Clearly making up with Luke does wonders for your skin. I recommend you continue a strict regimen of daily makeup sex. I'll let you know about dinner, and in the meantime, let's plan to finalize our install schedule before we leave. I'll work on getting more delivery time frames after I call Dillon. Oh yeah, that's his name, Dillon Peters."

"Wait a second, get back here," I said as he headed out the door. "Did you say Dillon Peters?"

"Yeah, so? Do you know him?" he asked.

I stared at him in amazement. "I'm surprised you don't. I know he's a couple of years older and went to a different school, but his family is very well known in town, and more importantly, he was a total jock stud in high school. He was a star lacrosse and hockey player, and by sophomore year, he was dating girls from the College of Charleston. No wonder he doesn't want to come out of the closet. His mom inherited a fortune, and his dad is the coach for the CofC basketball team. He has quite the reputation for being a hardass. I can't imagine a gay son fits into his life goals."

He scratched his head, looking surprised. "I guess if he was such a macho guy, he wasn't even on my radar. Also, most of the jocks I knew from other schools played football. I am surprised that I never came across him during my time at the hotel though. That does explain him being so secretive about us getting to know each other. I imagine if his dad is so hardcore, he didn't want to face his attraction to men. Sometimes it's just easier to try and play it straight. Didn't work for me, but I see it all the time. I mean, my dad wasn't over the moon about me not marrying Suzie Homemaker and having lots of babies, but he wasn't cruel. He eventually came around. I can't imagine having to hide who I am. Maybe it's a bad idea to get involved . . . "

"Oh, Chase, don't shut him out just because he's scared. Give the guy a chance. You never know, you could be missing out on someone great. Besides, you have such a big heart. If nothing else, maybe you could help him figure out how to ease into telling his parents and friends. Don't be so closed-minded. Call the guy. Even though he was a big-time stud, I never heard any rumors about him being a jerk. He seemed pretty cool. Also, I think you were underselling him. I remember that he was very, very hot." I grinned at him, and he waved me off as he walked out.

"I'll think about calling him," he threw over his shoulder.

It turned out that Chase did call Dillon. He was uncomfortable hanging out with us (couldn't say I blamed him, given the backstory), but he wanted to meet up with Chase afterward. Luke invited Ethan, but he had a date with his new girlfriend, who I found out was Liz Rutledge. I tried not to let my feelings show on my face, but I was not a fan. She'd hung out with Britt and Tad and their whole gang in high school. I would be surprised if they weren't still in the same social circle, given that their parents were all members of the same high-society "club." Luke mentioned that Ethan had invited us over, along with a few other friends to meet his new lady. Given that Ethan seemed to be serious about Liz, I figured I would give her the benefit of the doubt. Maybe she'd grown up and decided life was too short to look down on everyone else.

It turned out to be a fun evening with my two favorite guys, and I loved seeing Luke and Chase getting along so well outside of work. They actually have a lot in common, and there was some good-natured sparring about their rival college football teams. I had a moment of feeling nauseous, and Chase looked at me knowingly as Luke fussed over me and I reassured him I would be fine, excusing myself to visit the ladies' room. I was looking forward to telling Luke tomorrow because I was starting to feel guilty about keeping him in the dark. I could also sense in Chase's expression that he thought I should tell him already. But seriously, what was one more day? I wanted a little more time with no complications. I knew it was selfish, but Luke was so happy, and I hated that I was going to throw a wrench in his life.

Eventually Chase left to meet Dillon, promising to text me all the details no matter how late it was when he got home.

After he left, Luke scooted his chair around to get closer to me, and I giggled as he leaned in for a kiss.

"I've been wanting to do this all evening," he said as he put a strand of hair behind my ear and paused to stroke my neck.

I grabbed his hand, needing to touch him too. "I forgot to ask you earlier if we could go by Revival before we head back to your place? I promised Chase I would take a measurement for some artwork he wants to order tomorrow. Besides, it's been a few days since I was there, and I'd love to see the progress."

"Of course. I would love to show you around and get your feedback on some of the changes we made to the lobby area. I know Ethan ran them by you guys, but I think they turned out even better than expected," he responded. Just then, his phone rang. He looked at the screen. "It's Ethan. It's strange that he's calling during his date; let me see what he wants." He stood and left the table as he answered the phone. A few minutes later, he returned, shaking his head.

"What a moron," he said, chuckling. "Somehow he managed to drop his keys down a storm drain on Sullivan's Island. I think he was too embarrassed to say so, but I'm guessing he got distracted by his new lady and they fell out of his pocket. He asked if I could grab his spare car keys from his desk drawer and bring them to him. Do you mind going to Revival by yourself and I'll meet you there in a bit? You can get your measurements, take a spin through, and by the time you're done, I'll be back. I can drop you off on my way."

I nodded. "Of course. There are a few other things I wanted to look at while I was there, so take your time. I have plenty to keep me occupied," I said.

Still shaking his head over Ethan, Luke flagged down our waiter, and a few minutes later, he was dropping me off at the front door of Revival.

I let myself in with Luke's key and managed to quickly find a light switch inside the dark and deserted entrance. It was strange being here at night alone, but the lack of distraction was welcome. I wandered around the space, my creative juices flowing with ideas. Ethan and Sebastian had opened up the lobby area, but there were still several nooks and areas that would make for cozy spaces to hang out or meet with small groups of friends for a glass of wine. Luke and Ethan had a vision for a community that was more than just a cluster of condo homes. They were hoping to encourage interaction among the residents and their friends. A place they wanted to stay and hang out and areas they could enjoy outside of their individual unit.

The rooftop deck would be the last section to be completed, but already we had so many ideas for that space. Sebastian had managed to get approval from the city for a rooftop pool, which was a huge coup. Very few buildings in downtown Charleston boasted a rooftop pool, and there was no doubt it would attract buyers looking for that kind of lifestyle. I was looking forward to working with Austin on this part of the project. His pool designs were already legendary, and I knew we would have fun creating something unique for Luke and Ethan. The waiting list of potential buyers continued to grow, and I had no doubt that all the condos would sell out quickly once they were put on the market. Luke was a marketing genius, and he was deliberately waiting to sell to create more of a fervor and increase demand. His strategy was working because Revival on King Street was the talk of the town.

I decided to head upstairs to check out some of the units before Luke returned. Ethan and Luke planned to have a decorated model for each floor plan, so the focus of the construction schedule was completing the models and the lobby first. I made my way to the one-bedroom unit to check out the progress. I was pleased to see that the drywall was complete, and it looked like the carpenters would be installing trim any day now. The materials were lined up on the floor, and the space was neat and clean despite the construction that was underway daily. I wasn't surprised by how orderly things were; I knew from experience that Ethan ran a tight job site.

Chase and I had created vision boards for each of the decorated models, and with this being the smallest square footage, we were looking to keep a streamlined modern decor. All the condos included ample windows, so even this one-bedroom would feel light and airy in the daylight. Sebastian was a gifted architect, and this relatively small place felt spacious and cozy at the same time. Even without the finishes and furnishings, I could visualize how welcoming the space would be. I made some notes on my phone to talk with Chase about it tomorrow and continued on to check out the other future models.

Eventually, I completed my tour and looked at my watch. Luke had been gone for at least thirty minutes. I imagined he would be back fairly soon, so I headed back to the lobby to get my measurement. I reached the bottom of the stairwell and was confused by the unexpected smell of smoke. As I opened the stairwell door into the hallway on the first floor that led to the lobby, I was engulfed in black smoke. The air was thick with it, and I couldn't see my hand in front of my face. Instinctively, I brought my shirt up to cover my mouth and nose as I tried to make my way to the lobby, using my hands to feel my way along the wall. The smoke was so heavy, I thought it would be better to crawl along the floor. I was starting to feel lightheaded, so being on all fours was probably a better idea anyway. I made my way in the direction of the lobby, starting to feel queasy and even dizzier. I finally reached the opening to the lobby and saw flames licking up the far wall. I could see the front door opposite the fire, and I started to head in that direction. I knew it wasn't that far to the door, but it seemed that I wasn't getting any closer as I crawled toward it. Suddenly, I felt my mind get foggy, and I realized that the blackness crowding around me wasn't actually from the smoke. The last thing I remember was thinking about Luke and our baby as I descended into the darkness.

Chapter 23

JOE

"Few things are so deadly as a misguided sense of compassion."
Charles Colson

I was across the street from Revival, tucked in the shadows of an alley, watching the building that had caused me such bitterness over the last several months. A part of me realized it was ridiculous to be so focused on this one construction project in the city, but my common sense was overruled by an irrational anger toward Luke Coleman. The project had already been on my radar, as we had discussed the potential ramifications at the environmental nonprofit I worked for. The amount of demolition that would be needed to redo the crumbing apartments and create the vision that Coleman Grant had submitted to the city for approval was likely to cause a multitude of hazards for our fragile ecosystem in Charleston. I had seen other projects over the years, and I felt a growing animosity toward these greedy bastards who cared only about lining their pockets and not preserving the history and beauty of the Lowcountry. It was the same old story every time: money hungry developer promises care and environmental protections while creating a beautiful new building to be fawned over by the Charleston elite and frequent tourists. The city was won over by the possibility of more taxes, revenue from travelers, and a shiny new hotel/condominium/storefront to brag about. In the end, said developers didn't do half of what they said they would do, the ecosystem suffered, and—oh, goodie—we were left with something new that half the time didn't look as beautiful as the original. For me, this felt like the final straw.

When I found out through the grapevine that my ex-wife, Charlie, was not only handling the interior design of the project, but was also dating Luke Coleman, I think I just snapped. I mean, I shouldn't care, after all, I was re-married, and Charlie and I had been divorced for over two years. But hindsight is a bitch, and it didn't take me long after Charlie left me to realize what I had lost.

There was no doubt that I had fucked things up with Charlie. We'd had it all: great jobs, an amazing house in downtown Charleston and a fun group of friends. Charlie was a devoted wife, a beautiful girl, and she really loved me and our life together. I still can't figure out what possessed me to destroy it all by taking up with Michelle. I'd love to blame it on the fact that Charlie was my first and only and I just wanted to see what it was like with someone else, but when I look back at my life, I realize there was always a part of me bent on self-destruction.

My father was always miserable, and he took his unhappiness out on those closest to him. He made it clear that he thought my mom and I were useless and a burden to him. He never raised a hand to us, but his words cut deep enough, and by the time I was old enough to drive, I used every excuse to stay away from home. After I met Charlie, I spent as much time as possible at her house. Her parents were everything I had ever wanted, and she had such a joy for life. It was strange, but even though I told Charlie how I felt about everything else, I never shared my feelings about my parents or my home life. Maybe I was ashamed, since her parents were always so loving and supportive. I also think my mom and dad thought Charlie was a great catch, so none of our ugliness ever surfaced when she was around. We all did a great job putting up the front of a normal family. During high school and college, I was grateful to have Charlie and showed her how much I loved her as often as possible. There was never a doubt I would marry her. She was perfect—everything I wanted in a wife—and I knew our life together would help to erase the misery of my childhood, and then I could move on with the life I had always wanted.

Charlie and I had been married about a year when Michelle started expressing interest in me. At first, I tried to ignore it. I mean, I laughed with her and didn't exactly discourage her, but I never responded in a way that let her think I was into her too. I think my ego loved the attention from a beautiful single woman. One night, after a happy hour with several work colleagues, Michelle and I were the last of our group still at the bar. When she leaned in to whisper in my ear, her hand on my thigh, I didn't even think about the consequences. I followed her out of the bar and to her house, where I proceeded to tear my marriage apart. Maybe if I had just ended it there, confessed my indiscretion to Charlie, and begged her forgiveness, we could have repaired what I had broken, but no, I just kept on seeing Michelle. It wasn't until the moment Charlie walked in on us at our house that I realized the magnitude of my mistake.

I knew Charlie thought I didn't care, but I just didn't know how to fix what I had done. So I let her pack up her stuff and leave. I let Michelle claim me, finding it easier to move on with her rather than get on my knees and beg Charlie to give me another chance. Now, looking back, I realize all that I threw away. Michelle is a gold digger with no personal ambition. What I have with her doesn't even compare to the life Charlie and I had built. The life I trashed, which now belonged to Luke fucking Coleman.

Before I married Michelle, I did try to reach out to Charlie, but she wouldn't even be in the same room with me. I saw her at a couple meetings with our lawyers and at our divorce proceedings, but otherwise, she cut me off completely. In addition to that, our best friends, Chase and Everleigh, also dropped me like a hot potato—or the cheater that I was. Chase gave me the courtesy of a night out to tell me that his loyalty was to Charlie and, therefore, our friendship was over. Everleigh refused to take my calls and avoided me at all costs.

Running into Charlie with my former friends the other night was like a knife to my heart. A painful reminder of all I had lost. It was obvious after talking to her that she was more into Coleman than I had previously thought. I felt a growing anger as I imagined the two of them together. I had heard rumors of Luke's man-whoring ways, and I was sure that Charlie was too good for him.

I was shaken out of my reverie by the sight of a car pulling up in front of Revival. I was shocked to see none other than Charlie get out and walk up to the front door. "No, no, no," I said to myself, watching with dread as she walked into the building. I realized I was holding my breath, and I let it out with a whoosh as I watched the sports car drive away and Charlie disappear inside. *Maybe she'll only be in there for a minute and she'll get out before anything gets out of hand*, I told myself. I thought about the destruction I had put into motion. It would be a while before things got too out of control. It was after nine o'clock; what could she possibly be doing in there? I felt my agitation growing as the minutes ticked by and Charlie didn't reemerge. I imagined the small fire I had started beginning to grow, and I didn't understand how she couldn't see it and get out of there. What if she called 911? I should have left so I didn't get caught at the scene, but I couldn't seem to pull myself away without knowing she was safe.

I was just trying to draw negative attention to Revival on King Street; the last thing I wanted was for anyone to get hurt. Especially Charlie. It had been twenty minutes; surely she would be coming out soon. What in the hell was she doing in there? As another few minutes went by, I began to imagine different scenarios. What if she was trapped upstairs? Maybe she had tripped and fallen and was unconscious. I could see the smoke beginning to seep out of the windows and under the front door when I ran across the street. There wasn't time for me to go around back, where I had broken the lock earlier.

I grabbed the door handle and yanked on it. Of course, it was locked. Fortunately, it was a glass door, and I searched around for something to break the glass. I found a broken brick on the side of the building and quickly ran to the front door and hit it as hard as I could with the brick. The glass was thick, but it cracked, and after a few more swings, it shattered. I reached in and unlocked the door, then ran quickly into the smoke-filled lobby, looking frantically for Charlie. The smoke had filled the room, but it didn't take me long to locate a form curled up on the floor a few feet away.

"Please, God, don't let her be dead," I begged, reaching down to feel for a pulse. I covered my mouth and nose with my other arm, attempting to keep out the relentless smoke causing me to cough. I was relieved to feel Charlie's pulse, and I quickly bent down and scooped her up, running back to the door. My heart leapt in my throat as I saw the flames sweeping toward us, and I heard sirens in the distance as I approached the exit with Charlie in my arms. Just then, the door burst open, and Luke came barreling in, a look of terror on his face.

He nearly knocked us over due to the limited visibility and his haste to get inside. I kept moving toward the door; he approached me and reached out as if to take Charlie.

"Let me get her out of the smoke," I said, pushing him roughly aside with my shoulder as I breached the doorway, sucking the fresh outdoor air into my lungs. He was right on my heels, and as soon as we got across the street to safety, he reached for her again. Reluctantly, I complied. As he crouched on the ground, talking softly to Charlie and patting her cheek, I saw a fire engine come screeching around the corner. Unsure of what to do, I started to leave. Luke obviously sensed my intention.

"Don't you go anywhere until I have a chance to talk to you," he growled, still trying to rouse Charlie. I realized that Luke probably didn't know who I was. We had never met, and he was unlikely to have seen any pictures, unless he had decided to check into me after he started dating Charlie. I knew I could take off and he wouldn't chase me down if Charlie was unconscious, but a larger part of me needed to stay and make sure she would be all right, so I just stood awkwardly as he continued trying to coax her awake.

More fire trucks had joined the first one in front of Revival, and at this point, several firefighters were fighting the blaze inside and out. One ran over to us, and I attempted not to look guilty as he approached. He looked down at Luke and Charlie.

"An ambulance is on its way. Is there anyone else inside?" he asked.

I shook my head. "No, I don't think so. I saw her go in, and when I saw the smoke, I broke the door and went in after her. I found her unconscious just inside the entrance," I answered.

At that moment, Charlie started to move, and her eyes fluttered open. She looked up at Luke, confused and frightened. I felt a surge of relief as she reached to touch his face. And my heart twisted with her next words.

"Luke, what happened? Is the baby going to be okay?" My feelings were nothing compared with the look on Luke's face in that moment, and I realized with a jolt that he had no idea Charlie was pregnant.

Chapter 24

LUKE

This idea that we are our own saviors, our own heroes.
That's hard, but also incredibly uplifting.
—Reese Witherspoon

As I crouched on the pavement next to Charlie, I prayed in my head for her to be okay. She had soot on her face, but otherwise, she seemed like she was sleeping peacefully. But without knowing how long she had been breathing in the toxic smoke, I was still terrified for her. I had no idea who the guy was who had saved her or why he was even here, but that was the least of my worries. I stroked her face and begged her to open her eyes. My prayers were answered as she moaned in my arms and slowly opened her eyes and looked up at me. Her eyes were clouded in confusion, and I could see her trying to understand where she was and what was happening. When she finally spoke in a raspy voice, I nearly fell over in shock.

"Luke, what happened? Is the baby okay?" she croaked, her eyes looking pleadingly at mine. I could see she was a little out of it, and she began to cough. I struggled to maintain calm as my mind whirled, trying to understand her words. I had forgotten about the guy who had carried her out of the building, and I heard him clear his throat as he bent down next to us. The firefighter had returned to the truck to pass along the information about the building being empty, reassuring us about medical help being on the way before he left. I felt myself staring intently at Charlie, still trying to process her question. *Is she saying she's pregnant?* I thought to myself.

I could see her expression begin to clear, and she turned away from me to look at the other man, who was now on the ground next to her, reaching out to touch her shoulder. Her eyes widened in shock. The puzzle pieces fell into place as she looked up at him. "Joe, what are you doing here?" She looked back at me. "What happened, Luke?" As if in a dream, I watched her hand move down to her stomach. "Luke?" she implored. "Please tell me."

I managed to gather myself together and scooped her closer to me, almost shielding her from the man I now realized was her ex-husband, Joe. "I came back for you, and when I pulled up, I saw the smoke. You were inside." I tilted my head at Joe. "When I came through the door, he was carrying you out. Charlie? Is there something you need to tell me?" I asked gently. Out of the corner of my eye, I saw Joe stand and start to move away. I ignored him; I would deal with that bastard later. I had much more important things on my mind right now. As I waited for Charlie to answer me, I heard a siren in the distance and knew the ambulance was just minutes away.

"Please, baby, you need to tell me. Are we having a baby?" I asked her more firmly this time. The last thing I wanted to do was upset her, but I had to know. She nodded slowly, and I felt my heart rate speed up.

"Yes, I'm pretty sure we are. I have a doctor's appointment tomorrow to confirm it, but I took a home pregnancy test . . . " I could see she was getting emotional, so I waited for her to continue, trying not to push. "I was going to tell you tomorrow night, once I knew for sure. Please don't be angry, Luke. I haven't known for very long, and I didn't want to stir things up again if it was a false alarm. I'm so sorry you had to find out this way." My chest tightened as her tears began to fall and she started coughing again.

"Oh, sweetheart, it's okay. I'm not angry. I'm just trying to wrap my head around it all, and I'm scared and worried about you. When I saw the smoke as I pulled up, I was so afraid . . . " I hugged her to my chest as the ambulance pulled up in front of us and two paramedics came running over with a stretcher. I whispered in her ear as they approached, "I love you, Charlie, and I don't want you to worry. Everything is going to be okay. Let's get you to the hospital and check everything out, and then we'll talk through all of this. Just please know, I love you." I leaned back and looked in her eyes as I said it, and she smiled at me through her tears.

I reassured Charlie that I would meet her at the hospital. It was a short drive, but I wanted to make sure I had a car there for when Charlie was released. I also wanted to be alone to call Ethan and Charlie's parents. The phone call to Charlie's parents was a bit awkward, and I decided not to say anything about The pregnancy since I wasn't sure if they knew. Understandably, they wasted no time in heading to the hospital to check on their daughter. I hung up after reassuring them that Charlie was conscious, and I was sure she would be fine, and I would meet them there.

The phone call to Ethan included a lot more foul language and questions about the fire. I was in the hospital parking lot, and I was anxious to check on Charlie, so I left out the detail about Charlie's ex, Joe, being the one who rescued her. I told him I needed to keep it brief and get into the hospital. I asked him to go to Revival and talk with the firefighters and see what he could find out. We agreed to talk again a little later to fill each other in on both Charlie and the condition of Revival, and I headed inside, anxious to see my girl.

It didn't take me long to find Charlie. They had brought her into the ER, but unfortunately would not allow me in to see her until they were done with the examination. So, I was pacing in the waiting room when her parents arrived. They headed straight for me, both of their faces taut with concern.

Don Finley reached me first and held his hand out to shake mine, reaching out with the other to clasp my shoulder. "Luke, how is she, son?" he asked, letting go of my hand, but the other stayed on my shoulder.

"I wish I knew. They won't let me in to see her. Maybe you'll have more luck. She was awake and talking when the paramedics came. She was a little disoriented at first, but by the time they loaded her in, she seemed to have come around."

Judy had been listening intently, and I could almost see her mind churning as she watched me, her face a mirror of Charlie's with a few more lines and her auburn hair shot with a bit of gray. She turned to her husband. "Don, why don't you talk to the staff and see what you can find out? They may be stonewalling, since Luke isn't family." He nodded, gave my shoulder a pat, and headed for the nurses' desk.

Judy turned to me, her eyes softening as she looked into mine. For a moment, I felt an emotion I hadn't felt since my mom was alive. She smiled at me, almost as if she could read my thoughts. "I'm glad you and Charlie are working things out. I know you mean a lot to her, and it's been so nice to see her happy again." As she looked at me warmly, I was having an internal debate about mentioning the baby. I decided there had been enough secrets.

"Outside of the obvious mystery of who started the fire at the job site, a few strange things happened after I got there to pick Charlie up," I said.

Judy looked startled at my abrupt change of subject. "Okay," she responded.

I put my hand on her arm and gestured to a group of chairs. "Why don't we go over here and sit down, and I'll fill you in." She looked worried again as we sat, and I struggled with how to reassure her. Finding myself in the unique position of comforting my girlfriend's mother was certainly new for me at the ripe age of thirty-one. Despite the seriousness of the situation, I found myself marveling at the position I was in. I was surprised to find that I didn't feel at all uncomfortable and I just wanted to alleviate Charlie's mom's anxiety.

"I didn't mention it to you and Don on the phone," I began, "but I was not the one who rescued Charlie from the fire."

Her expression quickly changed from worry to confusion as she spoke. "If not you, then who . . . ?"

"I ran in the front door as a man was coming out carrying an unconscious Charlie. At first, I had no idea who he was; I assumed he had been a bystander. It was only later after Charlie woke up and recognized him that I realized it was her ex-husband, Joe. I'm still not sure what he was doing there, but I'm wondering if he had something to do with the fire. Can you think of any reason he would have to sabotage our project, Judy?"

Her expression was stricken when she responded. "I could never imagine him going to such lengths. Up until the day . . . well, he was always such a sweet young man." She paused and then continued, "I know that Don ran into him several weeks ago, and he was vehement in his feelings about your project. He's an environmental lawyer, and he seemed convinced that the renovation you had planned would adversely affect our ecosystem. Don tried his best to explain all of the precautions you were taking, but he didn't want to hear it." She shook her head and looked sad. "I just can't believe he would cause such destruction. And for what?"

I decided to tread carefully; despite my feelings of anger over the situation, I understood that this was her former son-in-law. There was history there. "Judy, I can't be sure he is to blame, but I will have to tell the police that he was there, and I'm sure he will be questioned. I only hope it was a terrible coincidence. And I am grateful that he went in after Charlie because much longer, and the outcome could have been even more serious for her." I reached over and laid my hand on hers, still wanting to soothe the worry from her expression. "On another note, Charlie also mentioned that she was pregnant when she woke up." I paused, giving her a chance to digest my words. I thought maybe she knew, and if so I also figured she was aware of the fact that I didn't know about the baby.

Her eyes met mine, still worried, but I could see that she was relieved she no longer had to keep Charlie's secret. "I am so sorry that you found out this way, Luke. It was important to Charlie that she made sure everything was okay before she shared the news. I know it wasn't in your plans, and I also think she was having a hard time figuring out how to tell you." She put her other hand on top of mine, clasping it between her own. "You have to know that no matter what, this is happy news for our family. We haven't gotten to know each other as much as we would have liked to, but you seem like a good man and I can see you care for Charlie. And as far as I'm concerned, if Charlie is happy, that is the most important thing. She deserves some joy after the way things ended with her marriage to Joe. I believe you can give that to her. I hope you believe that too."

I smiled down at her earnest expression, so much like her daughter's. "This much I can promise you, Judy: I fully intend to do all that I can to make sure Charlie stays happy. Maybe a baby wasn't specifically in the plans, and frankly, I'm still wrapping my mind around the idea, but I love your daughter, and I will love any child we make together, now or in the future." I felt my throat tighten as I said the words and saw the tears well up in Judy's eyes. We were looking at each other, smiling like fools, when I heard a throat clear behind me.

I turned around to see Charlie's dad, looking a little awkward, as he realized he had interrupted a sensitive conversation. Judy gave him a reassuring smile, and he seemed to visibly relax as he hurriedly gave us an update on Charlie. He was told that we would be able to go in and visit her very soon. They had finished up her exam and had run a few tests to make sure her lungs were okay and that there were no other problems. He fidgeted uncomfortably during the last part, and Judy interrupted him to let him know that I knew about the baby. I could see the relief on his face, and he went on to say that yes, it was confirmed that she was pregnant, and the baby's heartbeat was strong. They were also going to do an ultrasound to get a closer look. He paused and looked at me. "Would you like to be in the room for the ultrasound, Luke? I'm sure that can be arranged."

I felt my heart speed up, and everything was suddenly very real. I was going to be a father. Charlie was having my baby. I expected to feel a little bit of anxiety or some sort of reservation, but instead I felt a warmth in my chest. A contentment that I had never felt before surrounded me and I realized that I was happy and even excited. I noticed that both of Charlie's parents were looking at me with concern. I allowed myself a minute to revel in their parental warmth before responding. "I would really like that. Thank you, Don." He put his hand on my shoulder again, and we headed over to the nurses' station to inquire about going in to see Charlie.

It turned out that Charlie had been asking to see me, so the nurse escorted me to her room. She was sitting up in bed, looking pale but alert, and I was flooded with relief to see her smiling at me as I walked in. I could sense her nervousness, and I moved quickly to sit on the bed and reached for her hand. "How are you feeling, baby?" I asked her, yearning to scoop her into my arms.

"I'm actually feeling pretty good. I'm tired, and my throat hurts a little, but all things considered, I feel very lucky," she answered, giving my hand a squeeze. "Luke, they want to do an ultrasound to make sure everything is okay with the baby. Do you want to be in the room?" she asked tentatively.

I smiled at her and, unable to resist, I bent over to give her a quick kiss. I leaned back just a little so I could look her in the eye. "I would like nothing more than to see our baby." I felt her relax as I continued, "I love you so much, Charlie, and even though having a baby may not have been in my short-term plans, I can't say I'm upset about it. I'm still getting used to the idea of being a father, but at the same time, I can't wait to start my life with you and our child. For the first time, I realize I have everything I could ever want." I used my thumb to gently wipe her tears away as she smiled up at me.

"Me too," she whispered. "Me too."

Epilogue

CHARLIE

Love is an emerald.
Its brilliant light wards off dragons
On this treacherous path.
—Rumi

It was the perfect late spring day as I sat snuggled in Luke's lap watching my closest friends scattered around Ethan's cozy courtyard behind his Charleston single house. Normally, Luke would have been in his favorite position manning the grill, but since I left the hospital earlier that week, he had been stuck to me like glue. Constantly hovering over me and refusing to allow me to do anything for myself. I might have killed him if it hadn't been so adorable, so I was allowing it to continue just a bit longer. Unfortunately for him, I planned to put my foot down on Monday, when I intended to get back to work.

He nuzzled my neck, his hand firmly planted on my stomach, where it had remained from the moment he had seen the images of our tiny peanut on the sonogram screen. I spent the night in the hospital, but after all the tests showed me to be perfectly fine, I was released the next morning. A very tired Luke (he had slept in the chair in my room) drove us back to his place. He only allowed me to go home to collect some clothes and toiletries, which he insisted on helping me pack and refused to allow me to carry so much as a lipstick.

Poor Everleigh just shook her head laughing as we watched him pile everything into the back seat of his sports car. She had hugged me as I left, wiping away a tear. "It was a great ride, Charlie, but I'm so happy for you."

I squeezed her hard. "Stop being ridiculous, Everleigh. I'll be back in a few days."

She smiled indulgently. "No, I don't think so. There's no way that man is letting you leave his side, Charles. He's all in, and I think you are too. You deserve this, and I want it for you."

I felt myself tearing up, and deep down, I knew she was right. I loved living with Everleigh, but I didn't want to think about leaving Luke. I looked around our cozy little beach cottage and thought of all the good times we'd had there. Slumber parties with Chase and margaritas on the deck while we watched the sun set. We smiled at each other through our tears, and I squeezed her again. "Thank you, Ever. You are the best friend a girl could ask for, and you're right—we had a great ride here together." Before we could start with more tears, we were distracted by loud cursing in front of her house as Luke tried to shut the car door on my piles of clothes and shoes threatening to spill out.

My heart warmed as I looked at Everleigh, who was over by the grill laughing with Ethan. It was bittersweet to see that they had put their awkwardness behind them; a part of me still wished they would wake up and realize they were perfect for each other. I noticed Ethan's new girlfriend, Liz, was in the middle of a bocce ball game with Chase; his friend Dillon; and Sebastian's sister, Lily. I also noticed that despite the heated nature of the game, her eyes barely left Ethan, and she pursed her lips every time Ethan laughed at something Everleigh said. I was trying to give Liz a chance since it was obvious that Ethan was becoming pretty serious about her, but something about her still rubbed me the wrong way. Inadvertently, I let out a little sigh, and Luke squeezed me tighter.

"Is everything okay, sweetness?" he asked, his voice filled with concern.

"I'm so good," I said, leaning in for another kiss. "Just wishing that Everleigh would find someone as perfect as you."

He laughed, stroking his hand up my back and playing with my hair like he always did. "I'm sure that won't be too difficult. Maybe she should go hang out at your parents' inn and lock some poor, unsuspecting guy in a room with her."

I punched his arm as one of his friends yelled for us to get a room, and we both laughed. It felt great to be out of the house. Once we got back to Luke's after the hospital, he kept me in bed for another two days, except for when we had to go to the police station to be interviewed about the fire.

That whole experience was the only dark spot in an otherwise bright week. I didn't remember anything after making it into the lobby and then waking up in Luke's arms. Of course,

Luke told the police about Joe being the one to save me from the fire, and it didn't take long for them to track him down and bring him in for questioning. He quickly lawyered up, which was a wise move because the evidence was not looking good for him. They had found cached searches about household chemicals that can be used to start a fire on his computer, and a coworker had come forward to say that Joe had talked to him about sabotaging Revival on King. I was sad to think that Joe had been responsible for all the chaos and had been inadvertently responsible for my hospital stay. But I realized when I was able to quickly put it out of my mind that I had really and truly moved on. Joe had to deal with his continued mistakes, and I felt wistful for the boy I once knew, but mostly, I was just excited for my future with Luke.

As Luke spent the rest of the week spoiling me and juggling the fallout from the fire, he continually dropped hints about our future together. I let him talk, not wanting him to be too hasty just because we were having a baby, but inside, I was giddy with happiness at his complete turnaround. I caught the eye of his friend Austin, who was leaning against an oak tree, watching everyone with serious eyes. Of all of Luke's friends, Austin was the enigma. He was by far the most handsome, with dark, brooding good looks. He was the tallest of all the men, at least six foot five and built like an ox. I knew he had spent four years in the Army, most of it overseas, but Luke said he refused to talk about his time in Iraq and Afghanistan. These days he ran his family's very successful landscaping business. He had added on a pool building division which was flourishing, but yet, he never seemed content. Luke said he enjoyed the company of women, but I had never seen him with anyone, so he clearly wasn't interested in anything serious. As we eyed each other, a corner of his mouth quirked up in a small smile, and he tipped his beer bottle at me. I chuckled to myself thinking about when I had talked to him at the inn grand opening and considered him as potential to get back in the dating game. As sexy as he was I didn't feel the same pull as I did when I was near Luke. I nodded back and grinned, warmed by his small smile. I glanced over my shoulder at Luke, who was also watching his friends, and marveled at how much had changed in such a short time.

Sebastian had left the group playing bocce ball and had joined Ethan and Everleigh at the grill. I had known Sebastian for a while, having worked with him on my parents' renovation. He was the most laid-back of all Luke's friends. Just easy and fun, so comfortable in his own skin. I was surprised he was still single, but he was the youngest of the group at only twenty-eight. A child prodigy, he had graduated two years early and gone to college at sixteen. He had always wanted to be an architect, and his talent knew no bounds. He found beauty in even the most ordinary structure, and his services were in high demand. Lucky for Luke and Ethan, his loyalty was to Ethan Grant, and I figured it was only a matter of time before they convinced him to become a partner. They would make a formidable trio, no doubt.

Sebastian's sister, Lily, was so lively and fun. I had met her for the first time today, and I fell in love with her instantly. At twenty-five, she was a little younger, but she had been a fashion model and businesswoman since she was a teen. Despite her worldly experience, she was so down to earth and seemed to be the glue that held her small family together. She had left the world of modeling to start her own boutique line based right here in Charleston. Her mom had recently been diagnosed with cancer, and she and Lily were extremely close, so Lily didn't hesitate to drop everything and come home. It was obvious Sebastian adored her too, and I couldn't help but notice Austin watching her when he thought no one was looking. Hmmmm.

I felt Luke move underneath me. "I'm going to grab another beer. Can I refresh your iced tea?" he asked as he lifted me gently and put me in the seat next to him.

"Yes, please, that would be great." I watched him as he walked over to our friends at the bocce court. He joked easily with Chase and Dillon. Liz seemed to hang on to his every word, and I marveled at how relaxed he was in any situation. It was easy to see why he was so successful; people were naturally drawn to his easy charm. Chase had managed to convince Dillon to join our party even though he was clearly nervous about exposing his feelings for Chase, and surprisingly, Chase seemed okay with leaving their relationship in the friend zone for now. This told me a lot about how Chase felt about Dillon.

Luke leaned in, whispered something to Chase, and then walked over to the grill where the cooler of beer was stationed. As I watched Luke approach the group at the grill, I saw Chase head over to Austin out of the corner of my eye. Luke was deep in conversation with the trio around the grill. I couldn't hear what they were saying over there, but they seemed so cozy, I considered going to find out.

Just as I was about to get up, Luke started back toward me, followed closely by our friends. Before I had the chance to think this was strange, Luke was standing in front of me, a twinkle in his eye. He was smiling so broadly, I couldn't help but smile back at him. The next thing I knew, he was on the ground in front of me, his hand on mine. Wait . . .he was on one knee, and our friends, they were all around us wearing huge grins, and Chase had a camera. But Luke, he was smiling, his blue eyes sparkling, and at that moment, all I could see was him. He brought my hand to his mouth and kissed it. As I looked down at him, my eyes caught the glitter of the ring in his other hand.

"Charlie, my sweet firecracker, my love," he began, and my heart leapt into my throat. "Never did I think when you walked into that room and blew me away with your feisty words and fiery kiss that I would end up in this place. Here on my knees asking and hoping you will say yes. I never knew what I was missing until you walked into my life and slammed that door at your parents' inn. You stole my heart that day, and I am only sorry that it took me this long to realize it. To understand that was the moment—that first moment I saw you—that I wanted you right then. You own my heart and I can't go another day without knowing you are mine forever. Please, Charlie, say yes. Say you will be mine today and always. You, me, and our baby. Say yes."

Tears were streaming down my face as I heard his voice catch on the last few words. I felt as if my heart would explode. I hadn't imagined after Joe, that I would ever be here again and really it was unfair to compare what I had with Luke to anything that had come before. I knew without a doubt that I had finally found my soulmate. Somewhere, I heard Everleigh crying softly, but I only had eyes for one person.

I looked into the eager face of the man I loved and answered. "Yes, Luke, a thousand times, YES."

I hope you enjoyed Revival On King Street, *the first book in the Lowcountry Liaison Series. Everleigh and Ethan's story will be released in the summer of 2019. See below for an overview of their story and go to suziewebster.com/newsletter to sign up for our newsletter to get a sneak peek of the book straight to your inbox! You can also follow me on Facebook and Instagram for announcements, giveaways and release dates.*

Following Charlie's engagement to Luke Coleman, Everleigh is re-evaluating her romantic choices. Her best friend is going to get married for the second time and she realizes that her longest relationship with a man is with her gay best friend Chase. She takes a hard look at her attraction to unavailable men and why she can't seem to commit. She decides that it's time for her to grab her romantic life by the horns and makes a dating pact with Chase. The goal: 10 guys in 10 weeks. Together they each devise a plan to meet a new guy a week for 10 weeks to try and find Mr. Right. The only problem with Everleigh's plan is that the one man who managed to steal her heart and then break it, keeps distracting her from finding her soulmate.

Even though Ethan is trying to move on with Everleigh's high school frenemy, Liz, he continues to find himself drawn back to her. After losing his wife and unborn child in a tragic accident, Ethan let a warm and sympathetic Everleigh slowly bring him back to life. As his employee, she should have been off-limits as anything more than a friend, but Ethan had a hard time resisting her gentle charm. And in a weak moment, even though he knew he was far from over Jill's death, he let their friendship cross the line. That one night of passion cost him a good friend and a valuable employee. And while he couldn't deny the heat between them, at the time, he wasn't ready for her and he ended up pushing her away and breaking her heart. So why was it now when he was finally in a relationship with a seemingly perfect woman, finding out about Everleigh and Chase's 10 guys in 10 days pact was making him crazy. Suddenly, all he wanted to do was sabotage each and every date. As he continued to tell himself that he was just looking out for a friend, it was getting increasingly difficult to ignore the heat that sparked each time they were together.

ABOUT LOWCOUNTRY LIAISONS

The South has never been steamier as Luke, Charlie and their group of friends pursue their dreams by day and awaken their passions at night in the beautiful scenic city of Charleston, South Carolina. Each book is a stand alone romance about two of these friends, but the supporting players continue to pop up and add to the good times throughout the series.

CPSIA information can be obtained
at www.ICGtesting.com
Printed in the USA
BVHW041909160519
548515BV00010B/304/P

9 781641 112475